# THE OVAL AND THE OSPREY

## CELAENA CUICO

*Jodie Comer may not make it in Killing Eve, and well...that was a personal attack against all lesbians.*

*I apologize in advance if I do the same thing...*

## The Diadem

*Glass and Bone*
*Cages and Crowns*
*Moonlight*
*Oblivion and Ash*

## The Diadem Journals

*Elaenor*
*Tobias*

## The Belle and The Bird

*The Belle and The Bird*
*The Oval and The Osprey*

*"YUP."*
*SOMERVILLE 26:42*

# TRIGGER WARNINGS

The Oval and The Osprey features triggering themes such as graphic violence, gore, murder, physical abuse, rape, graphic language, sexual assault, child pornography, human trafficking, suicidal ideation, torture, confinement, and more.

Proceed with caution.

Or don't.

Your choice.

# CHAPTER ONE

## XYLA

Scream after scream tear through my throat as I kick and punch. Bruises and cuts spreading across my body like wildfire. Pain erupting through every nerve, every inch of my skin, every muscle on my body as I fight.

As I fight for my *life*.

There is no room for error, no space for mistakes.

Nails gouge, fists pommel, and feet dig into every single crevice they can possibly find as I pray to whatever Gods are listening that I—

"*For fucks sake, Xy!*" Oz curses as he steps back off the mat, essentially tapping out. Blood drips from his hairline, his shirt long gone after I tore it in half last round, and I glance down to see he's missing a shoe. Pure satisfaction rolls through me at the sight of his disheveled state.

"*Yes!*" I yell, throwing my arm up in the air and spinning around our underground gym, my bare feet sliding across the mat slicked with sweat and blood. His answering scowl is enough to make me laugh as he wipes drips of perspiration off his brow. I smirk and glance across the room at the horde of people pretending like they haven't been watching us spar the last hour.

They always like to wager which one of us will win, and let's face it, it's always me.

And anyone who bets against me, deserves the money they lose.

The Nest has increased tenfold in the last two years, and the size of our training room reflects that. We started with fifteen men, and now we host almost 200 across the entire country, and even a few collectives internationally. There is a daily rotation of teams and squads in this room, keeping all combat skills in pristine condition. Oz and I being no exception.

Our main base is now located in the heart of Washington, DC, just a few minutes' drive from my father, which is a far cry from the random warehouses The Nest used to acquire before. Now we live in luxury, or some underground dystopian novel. I am halfway stuck between the two, but as long as I have a waterfall showerhead and an espresso machine, I tend to be happy.

All around me, men and women in black clothing, train with various weapons, bags, and each other. Every single person in our employ has to train a minimum of two hours daily, unless on assignment. That training can be fighting, strength, martial arts, yoga for limberness and flexibility, or simply running. But two hours minimum of movement a day. It helps prevents injuries and keeps everyone in the best shape possible. They are also required to get physicals once a month and upon the return of every single mission.

An unfit and unhealthy bird will lead to death. And we have experienced way too much of that in the last two years, and even more since I joined.

Now that Osprey is in control of the Secret Service, those men train here as well, contributing to our growing numbers of irreplaceable soldiers.

Let me clarify, *only* the men we also have adopted into The Nest train here. Not all agents can be trusted, but those are the ones we keep far away from my father, who is on his second year as President of the United States.

All of the men who have adopted our lifestyle and morals have found themselves fast-track promoted in the ranks of the Service, because my father deserves only the best men watching his back. And having our men placed in strategic places allows both Oz and I to be in control of pretty much everything when it comes to national safety and terrorism.

Something we are both finding a lot harder now that Raven is gone. She could do all of this with her eyes closed, but it takes the two of us to steer the ship, to keep these men under control.

And yes, we are larger, but she could still do this. I am sure of it.

I turn back to Oz who is dabbing blood off his bicep with a rag where my long nails sliced through his skin, nails he repeatedly tells me I need to cut, but I like the feral cat look. He looks ragged, as if he was attacked by wild beast. Which I guess he sort of was.

"I created a monster." He mutters.

"I was a monster long before you met me, darlin'. Now I am just a more *efficient* monster." I smile and pat his cheek as I walk past, dodging his flailing arm swinging out in retaliation.

I step up to the wall of TVs showcasing every single camera we have access to at the compound, which is almost one hundred and fifty tiny, indistinguishable black dots in corners, plants, and other random places. A ridiculous amount, but only the bathrooms and sleeping quarters are blacked out. Every other inch of this place is well guarded and watched every second of the day to prevent anything from being thrown our way.

We are always prepared. Always ready. Always deadly—okay that was cringey. I digress.

I glance at the barrack hallway seeing people filtering out of their rooms, the dining hall where birds are snacking, and then finally the only floor above the ground, which looks like a generic office building fronting as a real estate agency, aptly named Bader Estates, because who doesn't want their name plastered on a luxury building?

Me. I don't want that.

The name was my father's idea, surprisingly, since he has been pretty instrumental and financially responsible for the growth of the operation.

This building took an entire year to construct, with five floors completely underground, that houses every single one of our men, armories, training rooms, dining halls, game rooms, surveillance rooms, and more. This entire compound is made out of five-foot-thick steel plates and cement, making it indestructible and bomb proof for the most part. Each floor has its own emergency security system to lock it down with all doors and elevators requiring biometric scanner clearance to access. We can cut anyone off at any time. No other entrances and exits aside from ones we control.

This does mean, however, that we have a pretty hefty electrical grid solely for the bunker. Three sets of generators that can back each other up, should the main grid fail. No bird will be stuck inside should we lose power, but we can sure as hell keep people out.

Every single person in this building is marked with a tracker in their neck, so we know where everyone is at all times. Not the same way Kestrel had tracked Raven, but in a way that if a case or mission were to go sideways, we can get our people out without fuss and with as few casualties as possible. Every single person also has an *'oh fuck'* button as Oz lovingly named it. This button is on their tracker embedded into their skin. If a bird is ever in a situation where they are not going to survive, they just need to hold down the button. This will alert us to cease all rescue attempts.

After a mission went sideways last year and we lost two trucks full of men and women, we decided to invest in that technology. This will save more lives. And every bird knows that their death is a promise not a threat. Most of us will not survive to see our hair turn gray, and so they take the tracker willingly, knowing the risks. However, I have been known, on occasion, to disregard the *'oh fuck'* button.

Because none of us have families. And none of us care if we make it out alive. But I care about my birds, so sometimes I break my own rules.

Due to the growth of our operations, we retired the required use of bird species for call signs and have allowed everyone to branch out, while still being called 'birds' in the general sense. Oz stayed Osprey, of course, and instead of *The Beauty*, I prefer the moniker of *The Beast*. Which fits because I only get sent in as a last resort. I may not be on the front lines, but I am the one our targets fear.

The last two years of my life have been nothing short of pure adrenaline and action. Ballet became a thing of the past, although as a second front, I own the Bader Ballet Company and employ various award-winning teachers, and Dalton, who manages it for me. When my father talks about his daughter, that is what he tells the world I am doing. Teaching and building the next generation of ballerinas that will win top marks in academies, international competitions, and someone who will eventually be the next prima ballerina. But he knows what I am really doing.

I took over for Raven, well *we* did.

Without her here, Oz was left to run The Nest, which as my partner in all of this, I wouldn't have any other way, but Raven's impact was undeniable and irreplaceable. And it is taking both of us to do what she used to alone. He couldn't do it by himself, so we partnered up. It was hard at first, as neither of us is very good at relinquishing control, but we found our rhythm. Now Oz is my best friend, my other half, and the only person in this entire world who understands what I feel.

He also trained me to be as close to Raven as possible. Not to replace her, that could never happen, but to protect me. As well as to protect him. If his partner couldn't protect him, have his back, I'd be a liability. He would be too worried about me to watch out for himself. We needed to be equals. But I surprised us both and became what we never expected.

I have mastered the art of blades, shooting, martial arts, and even archery. There is not a single weapon in this building I have not mastered, and I have gone against every single mercenary in our group—and won.

Even Oz.

I am no longer the child that fell in love with a protector, I became everyone's worst nightmare. I became what I was always destined to be, I just had hoped Raven would be a part of it.

But she's not. And that is something I have still not acclimated to.

But as the years pass, and my search for answers continue, I find myself tiring.

I find myself questioning the point of the fight. The point of all of this. Political safety? Control? What is the end goal?

What do *I* want out of life?

And with my father being the President, his own political agenda comes into question. My father is a kind and generous man, but too much power can corrupt a saint, and I worry every day what his team and advisors are spewing. I worry that one day the man in office will no longer be the father that fought for me.

The father that has always promised to put his family first, not politics. Not the country. The father that held me after I listened to my mother die in the room next to me. The father who flew across the world to find a group of mercenaries to protect his daughter.

That is the father I'll pray he always stays.

But until the day comes that corruption finally finds its roots, I will enjoy every second of normalcy I can muster.

I scan one of the screens to the right displaying our fake real-estate office, and like expected, Rena is there tapping away on her computer. I smile as I stare at her curly black hair pinned up into a messy bun, tendrils sticking out haphazardly. There is a pencil in her mouth, despite not needing one. She is a chewer, and if it wasn't a pencil, it would probably be her thumb, or any other random object she has near her.

She is one month away from completing her clerkship for criminal defense. After everything that happened two years ago, I told her the truth. Every single thing. And she switched her focus from litigation to criminal defense as a way to help. And now she is a full-on member of The Nest, just not a mercenary. She goes by the call name Fixer, because she thought it was cute, and she will eventually be the person we call to fix all of our mistakes before they even happen.

Plausible deniability she always says.

Her law degree will come in handy. It'll help us skirt the law, find loopholes, protect ourselves. Immunity from crimes is the only way we can operate, and with her clerkship, she's the perfect person to orchestrate that. To prevent any of us from ending up behind bars.

I tap the tiny mic in my ear and call out to her.

"Earth to Fix." I say in a sing-songy tone. Her head snaps up and goes straight to the camera. She taps her own ear.

"Yes, *Beast.*" She taunts, slamming her laptop shut and raising a brow.

"We have dinner at the house in an hour, yet you look like you just crawled out of bed." I scold. Her eyes widen and her jaw drops.

"And if I come downstairs right now, I should expect to see sweat and someone else's blood coating your less-than-ready face, right?" She teases back and stands, gathering her things.

"Hurry up and come find out, *Fixie*." Oz coos into the mic, his voice deep and throaty. I gag and roll my eyes.

Ever since Serena joined us, and left her loser boyfriend, her and Oz have been tiptoeing around each other. He flirts, she rejects him, she stares longingly, and he ignores her.

Back and forth.

Honestly, I just want them to get together already and leave me out of it, because whatever pining is happening is just annoying and I'm tired of seeing it.

"Gross." I say into the mic and then tap my ear, shutting off the comms. I glance at Oz, who's eyes linger on Rena as she disappears into the stairwell leading to the biometric elevator. His eyes are glassy, a subtle furrow of his brow. The same look I used to see in Raven when she looked at me. Love. Longing. Desperation.

*Fear.*

I take the earpiece out and walk past the screens, through the double doors, and to the stairs leading down to the very bottom floor.

The last floor is our surveillance room, armory, my suite, Oz's suite, our interrogation room, our holding cells, and two guest suites—one of which I should just call Serena's suite, because she's been there the last six months. This floor also houses our infirmary and surgical wing, which is completely stocked with supplies and medication as well as an on-call doctor who lives here for minor surgeries and wounds. We call him Stitch, because he spends half his time stitching us up.

For Halloween last year, Rena bought him a blue onesie with ears and made him wear it. We all thought it was hilarious, but Oz didn't laugh or even crack a smile. Only because he knows Rena and Stitch were a thing. A *very short* thing. Literally one night, but to Oz, he has a claim on Serena, and he'll kill anyone that touches her.

Toxic masculinity and all that. Even a man like Oz isn't above all that.

I set my hand on my suite door, unlocking it with our biometric systems, and the thick metal unlatches with a comforting *clank*. I step out of the sterile, gray hallway, and onto the plush rug. I toe off my sneakers, letting my bare feet sink into the soft blue.

My room is massive, as are all the suites.

When you first walk in, there is a sitting room, TV, and small dining table, that is usually covered in paperwork, although Miss Dolly usually keeps it pretty clean. There is also a kitchenette and espresso machine, which is the only thing I ever use in there. To the right is a door that leads to my private office.

I have another office on the third floor that anyone can come into, but I mostly work out of this one. Anything that is sensitive, top secret, or just personal, is worked on in there.

To the left is the bedroom and bathroom, which I modelled after my rooms in Celina. The pale neutrals, pinks, and yellows that make it feel bright but also cozy and warm. There is also a guest room in this suite that Miss Dolly has been staying in since we opened. I offered her a suite of her own, but honestly, we both prefer being together. It feels like home this way.

Miss Dolly, however, has been on a much needed and fully funded vacation. One she protested, but I figured she needed a break. And honestly, so did I. I spend a lot of nights in my office and while Miss Dolly is my family, her worried gaze and prodding has been making me feel helpless. Like what I am doing isn't worthy of the stress.

So, I lovingly sent her away.

Straight ahead on the blank wall, that unfortunately cannot house a window, sits a few frames. One with all of Raven's accolades from the marines that Osprey found, declaring Naomi Cross an irreplaceable soldier. I don't know where he found it, or where it came from. Naomi's existence was erased, but a year ago, after the compound was built, he walked in with a box, tears in his eyes, and left it on my desk without a single word. He still won't say where it came from, or who sent it.

There is no reason it should even exist, yet here it is.

And then, in the last shadow box, sits her gun. It was deep cleaned, polished, and placed delicately in a locked, bulletproof, box. I wanted to use it, but it didn't feel right. It's not mine. And I am *not* her replacement.

This wasn't the new one she had acquired, because that one had disappeared along with her body that night. This was the one we took off Kestrel's abandoned corpse with the small raven engraved onto the slide. The one she got from Goose her first year after The Nest was formed. Even if he was a traitor, he still meant a lot to her, and this gun was proof of that. He was her family, and he did what he thought was for the best in the moment.

I have to believe that.

For a short while, Goose meant a lot to me too. And that is how I'll choose to remember him, the father-like figure who kept everyone in line. The person who kept me safe...until he didn't. But I can't dwell on that.

One day, when we find Raven, she'll get the gun back. She'll get everything back. Because she *is* alive.

I just need to find her.

I turn away from the long list of pain I keep displayed on the vast wall, and head to the bathroom for a quick shower, knowing that we will have to leave sooner than later.

# CHAPTER TWO

## XYLA

It takes no time at all to shower, slip on a dress, and slap on some makeup so I look presentable. Rena and I exit our suites at the same time, her crimson dress complimenting her onyx hair perfectly. She has it smoothed into a sleek blow out, her eyes rimmed in kohl, and a brown lip. She gives me a spin, her heels clicking on the concrete, before gesturing for me to do the same with an impatient smile.

My black dress is made out of silk and liquid organza, making it fall to the floor like water. It has a deep V, exposing way too much of my body to be appropriate. My hair is pinned up into a faux bob. And the only makeup I have on is mascara and blood-red lipstick. I spin and smile and she claps before walking over and linking her arm through mine.

"Your dad is going to have a heart attack." She snorts.

"As his only child, I have to be the favorite as well as the troublemaker. It's quite a burden." I reply, pinching her arm.

"I think *I* am actually the favorite Bader child." Osprey's voice is loud behind us, and I turn around to glare at him. He is wearing an all-black tux, the tie and collared shirt the same deep hue. His leather shoes are shiny, freshy polished. His hair is gelled back and out of his face, his beard trimmed and groomed, and a small American Flag pin sits on his lapel.

Aside from that, he has a small scratch above his brow, and a small bruise forming on his jaw. Enough proof I kicked his ass to make me smile.

"Well don't you look handsome!" I exclaim, reaching up and tightening his tie until he chokes.

"*Xy.*" He groans, slapping my hands away before loosening it with a glare.

"Alright, you two, we are late. Let's go already." I push them both towards the elevator, neither really putting up a fight.

"Who's coming with us tonight?" Rena asks, pointedly ignoring Oz, even as he stares at her back like a love-sick puppy. I should invest in a shock collar, maybe it'll make him stop, or finally act.

The ooey gooey looks make me want to barf.

"Bog, Jet, and Shark are already on-site. Radar is waiting in the car." Oz replies, placing his palm on the scanner to take us to the parking garage.

Bog is one of our strongest men. Hailing from Louisiana, a total swamp rat who is built like a water buffalo. He could snap someone's neck with a single hand, and he is also Oz's right-hand man in the service, as he should be. He is quite literally Oz 2.0, and if I were to disappear, I would expect him to take my place, or at least take over a small part of The Nest so Oz didn't have to do it alone.

Shark is our lead interrogator. He's cold, malicious, and manipulative. He can get information out of anyone, even information someone didn't know they knew. He was a transplant from the CIA, one we may or may not have sequestered with a pretty paycheck and several international vacations. He oversees our entire intelligence team, and one of our key players in our operation. He works really close with our IT department, making sure our systems are as pristine as possible.

Radar is our tech-guy, the one in charge of said IT department. He was another kidnap victim out of Fort Brague. He was being trained up for some secret government sector, and we redirected his plane. When he landed, we gave him a choice, and he rightfully chose us, not that we gave him much of a choice. He controls all of our technology and equipment. He uses his engineering and computer science degrees to keep us safe, as well as to develop intelligence weapons for Shark.

Lastly, Jet. He is our lead pilot. He flew fighter jets and planes in the military and came to us willingly from the Secret Service. He is who we sent to kidnap Radar, and the one who takes us on all of our top-secret missions. Planes, jets, and helicopters. There isn't a single aircraft he couldn't operate. I'm convinced he would even be able to man a submarine if we somehow acquired one. Hence his very original name of Jet, but he chose it.

While our team is enormous, we have our dedicated people, and sometimes it feels just as small as it did before. But we are still missing our family. The ones we lost. Raven, of course, but I still think of Kite. The funny, goofy little brother. The one who put his body before mine. Who died to protect me.

He will never be forgotten either.

And then there is Goose. The cranky old man, who for a few months, was a possibly permanent fixture in my life. And then he chose his relationship with Kestrel over my life. Over Raven's life. And Osprey did what he had to do. I still see his face sometimes when I close my eyes. The bullet that went straight through his forehead. The blood spraying across my face. The taste—

I clear my throat and shake my head as the elevator opens and one of the blacked-out SUVs sits idling by the door. I see Radar in the passenger seat, laptop out as always as he types away. Rena and I climb into the back while Oz takes up the driver's seat, forever in charge of driving like the control freak he is.

I pull out my phone and send a quick text to my father, letting him know we are on our way, although, I doubt he'll see it. He's usually halfway through a bottle by this time of night when he's having a special event of some sort.

"Okay, spill." I turn to Rena and her brows furrow in confusion.

"What?" She asks, apprehension distorting her voice as she buckles herself in and quirks a brow. I see Oz glance at us in the rear-view mirror, no doubt assuming I am asking about a guy. His little jealous ears are probably on high alert.

"You have been working on some hush hush case for Dower and haven't spoken a word about it. I want to know everything." She chews on her lip, debating.

"Chief Public Defender Dower." She corrects and I roll my eyes at the ostentatious name, and at her stalling technique.

"I don't really care about his title." I retort.

"Okay, but it isn't related to The Nest, so I didn't think you would care." She shrugs and I want to slap her. I'll admit, I can be a questionable friend sometimes. I get so caught up in missions and tracking Raven, that Serena probably feels left out. But above all else, I care about her. And I care about what she spends her entire day on.

"Of course I care. *If* it's important." I clarify, because I don't actually care about any normal case. Only ones that could possibly pertain to us, but I will still listen. Always. I wink at her, and she rolls her eyes before nodding and picking at her cuticles.

"Alright here it goes. Dower has a witness to a huge case. She's a former CIA operative that was kidnapped out of Russia, drugged, manipulated, and forced to do the dirty work of some crime lord, who we have yet to identify. She has been arrested after a failed hit in New York. She says she has something big, and she wants immunity for her crimes if she comes clean. Dower has me looking into her past and any connections she may have had to Russia, since that's where she was. I haven't found anything; she was born here in Virginia and lived there until she joined the CIA after college." Excitement pools in her eyes as she talks about the high-profile case, her smile infectious under normal circumstances, but I focus on one single word.

"Russia?" I squeak, and her eyes soften.

"Yes, but it's not related to the Bratva. It's not related to Raven, which is why I didn't say anything. I checked, I promise."

She tries to placate, but I am instantly cautious of anything that could be connected to the Brotherhood of the Wolves.

"What is she being charged with?" I question, chewing on the inside of my lower lip.

"Multiple counts of international murder-for-hire, possession of illegal and untraceable weapons, treason, terrorism. Just to name a few. But the thing is, she doesn't remember all of it. We have surveillance footage of her committing some of these hits, but she has no memory of some of it she claims. So, she's not entirely reliable to a jury. Dower says she'll be seen as emotionally fragile and unstable. Her testimony and any big information she claims to have won't stick." Her voice trails off as she gets lost in thought. So, they'll plead temporary insanity and get her off.

"Drugs?" I ask, as that could aid in memory loss.

"Presumed at first, but tests have ruled that out. She's clean now, but I guess that doesn't mean she was during the act. We think some sort of brainwashing or manipulation." She frowns, as if she's still trying to figure it out, chewing on her inner cheek.

"Has she named anyone? Said why she was doing it?" Osprey says from the front of the car, interjecting as always.

"Just that she was forced. She won't give up anything else without a promise she'll be free after." Rena responds. I ponder, leaning back in my seat.

"It makes sense." I shrug.

"What does?" Oz asks.

"She wants protection, but if she truly is being manipulated by someone, she has to know that she'll be killed by whoever that is if she walks free." I supply.

"So, what are you saying? That she's willingly sabotaging herself? What would be the purpose?" Rena presses, leaning forward.

"I'm saying she *wants* to die."

# CHAPTER THREE

## OSPREY

I pull the SUV up to the back gate of the White House, flashing my badge at the guard manning the controls. He gives me a once over before shining a flashlight into the back seat window. The girl's chatter doesn't falter as they ignore him. Despite being very well known, *and* this fucker's boss, we go through this every single time.

Badge check, vehicle check, heat signature scanning, and then—

"Sir, welcome back." He nods, before hitting the latch that opens the gate. I drive through and go straight for the underground parking garage, passing another set of guards who nod as well.

The second we park, Jet and Shark are there opening the doors for the girls and helping them out. Each of them offers an arm to escort them in, never letting them out of sight. I follow behind with Radar, who hasn't stopped tapping on his tablet.

"Report." I instruct as the elevator doors close.

"The President is in the ballroom with members of congress. It is rumored that his new Chief of Staff will be presented tonight." I see Xyla's lip curl from behind as she listens.

She hates Adrina Coral. Not only does she consistently say her name is ridiculous and sounds like something a stripper from Miami would have, but she is a middle-aged woman who has been all over her father since his election. Which is just unprofessional. Xyla repeatedly says you shouldn't shit where you eat, but then she is always pushing me and Serena together, so maybe that only applies to her father. Adrina Croal was rumored to be the new Chief of Staff about a month ago, after the last one stepped down due to ongoing health issues, so this isn't entirely a surprise.

Lincoln needs an aide, that much is true, but that new aide being Coral was never part of the plan. However, she is well-loved by faculty, just not his daughter. Xyla will have to get used to it, or she'll force her out and then Lincoln will be in search of another person to answer his beck and call.

I just think she's worried her dad will fall for her, and she'll end up being her new stepmother. I think Xyla would actually kill her before she'd let that happen.

"Delightful." Rena mutters, also hating Coral, but she shows more decorum than the little beast ever does. She'll shake her hand, offer pleasantries, but Xyla? She'll ignore her.

"Behave." I warn them both and Xyla turns to glare at me.

The elevator doors open and the sounds of clinking glasses, chatter, laughter, and squeaky footsteps cascade around us. I take a deep breath and step through first, leading the pack. I always assume this position as a safety precaution. Xyla hates it, saying its sexist, but honestly, I don't know how much use she'd be in her stilettos right now.

And if I ever told her I thought that she'd send her heel straight through my gut. Or my eye. Or my temple. Honestly, she'd send it anywhere that would prove a point.

The girls follow behind, Jet and Shark melting into the crowd, assimilating into their positions along the wall with the other members of the service.

People stop Xyla, introducing themselves, asking about her ballet company, and more. I stay by her side, hers *and* Serena's, because those two always stick together. Never letting them out of reach. She mingles, placating every old man wanting her attention, same routine as every single time we come to one of these dinners.

Eventually, Lincoln's booming voice cuts through the crowd and I relax slightly, getting my eyes on him. Bog is behind him and gives me a shallow nod as he follows the President forward.

"My darling daughter!" He exclaims, pulling Xyla into a hug.

"Daddy." She says softly and melts into his arms, a look of homesickness flashing through her eyes. He pulls back, kissing both of her cheeks before doing the same to Rena.

"I fear you are both late." He scolds, but his glare lands on me, because of course I am the keeper of the women. I fight the eye roll and muster an apologetic smile.

"You can thank your daughter's need for primping, sir." I respond, switching to a smirk, only to end up with an elbow in the gut from Serena, surprisingly.

"Well, as to be expected. Come, come." He grabs the girls' arms and leads them to a group of people. One of which, being Adrina Coral. "Miss Coral, you remember my daughter, don't you?" Her eyes widen as she scrambles forward.

"Hello, Miss Bader! It is so wonderful to see you again." She clasps Xyla's hands and shakes them, albeit a little too enthusiastically. Xyla's smile is forced as she pries her hands from Coral's, refusing to give her a response.

I glance up and see Dower step into Rena, whispering into her ear. Her face pales as she pulls back and nods, my fists clenching in response. He steps away, blending into the crowd as if he was never there to begin with. I meet her gaze, giving her a quirked brow, and she shakes her head once, telling me to drop it. My jaw tightens at the deflection, and I turn my gaze back to Lincoln as he leads us to the dining hall.

My men are stationed around the walls, their black figures standing out amongst the politicians donning vibrant shades of blue, cream, and white. I meet their gazes, giving them nods of acknowledgment, before I take my place at the table with Xyla, Rena, Lincoln, and a few others. Lincoln taps his champagne flute and stands, causing a widespread silence.

"Thank you all for coming tonight. I know dinners at the house have been few and far between lately, with the goal to host at least weekly falling short. But tonight is due a celebration, so having you all here to enjoy our fine chefs is perfect timing. A huge win for our country has occurred today!" He pauses and glances around the room, as if trying to build anticipation. "Chief Public Defender Dower has put the international disaster from the last few weeks to bed, and we can rest easy knowing everything is right again, and that our administration is free from negative infliction." My eyes go to Rena's, as she looks down at her plate, messing with her napkin uncomfortably. I see Xyla do the same thing, staring at her best friend in disbelief.

This has to be about the woman she was just talking about. Clapping ensues around us as Dower stands and nods, gesturing his thanks. It seems everyone around us knows about the trial and the former CIA operative. What actually happened?

The sound of everyone cheering is deafening, and I tap the mic in my ear once, sending a beep to the birds, a sign to stay vigilant during the ruckus.

"Now, let us enjoy the feast!" Lincoln yells to the crowd before he sits. His eyes slide to Dower's and they nod at one another.

Not in a we got the answer we were looking for nod, but in a we won sort of way.

What did Lincoln do?

# CHAPTER FOUR

## XYLA

My eyes keep going back to Rena's, but she stays immersed in conversation with Dower and his friends as they talk about a case. Whether it's the one I am eager to learn about, or another one that Rena might deem not important again. I inwardly roll my eyes at my own petulance. She has a life outside The Nest; her cases aren't my business. But everything around me presses in, making me feel like a paranoid conspiracy theorist.

I take a deep breath, fighting the ache in my chest that everyone knows something I don't.

My father, Coral, and Oz are discussing the security measures at the upcoming international summit the U.S. is hosting in a little over a week, but I have no desire to pitch in. So, I sit here in silence, picking up small pieces of everyone's conversation while I pick at the steak and lobster in front of me. Not going to lie, the chef here isn't the greatest. I think Miss Dolly makes better meals than this. But despite the desire to put my thoughts about that woman aside for another hour, I can't.

What was the speech about? What did Dower make disappear. What did my *father* make disappear? I guess I should be wondering *who*, not what. They had to be referring to the woman currently under their care, the huge case Rena was talking about, but this doesn't feel right.

At all.

And who is my father becoming if this is all related? I chew on the inside of my cheek, questioning whether or not it's my fault he's changing. Is it because of my line of work? Or is my line of work why I am just now seeing the signs of who he might really be under the surface of the perfect politician?

Dinner lasts forever, and by time dessert is brought out, I stand, unable to shovel another forkful into my mouth, or force another smile. Everyone around us immediately glances at me, no doubt for breaking some unreasonable rule of etiquette by leaving before the host, but who honestly cares?

"Daddy, I thank you for a lovely time, but we have an early mornin'." My twang is in full effect as I give him a sweet, innocent little smile. His brown eyes drop in disappointment for a fraction of a second, before they quickly perk up.

"Of course, my darling girl." He stands, as does everyone else at the table and I give them all a small smile. I don't wait for a dismissal or a hug, I just grip Rena's arm and lead her away, Oz close behind as we scurry towards the door.

"Talk. *Now*." I spit as we exit the dining hall.

"In the car." She whispers back, her voice wavering. But I can't tell if she is scared, nervous, or excited. Honestly either of the three would be enough to make my stomach roll given the circumstances.

Our steps are quick as we reach the elevator, Jet and Radar meeting us there and slipping in just before the doors close. We descend into the garage, stand in silence as we wait for Oz to retrieve the SUV, and then climb in. Serena doesn't start to talk until we exit the grounds, passing by both security checkpoints.

"She's gone." She says softly.

"What?" I say, louder than necessary, making myself flinch.

"The courts made it all disappear. The case, the evidence, *her*." My lips part, a sharp inhale rushing in. *I fucking knew it.*

"How is that possible? How can they just make her disappear?" I demand. I hear Radar tapping away in the third row behind us, no doubt looking for something. My guess is he won't. I have a feeling all of this is off the books.

"Your father, Xyla. He paid off the judge and Dower to get rid of everything. She is gone, literally vanished. I don't know what they did to her, but my guess is they killed her to make sure there were no loose ends." I scoff.

"My father did not kill someone." I rebut.

"I didn't say *he* did, Xy—" She starts, but her even suggesting it pisses me off.

"He wouldn't be *complicit* in it either. What reason would he have? What would he gain out of it? Wouldn't he get more glory for his administration catching a known international mercenary who was a former government operative? He'd get a damn medal."

My voice raises in volume, and I take a deep breath, shutting my eyes briefly. There is no way, no way at all my father would do this. The sweet, gentle man who was always there. The person who treated my mother and I like queens. Who never harmed another soul. That man wouldn't be a part of this.

But what if that man is gone?

"They got her to talk." The car goes silent as I stare at her. Even Radar stops typing.

"What did she say?" I whisper.

"She said she was standing in for The Black Bird. She said that the orders came from *inside* and that she had no choice. She knew something."

"The Black Bird?" I say softly. There is no way. No *fucking* way that this is *actually* circling back to us. To *Raven*. The idea that it was connected because of Russia was a delusion.

Not something I thought would be a reality.

"She said she was a decoy. That the orders were passed down from our government. She had names and was all too eager to provide them." She sighs, falling back into her seat.

"Who? What are their names?" I push, my chest pumping in tune to the racing heart underneath. We can catch th—

"I don't know, Dower didn't tell me that. But she's gone, he said that as much. Any evidence, any tapes of her interviews, any notes, *everything* is gone."

"What exactly did Dower say?" Osprey asks from the passenger seat.

"He said everything has been disposed of, and to drop it." She responds quietly. I know she was excited for this case, but if it was this dangerous maybe it's good she wasn't involved. "It didn't sound like a suggestion." Serena adds.

"If she was a decoy—a decoy for The Black Bird—you don't think...?" Jet starts as he turns down the street housing our base.

"It's not Raven." I snap. "My father wouldn't keep her from me." But we are all thinking it.

It would be stupid of us to disregard the possibility.

"I don't think we know what your father's true agenda really is right now, Xy." Rena says softly, her hand resting on mine from across the seat. I pull it away and glare at her.

"My father is not a monster. You are wrong." I turn away from her, looking out the window as we descend into our hidden parking garage.

"Xyla. Don't let this rattle you." Oz starts but I ignore him too.

They are wrong.

They have to be.

This isn't my father.

# CHAPTER FIVE

## XYLA

The compound is empty once we return, either everyone is on a mission, holed up in the game room, which is honestly the only form of non-work-related entertainment we have here, or they are asleep.

The SUV enters the garage, the door closing behind us and disappearing into the wall as if it was never there. We pull into a spot in line with the collection of other matching vehicles, and Jet leaves the keys in the center console. All of the keys stay in the cars, makes it easier for a fast getaway.

I unstrap my heels and let the balls of my feet touch the cold cement floor as I exit the car, Rena staying close behind. I can tell she wants to say something, but I don't spare her a glance. I don't want to talk about it.

Her arm loops through mine anyway as we reach the steel door that opens to a stairwell. My hand is placed on two separate palm scanners before we are finally stepping into an elevator, dropping to the bottom floor.

Rena's eyes are glassy, half-lidded, as she leans against the wall. No doubt the result of a lot of wine and cocktails, which I saw her indulge in, but also from her revelation. I can't imagine how exhausted she must feel, but also disappointed. She worked for weeks on this case, only for it not to be needed.

I, on the other hand, don't drink. I will hold a glass and fake a few sips, but I always need to be aware. Being sloshed on expensive liquor would no doubt result in some unintentional deaths should the need for protection arise. Or honestly, if someone pisses me off. I am sure alcohol and drugs will make my trigger finger a little too happy.

The elevator dings and our arms slip. A short wave goodnight, and we are entering our separate rooms. I shut the door behind me and let my back rest against the frame. Deep breaths. Over and over. I let everything wash over me, facts and evidence piling in my mind as I try to decipher what the hell is going on.

My father is not a monster. My father wouldn't stand by while someone is disposed of.

Would he?

Isn't that what I do? What my entire operation does?

Am I just being a hypocrite?

I take a few steps, entering my office, and let my eyes stay focused on the ground. The soft plush rug in the entry way feels comforting on my feet as I chew on the inside of my bottom lip.

She is sending us a message. She has to be.

Or *someone* is.

A decoy for a black bird. A woman who was a murder-for-hire. She was kidnapped and manipulated. She was a former CIA operative.

Another deep breath.

My chin lifts, as does my gaze, fixing on the wall behind my desk. Polaroids, printed articles, maps, and strings of every color cover the entire wall, edge to edge. Two years of work.

Two years of tracking.

And this might be the biggest clue we have.

I walk around my desk and let my finger flick one of the red strings. I follow it up to a polaroid of her and I, before everything. Dalton had taken it and gave it to me last year. It was of me dancing, I was on the stage, practicing. And in the back, dark and broody, was her. Watching me. Her focus never wavering.

Under the picture, the word *recital* is written. Just documenting when the picture took place. I follow the string back down to a map of Celina. I follow the strings connected until I am walking back and forth, following our journey. Until I reach the night.

The night she died.

Although the item marking that moment is a polaroid of Kestrel's dead body.

The night we thought we would finally be free, but that didn't happen.

The strings don't stop.

I follow the blue string, the one marking the unknown, the potential, movements. It travels across a few articles and stops on a picture of Norilsk.

Two hours after Raven's death and/or disappearance, a one-man chartered flight left Nashville and landed in Siberia. It was said to just be a single pilot, no passengers. But no records show who hired the pilot, or why they were going there. Oz couldn't even hack into the plane's system to figure out what exact destination they were achieving, but it landed in Siberia.

Kes was from Siberia, a small village called Norilsk. And I have no doubt that is where she ended up, but who took her is the question on hand.

I follow the string from Norilsk to a map of Romania, focused on Bucharest. Six months after that plane landed, a string of bodies were found in Bucharest. At first it was some low-level crime lord, and then what we assume was their chain of command, until their leader was found hanging from a flagpole in the town square.

There was no reason for this to even make us think it was Raven, and not just a rival gang or mafia, or whatever. Except for what they left behind. It wasn't a feather; it wasn't a bird.

It was a ribbon.

A pink, silk ribbon.

Tied around the neck of her victims. Every single one.

And I say her, because it is her.

It has to be.

I spin on my heel and open the top drawer of my desk and pull out the only thing in there, a manilla envelope with Romanian on it.

I don't know who Oz knew, but this was overnighted that same day. I pull apart the tabs and open it, before flipping the envelope upside down.

A pink ribbon flutters into my hand, speckles of dried blood staining it a rusty brown in some spots.

I lift the ribbon to my nose and inhale, chills running down my spine. Gunpowder and leather. *Her* smell.

If this is just a coincidence, one that has nothing to do with us or her, I don't know what I'll do.

"Believing she is out there is the only thing keeping me alive." I say out loud, my voice cracking, as I look up at Oz standing in my doorway.

I heard him, obviously. Before I even lifted the ribbon to my nose, I knew he was there.

"You don't mean that, Xy." He responds, crossing his arms.

"I had no purpose other than to fulfill my mother's dreams. She gave me a future to look forward to." I admit.

"Scotland." He says, not as a question, but as an understanding.

"Scotland." I repeat back. I slide the ribbon back into the envelope and return it to its place in my drawer.

"Do you think this woman was a message?" If I didn't know any better, I'd think his voice sounds slightly hopeful.

"I do. I know you think all of these are just coincidences, but Russia, the ribbon—"

"Just because it's a pink ribbon doesn't mean it has anything to do with you. She would have just put a—"

"Unless she's *running* from someone." I interrupt. "She knows putting a feather or bird marker on anything would lead back to her, so she had to pick something else." He silent for a second.

"They call her *Zea Ros* in Romania. The Pink God." I snort at the term.

"Creative." But she was a God. She was *mine*.

"*If* it's her." He adds softly.

"It's her, Oz. It has to be." I turn back around my eyes focused on the string that flows from Romania to Paris, where it stops.

I go back to my desk and pull out some red string. I unravel it a few times, ripping off a piece. I reach up and tie it to the tack under Paris, before reattaching it back to Russia.

Where it all started.

"This is a clue, Oz. It has to be."

"And if it isn't? Do we ever stop?" He asks.

"Then we keep looking until we find one that is. We don't stop until we have her bones." I say matter-of-factly.

"This is starting to feel like a hunt." He supplies and I can hear the smile in his voice without even seeing it.

"It is." I turn to look at him, seeing that grin. "She's ours, Oz. And I will hunt down whoever took her from us."

# CHAPTER SIX

## OSPREY

Two days pass and we have a plan.

Finally.

Jet is taking off with Radar and Shark tonight, along with a few men for back-up. Bog is staying with Lincoln, and I am staying with Xyla until it's time for us to move. The private plane flown by Jet is headed straight for Siberia, where our men are already stationed on the ground in Russia will take them to Norilsk to command our headquarters there. We have Radar on the ground there just in case we need some security hacking in the surrounding areas.

"We are starting from scratch." Xyla states, looking over the stairway railing at all of our men assembled below in the training room. Silence ensues as they all look up at her. Their eyes determined and focused as if she is a Queen and they are but her subjects.

Sometimes it feels that way. But that means I'd probably be the jester.

"There is a chance our target is alive." I add and whispers ensue, but a quick whistle from Bog has them shutting up.

"Whether that target is in Siberia, Paris, or Bucharest, we are not sure. But we had a lead. A lead that was solid and was claimed to be the decoy for The Black Bird." Xyla continues and I can see the wheels turning in everyone's brains.

"We are starting fresh, like Beast said. We will start with evidence from the night of Raven's death. We will trace all steps connected to Kestrel and The Brotherhood. We will start from the very beginning of all of this." I add.

"Radar, Jet, and Shark will be on their way to Siberia to meet with our spies on the ground tonight. Radar's team, you will be in charge of going through surveillance from the last eight years. Follow Kestrel, Raven, Goose, and any single person that can possibly be connected to them. This will be a lot of work, but it is imperative we comb through every camera, correspondence, potential leads—anything at all that can be of use." Xy glances at me and I nod.

"Shark's team. You will be pulling all individuals Team Radar supplies. Interrogations and questioning will begin immediately under the guise of the Secret Service or the FBI. You will work with Bog's team to ensure everything is done up to code and to look as if it is the work of the government." I pause, watching as people shuffle around into their designated teams.

"Team Black Bird—" Xy starts. Because the word itself is hard enough to say, but knowing the codename we have used since Raven went missing two years ago was also being used as a decoy name from a random operative? That alone adds a new meaning.

A meaning that Xyla might have been right all along.

"Team Black Bird, you stand by. You train. At any point we will move out to our next location. We need supplies packed, planes organized. We need to be ready to leave at a moment's notice. But not all of us will be going. Osprey and I will be hand selecting a few on each team to accompany us on any of our travels. The rest of you will remain here, protect The President, and work from HQ to ensure we are fully supported. But that doesn't mean you won't see some action." Small chuckles float up to us as the men smile. They truly are little adrenaline junkies. "I need all of you, regardless of your team, to be ready to move at any point. We don't know what we are truly up against or how many of you we will need. Does everyone understand?" A chorus of confirmations ensues, but no one moves an inch.

"Team Stitch," I add, glancing over at the men standing by our doctor. "We will need medical supplies pulled and included in all of our go-kits. We will not be travelling with any medics, aside from Stitch, so ensure we have everything we need on us at all times. We need these on the plane before the end of the night. Dismissed." Movement as everyone shuffles to their designated locations. It takes half a second before the sound of muffled gunshots echoes through the cement walls and people pair off on the training mat.

I turn and face Xyla who is watching everyone below.

"How many will we be bringing with us?" She asks me.

"Each smaller jet can hold twenty. I think we should bring Bird #13 as our HQ since it can hold more and has a larger cargo space. We can have Birds #5 and #27 holding any remaining soldiers and gear we need." She nods.

"So, fifty men, give or take, headed with us?" She questions.

"Yeah. Might be overkill, it isn't like we are going to war. But this gives us more men just to have as protection. We can also split up." I add, chewing on my lip. Her eyebrows raise.

"One plane to Paris, one to Bucharest, HQ to Siberia?" I nod and she smiles. "Sounds like a solid plan, partner. Men on the ground in all three locations. Get HQ's set up at each of our safe houses, that way we are ready to move without needing to worry about set up." And it gives Jet more men. I always feel a little suspicious of the men we keep permanently stationed in Russia.

"Exactly." I smile, pride fueling the blush to my cheeks as I stare at the former ballerina. "You've come a long way, Beast." I supply and pat her on the back before walking past her, but she grabs my arm.

"Wait. We have one more person to discuss." I sigh and turn around, her hand slipping off my bicep.

"She isn't coming." My voice is stern, edged in malic because I sure as hell will not condemn Serena to any of our untimely deaths, or her own.

"Not Rena, although she *is* coming. She would kill us both if we left her behind." She rolls her eyes before taking a deep breath. And fuck if she's right, but I will still put on a good show of fighting her. "My father. What are we going to do about him?"

"Bog's Team—" I start, but she cuts me off.

"No, Oz. He was a part of the hit on the decoy. He was a part of ruining any chance we had of learning who she was talking about. I don't think we can trust him." Her eyes search mine, and if I didn't know better, I would think they were starting to water.

"Well, I didn't expect us to even tell him where we are going." I try and joke, but she isn't having it.

"That isn't what I mean, and you know it." She spits, her brows furrowing. I sigh.

"Your father is a politician. We won't know his motives, probably ever. It's very likely he was trying to protect the country, or he could have a personal stake in it. We don't know and I doubt we ever will, regardless of how much we try. What he did is not important right now. With or without the decoy, we have a lead to Raven's potential location, or at least a location on a potential new threat. Let's focus on that for right now. Something we can control."

"It's not as easy for me to compartmentalize on this, Oz. He's my father."

"One day at a time." Her eyes soften as she recalls that Raven used to say that. She copies my deep breath and then nods.

"One day at a time."

# CHAPTER SEVEN

## XYLA

I awake to the sound of my front door closing. I am out of bed, armed, and throwing open the door before I can even take a breath. I spot ginger hair and muted green eyes through the sight on my pistol.

"Let's go." It's Oz.

"What happened?" I ask, tossing the gun on the dining table and slipping a pair of sweatpants on over my underwear.

"Conference with Jet." I stick with the pink camisole and bare feet and follow Osprey to the stairwell and up to the third floor. We make it to the conference room, and I see Jet on the big screen. He's on the plane and has blood along his hairline. But despite his sad state, he still quirks an eyebrow at my clothing.

"Jet, report." I command as I grip the back of one of the chairs tightly, ignoring his skeptical look. What the fuck happened?

"We landed in Siberia, the private hanger like always. But we were ambushed. All of us made it out, but we were expected. They knew we were coming. All of our men, the spies on the ground, their bodies were strewn around the hanger in various positions. Hanging, dismembered, disemboweled—"

"Enough." Oz says, and I hear him swallow.

"They knew we were coming." He repeats.

"Who did?" I ask.

"It was the Bratva." Jet says matter-of-factly.

"You mean the Red Feathers?" I inject, because the Bratva is done with. They were gone before the Red Feathers even joined the party.

"No, the Brotherhood of the Wolves. They are back." Silence. That's all that sits on the other side of the call as Oz and I stare at each other.

"It's not Kestrel." I point out. We have his body frozen in the morgue next to our suites.

"It could be Raven." He says, tilting his head.

"Running the *BRATVA*?" I screech at the blatant disrespect on her name. "She would rather die."

"Someone resurrected them. The Red Feathers are gone, but the Bratva was their originator. *Someone* brought them back."

"So we go to Siberia, to Norilsk. See if Kestrel has any family, or even Raven. Someone who could have brought it back and known about the last three years." Plans and maps start flicking through my mind like a picture book as I try and figure out what our next steps are.

"We are not going to Siberia." Oz spits, his glare fixing on me.

"Guys, I need a destination." Jet says, his voice loud over the plane engine.

"Meet up with the crew in Romania. We will meet you there." I disconnect the call and look up at Oz. "Get a jet ready. We leave in ten." I don't spare him a glance as I walk past, but his grip around my upper arm is firm.

"We are partners, Xyla. We make these decisions together." I stare at him and unclench my jaw.

"What would you have us do?" I push, hoping for peace.

"I say we go to Paris. We have three destinations. Three bases set up. Our one in Siberia is compromised. We send one of our planes to Romania and the other to Paris. We can be on the one to Paris."

"Why?" I question. Not because I doubt his logic, but because I want to know why he chose *Paris*.

"She always said Paris." He says with a smile.

"What?"

"She always said Paris was her favorite place in the world." I literally have never heard her say that, but I can't discredit the years they spent together before me.

"So, if she's alive..."

"Then how romantic would it be to find her there." I scoff, but it morphs into a laugh.

"I am not looking for romance right now, Oz. I am looking for a sign of life. And if she is alive, I think you're right. Paris would be a good start since we can't make landfall in Siberia. Paris or Bucharest are our only options."

"Paris it is." I nod and he turns to make the call, getting the three planes ready to depart.

"Serena—"

"No, Xyla." His voice is stern, harsh as he spins around.

"She's coming, it's not up for discussion. I just wanted you to know." His face turns an angry shade of red, and I pat his shoulder. "Buck up, soldier. She won't be a liability. She'll keep us safe." He rolls his eyes, and I take that as my cue to leave.

On my way back to my suite, I knock on Rena's door.

"Wheels up in ten." I yell and then walk away.

Exactly seven minutes later, I am packed and staring at the blank wall in my living room with Raven's accolades. Stars, medals, and the gun. The stupid, fucking gun. The one thing she considered a prized possession.

Angry tears spill down my cheeks, my fists clench, and then one is flying through the shadowbox.

Glass sprays everywhere, slicing through my knuckles. The shadowbox falls off the wall, the gun hitting the ground. I wipe my bloodied fist onto my pants, bend down, and pick up the gun. I give it one look before I shove it in the holster on my right thigh.

Hand wrapped and hidden under leather gloves; I take my seat on the jet with one minute to spare.

# CHAPTER EIGHT

## SERENA

Three hours in the air, and Xyla is passed out. Her hand resting on the gun she thinks we don't see. Osprey and I share a look, my gut twisting as I turn to look out the window. The sky is pitch black, clouds barely visible as they brush past the glass.

"Fix." He says as he moves to the seat across from me.

"Osprey." I respond, not letting my gaze drift over to him.

"You shouldn't have come." I suck on my front teeth and turn to face him.

"It's not your choice. And besides, I will be safer with you in Paris than I will as a sitting duck in DC." I spit, narrowing my eyes. His own lighten and a smirk follows.

"So, you think you're safe with me?" He leans forward and I feel my stomach flip as he rests his forearms on his knees.

"You wouldn't let me get hurt." I deflect. "You're too scared of Xyla." He snorts and shakes his head. Feeling bold, thanks to two glasses of champagne, I lean forward, mimicking his position.

"Am I wrong? Am I *not* safe with you?" I tilt my head, my tongue running across my lower lip. I watch as his eyes track the movement.

"You're safe from the outside world when you're with me, but," He stops, swallowing.

"But?" I whisper, leaning ever so slightly closer until I can feel his breath cascade across my face.

"You're not safe *from* me." My eyes flick down to his lips before returning to his eyes. So close. He's so close, yet I can't go there.

I can't jeopardize their partnership.

"Well, alright then." I lean back, crossing my legs and picking my book back up, ignoring the flutters in my chest. His eyebrow quirks and I hear him sigh before he gets back up and returns to his seat.

I bite my lower lip, hard. I feel the prick of my teeth and then taste the copper tang of blood, but I keep biting down.

After my ex, after feeling like such a burden, being anything but a one-night stand for a hot mercenary is out of the question. So, I have slept my way through Xy's men. It isn't a secret. But Osprey, he would be a different level. A level I can't cross unless I am sure it's something I want.

Something that would last.

Because with him, it could mean something. He's not a dumb brute who I admire for their body. Osprey's brain, his heart.

That is what I admire about him. The way he commands an entire militia of men but still jokes around and smiles when they aren't looking.

I glance up at him, watch as he drapes a blanket over Xyla and reclines her chair so she's more comfortable as she sleeps.

He's perfect.

And that's why he can't be mine.

And I can never be his.

# CHAPTER NINE

## XYLA

Jet, Radar, and Shark beat us to Paris, even after rerouting mid-air. Their flight only taking four hours compared to our seven. Jet is there, waiting by an idling SUV, when we step out of the plane and onto the tarmac.

"Report." I say as I walk past him, a yawn creeping up my throat. He keeps pace, opening the door for me.

"HQ is set up in an abandoned warehouse. Men stationed at the perimeter for look out. We have three undercover in various locations across the city. We have had no sightings of anyone that could resemble Black Bird. We have, however, noticed a string of robberies along the Seine." He shuts my door and climbs into the passenger seat.

"What kind of robberies?" I ask as I pull out the tablet from the back of his seat.

"Illegal weapons, grenades, ammo. Black market arsenals mostly." He adds as I pull up the reports.

"Gangs?" I question, looking at surveillance footage. I see darkness, but that's it. No defining features. And no vehicles.

"No, the gangs are the ones being robbed. We have made a connection with *La Morsure*, it's them being robbed." I pause.

"The Bite?" I question. They are the largest mafia syndicate in Paris. Their name comes from the phrase "*la morsure du serpent*", which means 'the serpent's bite'.

"Correct. Étienne Veyrac confirmed he will meet with us." My mouth falls open.

"You got a meeting with the *don*?" I squeal. I turn to look at Oz, who had climbed into the driver's seat.

"Yes, boss. Figured we shouldn't waste time." Jet says with a smirk.

"God, I love you." I tap away. "What do we know about them?"

It's Radar who speaks, his voice piping up from the back.

"Étienne Veyrac is fifty-two years old and carries around a serpent-shaped cane which is believed to have actual poison in the fangs. His team prefers poison to bullets because its silent and easier to hide, however they aren't afraid of a little gun play. He grew up in Marseille, where he started *La Morsure* as a Corsican smuggling ring. Humans, weapons—you name it. He moved to Paris simply for access to docks and the endless tunnels under the city. This is where he chose to build his empire. He isn't known for being rash, he thinks things through. You always know he's coming, but you never know when, or how. He likes to catch people by surprise. He has no children, and no wife. His mafia are his family." He finishes and I stare at the old man on the screen before me.

He's handsome, as handsome as a disgustingly rich old man can be. This picture appears to be taken by someone on the street. His muted gray suit is tailored perfectly to him, and I can barely make out his serpent cane, partially hidden behind his leg.

"Where are we to meet him?" I ask.

"The edge of the Sienne in an abandoned crypt that used to be a wine cellar." He responds, and all I can picture is a decrepit dungeon we'll never leave.

"Lovely." I scoff as we drive through the darkened streets, the sun starting to rise.

"When is this meeting you scheduled without a direct order?" Oz pipes up as he turns into an alleyway, anger coating his voice. He'll have to get over it. Jet's rash decision probably just gave us the best lead we've ever had.

"Tonight. Midnight."

Despite some protests, only Osprey and I head to this clandestine meeting hours later. Serena had the most to protest, saying she was safest with the two of us. However, we reminded her that almost seventy trained mercenaries outside her door are probably going to keep her safer than going to a meeting where we are walking into only the Gods know what. She pouted and locked herself in the fourth-floor room we are using as the main suite and office for the three of us.

So, Oz and I left, walked almost a mile in the direction that Jet pointed, saying we'll know it when we get to it. And we did.

We spy a small boat, anchored for us off the edge of the Siene. We both look at it for a brief second, before I shrug and jump in from the sidewalk. A resounding boom echoes over the silent night as my feet land in the center of the boat and I hold my arms out to keep it steady. I have no desire to fall in the cesspool of this dirty ass river.

Oz joins me, with less grace obviously, and then takes control of the oars. We use the small boat to approach what looks to be a covered archway, another thing Jet told us to look out for. The water is quiet, lapping at the sides of the rotting wood and I find myself curling my lip in distaste. We are going to either sink in this shitty boat or get locked down there.

The archway is crumbling, small rocks falling from it as the breeze dislodges loose debris. The whole thing is abandoned, but out of the corner of my eye, I see a glint of metal in the darkness.

"There!" I whisper and point. Osprey turns the boat so we are level to the archway and reaches forward, pushing open a metal gate leading to a landing and then stairs going down.

I grip the edge of the boat and throw myself over, fighting against the small current of the river, before landing on the concrete. Oz joins me, ties the boat off, and we stare at the darkness below.

"Think it's a trap?" Oz says as he peers cautiously.

"Only one way to find out. At least Jet will know where to retrieve the bodies." I joke, earning me a sidelong glance of annoyance.

Oz goes first, his footsteps echoing on the stone as he slowly descends. We turn the corner and see lanterns appear, their flames licking at the damp walls, finally illuminating the space. Wet stone, mold, and smoke fill my nose, and I crinkle it. It smells old and rotten.

I feel an overwhelming sense of claustrophobia and dread as we descend even further, until we reach the very end of the steps. Right before us a fairly large circular room opens up, and we both take a second to scan it.

There in the center of the room, sits a table with a white tablecloth, wine glasses, and none other than Étienne Veyrac. In the candlelight I can see a deep purple scar running from his jaw, down to his jugular. He's wearing a dark suit, a white shirt that is unbuttoned enough to show off the bright, gold necklaces around his neck. He's wearing a mobster looking top hat that makes me want to snort in the irony, but I bite my lip to hold it in.

Movement out of the corner of my eye has me also fighting a flinch as five men step out of the shadows in unison, letting us know we aren't alone. Their hands stay clasped in front of them, their bodies rigid in their black t-shirts, jeans, and boots. Damn, they must be cold. I can feel the icy, wet air even through my jacket.

Étienne is all smiles as he stands, taking a fat cigar out of his mouth and setting it on an ash tray, before clapping his hands in one resounding *smack*.

"Oh, *ma chère*!" He exclaims, stepping around the table and towards us. "Xyla Bader, you are more beautiful than I could have predicted." He reaches for my hand, and I hesitantly give it to him, readying for any funny business he tries. He presses a kiss to the back of it before letting it go and offering his hand to Osprey to shake.

"Nice to meet you, Étienne." Oz says, no ounce of diplomacy in his voice as he stares the old man down.

"Interesting meeting place." I add, giving him a light smile.

"Ah. Paris keeps her secrets best in the dark, and the Siene is known for hiding the truth." He says cryptically and then gestures to the table. "Sit, sit." I move first, following him further into the chamber and watching as he pours a rich, red wine into three crystal glasses.

"I know why you are here, *ma chère*." I raise a brow and take a seat. "Whispers of a missing bird, a *perle rare,* have come even to us in Paris." He smiles, and his eyes glance at Osprey behind me. A rare pearl. He knows we are looking for Raven. "And of course, you brought *ton chien fidèle*. A queen should never walk alone, hm?" He adds.

"What did he just call me?" Oz says, his voice dropping in octave as he leans closer to me and this time I don't fight the snort.

"A loyal dog, are you not?" Étienne smiles at me and I gesture for Oz to sit, but he doesn't move.

"Thank you for meeting with us." I say as sickeningly sweet as possible.

"It is my pleasure, *ma chère*." He takes a sip of his wine. "Now about your missing bird." He cuts to the chase, and I find I like that about him.

"Do you know of her whereabouts?"

"Patience." He scowls, waving a hand in the air. "Don't you want to know about the missing shipments of weapons? I believe that is why the other dog demanded such a meeting?" I bite my tongue and nod. It technically was, but he was the one who brought up a missing bird.

"Over fifteen cargo shipments have been taken from us. Men killed, men with families." He starts and I almost think I hear his throat catch.

"What were in those shipments?" I ask.

"Weapons, rifles, materials for bombs, you name it." He gestures wildly with his hands. "We had assumed it was someone else, but now we are thinking it has something to do with your bird." He purses his lips and looks at me accusingly.

"You think Raven is the one stealing your shipments?" I say with disbelief.

"Naomi Cross is not stealing my shipments, no." He retorts as if the name is nothing more than idle gossip. I gasp and Oz tenses behind me, his hand resting on my shoulder.

"You know her? Her real name?" I stand, the chair scooting back as my voice turns into a shrill sounding yell. The men in the shadows reach for their weapons, but I ignore them. "She's *alive*?"

"Yes, she is. Missing no more! *Ha*!" He laughs as if he made a joke and I glare at him, my lips curling in irritation. He chuckles to himself and then sucks on his cigar again. He's blowing out a long line of smoke as Oz breaks the silence.

"What does she have to do with your shipments?" Oz pushes, and Étienne shuts his mouth.

"Your rare pearl, the missing bird. She is not working alone, no? How could she have faked her death without help? I bet you are wondering who it is that stole her away in the night." He smiles, and I fear he'll make us beg or give something up for the information. But to my surprise, he offers it up. "The one stealing my shipments is her brother. Nathan Cross. But I believe you knew him as Crow?"

# CHAPTER TEN

## OSPREY

The silence is thick enough to cut as we both stare at Étienne. Xyla is barely breathing, and my own heart feels as if it'll explode out of my chest. Even though she is standing, my hand still rests on her shoulders. Either to hold her back, or shove her behind me for protection, I am not sure.

"Explain." She says through gritted teeth, and I feel her back tense.

"All in due time, *ma chère*." He says to Xyla. I squeeze her a little harder, definitely leaning more towards restraining her.

"So, neither Raven nor Crow are dead." She responds.

"Correct." Étienne's air of nonchalance is going to be the death of him. If I don't get to him, Xyla will rip him to shreds. Either way, he won't make it out at the end of all of this.

"How could you possibly be involved with him?" I question, hoping for more answers. But he strikes me as the type of man who wants you to ask the right questions, otherwise he won't give you the answers.

"*La Morsure* has three outposts. Conveniently in the same locations as you. How interesting?" His voice trails off before he smiles and starts ticking off his fingers. "Bucharest, Paris, and Siberia. Bucharest is where our human...*dealings* lie. Paris is where we rule from, and Siberia is where I have outsourced my mercenaries."

"The Bratva." Xyla whispers, sitting back down. "You brought them back?"

"Yes, *ma chère*. Brilliant, you are." He smiles at her as if she's a prize. "But I never brought them back because they were never gone. Just hidden. Operating under a new name. I just employ their services."

"I don't understand how this has to do with Raven right now?" Xyla questions.

"Nathan needed a way to hide his *perle rare's* movements. It was my serpents who caught her, and we struck a deal. He can use my channels to keep her hidden, and in exchange, I get use of his men and information about U.S. intelligence."

"But *why* is he using her?" Étienne shrugs, as if the question never even crossed his mind.

"That is of no consequence to me. I benefit from his men and information, and he benefits from mine. He is reckless and brash, merely a child with men stupid enough to follow him. He gets what he wants, he just doesn't know he is giving me what I want." And I was right. He doesn't care about Nathan's end goal, only that he is getting something out of it. A businessman in all aspects, I guess.

"What I don't understand is why you think Nathan is stealing from you." I lean back in my chair, the question burning in my mind. Yeah, I can think of a million reasons why they would need weapons and bombs, but why steel from presumably the only ally you have?

"Nathan is using me. He doesn't want a lasting partnership; he wants my job. I am the Parisian kingpin, and he is merely," He pauses and looks right at me. "*Mon chien fidèle.*" I roll my eyes. *His* loyal dog. Although loyal he is clearly not.

"Why are you telling us this?" Xyla asks.

"Nathan is setting me up to take the fall. He thinks he can weasel his way into my men and then turn it around so I go down for his crimes. And I guess mine. This world you are carelessly entering is a chess game, *ma chère*. One that was started a long time ago. We have been playing for so long, yet neither of us have had the ability to check the other king. I need a queen. And that is the position I offer you." Xyla snorts and I turn to look at her.

"You want me to marry you?" She spits, cackling into her hand.

"On the contrary. I have no desire for a wife. I just want your aid. Your partnership. I want you to help me take Nathan down, in exchange, I will help you recover your bird." He offers and fuck if it doesn't sound too good to be true.

I watch her eyes flick back and forth as she thinks, and I bite my tongue. My choice would be to say no, but this whole hunt for

Raven has been hers from the beginning and for once, I'll follow her lead. I will let her make this decision.

"Better to accept the bite willingly than to wait for the fangs to coat in poison, no?" Étienne's voice is laced with sweetness as he doles out a poetic threat, and Xyla just stares at him before turning to me.

"Oz?" This could be our chance to find Raven and to take down the Bratva, but we would be aiding an even bigger monster.

But what if we could take them both down at the same time?

I hold her stare and see a little gleam in her eye that tells me she knows what I am thinking. We nod at the same time.

"We accept." I answer and Étienne's smile turns sinister.

"I cannot wait to have fun with you, *ma chère* and *ton chien fidèle.*" We all rise as one, no hands are shaken.

Xyla and I step back towards the entrance as Étienne and his men disappear in the shadows, obviously exiting another way.

"We will be in touch!" He yells out as I push Xyla towards the stairs. She takes them two at a time, no doubt feeling a little untrustful in the ease of everything. As am I. This doesn't feel right.

We break out of the damp air and onto the edge of the river. I step into the boat, helping her in behind me, and start paddling away from the cellar as fast as I possibly could.

"There is something we forgot to ask him." Xyla says and I look at her, confused. I feel like we got as much information as we were ever going to get in one evening. Maybe even more than he had planned to tell us.

"His connection to my father. There has to be one." I ponder, because she's right. There is a connection between Étienne, Lincoln, and the decoy. Maybe even a connection to Nathan thrown in there. And for once, I agree with the bad guy. This is a chess game we just entered out of nowhere. The game has already started, and we will be left to figure out who to play and who to survive.

"One step at a time, Xy. Right now, we just found out both Raven and Nathan are alive. I would call this a win. It's sure as hell a win in my book." I say, trying to lighten the mood. The last thing we need is her spiraling about her father right now. Our issues and distrust with him will be there tomorrow. And the next day.

Honestly probably forever. You can't trust any politician.

"What are we going to do about *La Morsure*?" She asks, her chestnut and gold eyes staring into mine with naivety. With hope.

"Play the game."

# CHAPTER ELEVEN

## XYLA

The walk back to the warehouse is silent. Both of us pondering whatever the hell we just got into. But even though Oz called this a win and said we should play the game, I still feel hesitance coming from him.

"What's the next step? It's not like he gave us a phone number." I mutter and feel Oz sigh next to me.

"I don't know, Xy. I don't know." I stop, the dark alleyway barely illuminating his face as he passes me.

"What is it?" I ask. He stops and turns, his face impassive.

"I don't know if I believe him." My breath catches.

"Believe him about...what?"

"Raven being alive. Nathan being alive. It just doesn't feel right. Like it's too good to be true. Like this is a trap." He says softly.

"We knew she was alive. We always knew."

"I didn't. I didn't believe it. And now—"

"Now you feel like you failed her because you stopped looking." I finish his sentence, because that is what I feel.

I failed her.

We both did.

We didn't find her. We didn't save her. We didn't prevent her from being a pawn. We moved on.

But one thing doesn't add up.

She's a pawn, but why?

Why is she doing this willingly? Because the Raven I know would have fought like hell to get out of whoever's grasp, yet she has been gone for two years. Two years is a long time to bide your time, and a long time to spend fighting.

So, what is she doing?

"Why is she cooperating?" I ask, breaking the silence, his gaze never leaving mine as I rifle through the thoughts in my head.

"What do you mean?" He quirks a brow.

"She hasn't fought. She hasn't broken free. She's willingly being Nathan's puppet. If she were fighting this, we would have heard about it somewhere. We would have heard from her. You think she'd go this long without contacting us? Why is doing this willingly?" I take a few steps, catching up to him.

"We don't know that for sure. But if she hasn't, there has to be a reason. She would never abandon us, Xyla." His voice turns soft as he looks down at me.

"So, next steps should be finding that reason." I add, swallowing any ounce of hurt that threatens to bubble up.

"Not finding her?" His brows raise again as he looks at me with surprise.

"She's hiding. Evading us. For a *reason*. So, we can't waste our resources looking for her if she doesn't want to be found. Trust me, all I *want* is to find her." I stare at him deeply, trying to convey the longing and hopelessness in my eyes. "But we need to work with Étienne and find out what Nathan has over her. And then, then we can break her out, release her, whatever the correct term is for her current predicament."

"One day at a time."

"One day at a time, Oz."

We get back to the warehouse a little after three in the morning, the October air slightly frosting the cracked windows. Unsurprisingly, the previously abandoned building is still bustling. Men filing in from hidden rooms, computers set up everywhere, an entire wall of TVs showcasing our endless supply of surveillance across the entire city.

"Jet!" I call out into the warehouse. One single word and he walks over with Radar in tow, his head in a tablet as always.

"Boss." He gives me a curt nod.

"Are the planes hidden?" He nods again. "Good, work with Radar's team on the drones to make sure visuals are always on. Radar, make sure your men are looking into any bank correspondence between Nathan Cross and Étienne. I know they have a financial connection, and I want to see how much money we are talking. They are smart, so finding their accounts, offshore and local, will take a bit. I want you on that ASAP." I instruct. He also nods, and both men walk away.

It's Serena that walks up next.

"Rena." I smile and squeeze her hand.

"How did it go?" She asks, worry in her eyes as she searches Oz up and down. Their gazes meet and she turns back to me.

"As to be expected. I'll fill you in later." I look around the open room and see a set of iron stairs to the back right. "I am ready for bed." I groan and she tilts her head, gesturing towards the stairs.

"Everyone else is set up in barracks in the basement. Our rooms are set up upstairs in the observation deck on level four." She explains as if I wasn't here earlier.

"Why are you calling it an observation deck?" I ask and look up to see the floor that has a glass lined wall overlooking the warehouse. Oh, because the room quite literally observes the entire room. "Got it." I look back at Oz.

"Go on. I'll make sure everything is good down here and then meet you." I nod and pull Rena with me towards the stairs, exhaustion making my limbs heavy. I am also starving but honestly sleep and a shower sound better than food right now. I'll have to eat something when I wake up in a couple hours.

"Boss!" I hear someone call and turn to see Radar walking over with a tablet. "You have an encrypted message."

"From who?" I ask, taking it from him. A few taps later and I groan. It's from my father. "*I need you to return to the states for a summit on international affairs, particularly our relationship with Russia. Non-negotiable. Love, Daddy.*" I read aloud. I scoff and hand him back the tablet. "No time. Sorry." I say to no one in particular, turning back towards the stairs and making my way to our suite.

By suite, I mean very drab room with bunk beds, desks lining the windowed wall, a private bathroom, and that is quite literally it. The ceiling has various mold spots, damp air making me scrunch my nose. We could have at least sequestered a less abandoned looking abandoned warehouse.

I claim a top bunk, tossing my cell on it, and then drown myself in scalding water in the arguably decent shower. My bags are sitting in the bathroom, and I quickly change before heading back out to the bedroom, counting down the seconds until my head hits the pillow. I have on a pair of pink sweatpants and a gray henley. The warehouse has a slight chill, and the frost keeps growing unseasonably fast. So, long sleeves and pants will help me *not* freeze while I am trying to sleep.

Rena is sitting on the bottom bunk under mine, scrolling on her phone when I approach. She's chewing on the edge of her thumb, and I can see some new scabs along her cuticle. She only chews when she's nervous or stressed, but I guess considering our current situation, both are appropriate.

"Do you think we will have time to explore a bit tomorrow?" She asks without looking up and I see she's searching a map on her screen. "If you can't come, I'll take one of the guys. I just want to see some of the city." She says it so nonchalantly and it breaks my heart. She expects me to not spend any time with her.

Because I usually don't.

I smile, the tilt of my lips not meeting my eyes. She endures these travels yet ends up stuck in the hotel or headquarters the entire time. She's the one who chooses to go, but we are still both so young and the urge to explore is pressing. She deserves to see the world she travels too, and I need to be a better friend.

"I plan on sleeping in a little bit, just to catch up, and then why don't you and I get some breakfast and then see the catacombs?" Her head whips in my direction, heart wrenching surprise on her face.

"Wait, really?" Her voice is coated in disbelief, which just makes me feel like shit.

"Yes!" I exclaim, jumping on her twin size mattress. "I have always wanted to see them too, might as well. I mean we have a lot to do here, but I can spare a few hours." She claps enthusiastically and throws her arms around me. I really would love to see the catacombs. The amount of horror movies we have binged that surround the catacombs is insane, but we both have a little bit of an obsession with them.

"What is going on up here?" Oz asks as he steps into the room, eyes wary.

"Xy and I are going to see the catacombs tomorrow." Rena responds, glaring at him as if he interrupted something important.

"Oh really? Nice little vacation treat?" He teases and she throws a lumpy pillow at him.

"I told her I could spare a couple hours tomorrow morning. You are more than capable of taking care of things here." I supply, throwing in a little praise.

"Your faith in me is appreciated, little beast."

"Har har." I say sarcastically. "We'll take Shark with us."

"I wish Bog was here." Serena pouts and I see Oz's face flame. Her and Bog have never done anything but do have a healthy flirting relationship.

"He is definitely bigger than Shark, but between him and I, we got you covered." I quickly add, making it seem like it's because Bog is a heartier male who can literally hit people with the force of a battering ram, which he can. The dude's a tank.

"Mmhmm." Oz says as he closes the bathroom door a little too forcefully.

"You are breaking him." I scold as I smack her knee.

"Listen, if he can't handle me than he doesn't deserve me." She shrugs before tossing her mass of onyx curly hair over her shoulder.

"You know just as well as I do that there is no one in the world better for you than him, Serena." I say quietly so Oz doesn't hear. But *she* needs to hear it. Because I am right.

"It would never work, Xy. It's too dangerous. This line of work always results in loss and casualties. Just look at y—" She clamps her lips shut, her eyes widening in surprise that she just said that.

"Look at me and Raven?" I finish for her and her brows furrow, regret washing over her.

"I didn't mean—"

"No. You did." I cut her off, a little too harshly, so I soften my voice. "And you're right. But Raven saved my life. She loved me so much she took a bullet for me, multiple times. She was tortured and then died in my arms. That kind of love, even if it's short, you don't want to miss out on. It's life changing. I could never settle for anything less than that. Anything less than what she wanted to offer me. And Oz? He would love you so fiercely, you couldn't breathe. He would never let you get hurt, he would defend you until his last breath."

"That's what I am afraid of." She whispers, glancing back at the shut bathroom door.

"What do you mean?" I lean closer.

"He already is overprotective, trying to prevent me from doing things, going places. He didn't want me to come here. He doesn't ever want me to travel with you, and sometimes I feel like he wishes I wasn't at The Nest, but then I also feel like he would be worse with his stalking if I lived somewhere else. We aren't even together and I feel suffocated. What would it be like if we were?" She makes a good point, but I think what she sees as an incredible trait as a negative. Having someone love you and care for you so much that their entire life revolves around you is rare.

"Oz is a trigger-happy golden retriever who wants his people safe. Anything he does or tries to do isn't in malice, it's not from a desire for control. It's in fear. It's in his desire to keep you safe. His choices and actions are based on love. For you. For me. For Raven. Oz and I haven't known each other long, but he is my other half. He is the other half of my soul in a way Raven wasn't. With her, it was romantic love, sexual tension and a need for each other. But with Osprey, he is my brother. My partner. My platonic soulmate. For him, I would risk everything. Just as I would for you. Just as he would for me and just as he would for you. Whether you are with him or not, that won't change."

Tears prick in her eyes, lining them silver as she stares at me, absorbing everything.

"I want that kind of love. The love you have for Raven and Oz. I want that feeling. I want those connections. You and your dad are all I have ever had. And seeing you with Oz and how you were with Raven, I got jealous. Literally green with envy, when you were fighting for your life and watching people you love die. And I was at home pissed off because my boyfriend didn't look at me like that."

"Then stop limiting yourself." I reach forward and squeeze her hand. "Take a chance for once."

"What if it doesn't work out?" Her lip trembles.

"There is no dimension in the universe where you two aren't endgame, Serena. That man is so in love with you it makes me sick." She playfully slaps my hand away and wipes at her face. "Take a chance. On yourself. On him. And as cliché as it sounds, take a chance on love." She inhales slowly and then nods, just as the bathroom door opens.

We both swivel our heads quickly and Oz freezes, his eyes widening.

"What?" He says sheepishly and despite the tense conversation, we both erupt into a fit of laughter. "I hate you both."

# CHAPTER TWELVE

## XYLA

The night is both long and short at the same time. The cold seeps through the thin blankets and I miss the lush pillow top mattress at home. Osprey's snores echo through the room that is 90% cement, so everything echoes, and I can hear Serena's music filtering through her headphones. Not to mention I can hear everything going on downstairs since the windows are a far cry from soundproof. Last but not least, I couldn't stop thinking about Raven.

Alone.

Somewhere here in Paris.

Crow—or Nathan—must *have* something on her. Something he could threaten her with. She would risk her life to break free from a tyrant, she did it with Kes, so why isn't she walking away? Why didn't she just kill him already? What could possibly be at risk? Or what is he holding over her?

Is Étienne right? Or are we truly chasing a ghost?

I roll over again, peering over the rusted metal edge of the top bunk. Oz is asleep on the bottom bunk across from us, his positioning mirroring Serena's. Both of them are on their sides, knees tucked close to their body, blankets burrito'd around them. I roll my eyes and sit up, already missing the warmth from the mattress.

The sun is barely peeking out over the horizon, lighting the room slightly. The top of the walls feature some cracked and stained windows that are so small, a person couldn't fit through them, but at least they offer some light.

I quietly slide off the bed, using the frame as a makeshift ladder, the metal so cold it stings my bare feet, and walk to the glass wall. I cross my arms over my chest, rubbing my hands up and down on my upper arms as I look down.

Men and women are bustling about below, moving through chairs and desks with ease. Some on computers, some training, some organizing and cataloging weapons, some eating at the makeshift kitchen. Some are drinking coffee and laughing as if they are at a standard nine to five. Despite this being an organization built on grit and stamina, these people have created a family within one another. People they would die for.

I look back at Osprey and Serena peacefully sleeping in their bunks. Despite everything, *they* are my family, the ones I would risk everything for. I have my father, yes, but his duties are no longer certain. His morals and agenda are up in the air, and I haven't had a moment alone with him to try and get him to divulge whatever it is he's hiding. Between making a prized piece of intel disappear and not divulging anything with us, he is no longer the man I know. The man I know wouldn't have erased a woman. He wouldn't have been complicit to murder. He is working with someone and with Étienne saying Nathan provides U.S. intelligence, it makes me question whether or not my father is working with him.

Could he be? Could Nathan have been literally right under our noses this entire time? Just an arm's reach away?

And if he is working with him, does that mean he knows Raven is alive? Does he know that the woman I fell in love with and who died so that I could live, is out there? Is he willingly keeping her from me? Because I think that would be the one thing that would truly destroy the image of my father in my head. The one thing that would ensure I never forgave him.

I shake my head and turn away from the glass, gritting my teeth in anger. I quickly change into the bathroom, lacing up my boots as tight as they can go, before throwing my hair in a braid and racing down the stairs. I need to work off this anger. I need to do *something* other than sit there.

"Shark!" I yell and in seconds the brick wall of a man appears as if he can teleport.

"Boss." He gives me a curt nod.

"I *really* need to punch something." I say and I can't help but smile at the wicked gleam in his eyes as he foresees just how dirty it's going to get.

We spar, and by spar, I mean we go to death. That's what we all do. We never hold back. Never. I get a sharp kick into his knee, but soon after his fist clips my ribs. I feign to the right and then send my fist flying into his cheek, sending him to the ground. He gets to his knees quickly, but my boot hits him square in the stomach and he gasps for air as he rolls onto his back, tapping the mat to yield. Cheering erupts around us and a bow dramatically. Shark stands, shakes my hand, and steps off the mat, collapsing into the first chair he finds. I hear the cheers from others and the feel the footsteps on the mat as another takes his place. When I turn, I see it's Oz and I know it's about to be fun.

"Morning, sleeping beauty." I say with a grin.

"Oh, how original." He mocks. "Come on." He gestures forward and I cock a brow. We start our slow circling of one another, our booted feet silent on the mat. My hands are loose at my sides, as are his. Our usual dance since we spar so often.

He flinches forward, but I don't fall for it, and he smiles in response, his brows furrowing as he concentrates.

"It's always boring when they fight." I hear someone mutter and I snort. Oz shoots someone a glare and I take that moment to lunge.

My arm goes around his neck, and I kick myself up in the air, flipping backwards. He falls forward, landing on his hands as I land on my feet.

"Alright, *Natasha*." He mutters, and I quite like the reference to the *Black Widow*. He pulls himself up and lunges forward, grabbing my arm that wasn't tucked into my side enough. *Rookie move, Xyla.* He spins us around, bending my arm at an unnatural angle, shoving my hand up towards my neck.

I can feel the tendons and muscles stretching, the burning making my fingertips tingle. He wrenches my wrist up, forcing it even harder against my spine. One might think that would be it and I'd tap out, but Oz has one disadvantage when he's fighting me.

His size.

I swing one leg back, forcing my entire body weight forward as we both come to the ground, using the momentum to knock off his balance. He lands on my back with a grunt, and I ignore the pain. I use the one knee I manage to slip under me to throw us up, my quads burning. He lands on his back this time, and I end up straddling his chest with a knife pressed against his neck, my other hand threaded through his hair to keep him still.

"Checkmate." I whisper, panting. He smiles, and then I feel it. The prick of a blade at the bottom of my ribs, just barely cutting into my skin. I glance down and see his own knife angled up. If he were to break through my skin, push up just a few inches, he'd hit my heart. Even with my vest, the knife could easily slip in without restraint.

"Checkmate." He says back and I smile. God, I love this man. He truly is my equal. I sit up, pulling my knife off his neck, making sure to scratch him a little, before getting to my feet.

"My turn." My hand freezes in the air as I offer it to Oz and we both look over in shock.

Serena is pushing her way through the crowd wearing *my* clothes. She is a lot curvier than me, so the sleek black tank top and leggings do little to hide her perfect figure. Her hips are wide, her waist small, but sloping into breasts that are no doubt everyone's wet dream. She has always been prettier than me. I smile as I look her over. She has on my spare vest over the tank top. Her curled hair is pulled into a bun atop her head, but that one unruly tendril is still dangling in front of her face. She has on a pair of boots, laced up to mid-calf. Her tanned skin is slim, toned, but not muscular like mine.

But that's something we can fix. Excitement bubbles its way out of my chest, and I give an excited shrill as I clap.

"No." Oz says, slapping my clapping hands out of the way and pulling himself up to his feet.

"Damn, Fix." I hear someone call out with a whistle. And I have to admit; she looks fucking hot. She looks *deadly*.

"Fuck, yes." I say bounding over to her. "Ready to get dirty?" I say with a devilish smirk, grabbing her arm.

"I've been ready. You know I have. But I don't want to fight you. I want to fight him." She points at Oz, and his face grows red, anger filling his features as his eyes narrow.

"I am not fighting you." He says it slowly, enunciating every word as he stares her down. But my best friend, my very hot best friend with a death wish, doesn't flinch.

"Fine. Anyone else care to take me on?" She spins in a circle, giving the men her deadliest smile, and I slap my hand over my mouth to hold the laugh in.

Oh, she is definitely going to get it.

"If anyone takes one fucking step, I will send a bullet in between your eyes. I don't fucking care who you are." Silence spreads as no one dares to breathe. I step off the mat, backing into Jet who steadies me, and watch Serena get closer to Oz. Her prance is cat-like, lithe, as she reaches him. She lifts one hand, her finger tracing his bicep, her short nails leaving a red line as she scratches him.

"Don't worry, Ozzy baby, you won't hurt me. I like it rough." She peers up at him through her lashes and he freezes.

"Fuck." He whispers in an exhale, and I feel every single person around me stiffen.

Oz is always scary, but when it involves Serena, he's fucking terrifying.

# CHAPTER THIRTEEN

## OSPREY

I can already smell her. Floral and musky. Like a forest after it rains, it cascades around me and I inhale. I can feel the sting of her nail from where it slid down my skin, knowing she left a mark and goddamn I really hope she did. I can feel her heat as she steps closer to me, begging me to fight her. Her breasts press into my ribs as she looks up and I look down. Our gazes hold and I can feel the tension, the tension that's been there for years.

Fuck it.

I grip her wrist and spin her around, forcing her against me. The generous curve of her ass presses into my quads, and I try to ignore how good it feels, but she shifts, rubbing against me slightly. She's playing extra *dirty*. I keep my grip light to keep any bruises to a minimum, also allowing her to slip out of my grip if needed. She leans back against my chest, tilting her chin up so she can look at me, giving me her softest doe eyes.

"So gentle, Osprey." She chastises and rips her arm from my hand, spinning around to face me. "Treat me like you treat Xyla." She orders and I shake my head.

"Xyla has had training." I argue, putting my hands on my hips.

"Then train me." She pushes, her brows furrowing slightly as she becomes incensed. An emotion I quite like on her. She steps back into me, her hand coming up to touch my face. But before it can, I slap it away and kick her feet out from under her.

She bounces on the mat as her back hits it, a very unglamourous *oof* escaping between her lips as it knocks the air out of her. She shoots back up, her tiny fist flying through the air. I catch it easily and shoot her a wicked grin.

"Getting angry are we, Fix?" I tease and her frown deepens as her jaw clenches. She spins sloppily on her heel but successfully sends her elbow into my sternum. I sputter and she reaches forward to grab my hair—a cheap shot, one she probably learned from watching Xyla. My arm goes around her waist, lifting her off the ground easily, before I throw her back to the ground.

I land on top of her, my teeth clenching together as I pin her down. One of my arms rests lightly on her neck, the other holds her arms above her head. She looks up at me, breathing heavily as I sit on her.

"You're enjoying this." She hisses, her breath cascading over my face.

"You have no idea how much." I whisper, feeling like my chest is going to explode. My eyes land on her lips as she licks them before I meet her gaze. Her eyes lock on mine and then I let out an involuntarily girlish yelp.

I roll onto my back gasping with breath. She kneed me in the dick while I was distracted by her mouth. I fight for air as my hands cup my very wounded manhood. The pain unimaginable.

"That was a cheap shot." I spit out, barely able to form the words as I roll around in agony.

"I won, right?" She asks, but I know she isn't asking me.

"Yeah, you fucking did." Xyla chokes out a laugh and I fucking hope they are far away once I catch my breath because they are both getting their asses kicked.

# CHAPTER FOURTEEN

## XYLA

Four days have passed, and we haven't heard anything from Étienne, nor have we had any success in finding Nathan and Raven. Not a single new thing has been discovered or found. Different shifts of men scour the city during the night and the day, but nothing is happening. Our men in Bucharest are doing the same thing, but again, *nothing*.

We are at a dead end. A stalemate. A standstill. And every single other word I could think of as I glare at nothing in particular.

"Boss." Someone calls and I turn to see Radar. "You have three more messages from the President." He hands me the tablet, and I read through them. All requests to come home for the summit, getting increasingly more aggressive and desperate. Why the hell would my presence at this summit be so important? I hand the tablet back.

"Message him back and say that I am mid mission and cannot abandon my post." He looks unsettled, glancing around us. "What?"

"I said that last time and he didn't take it well." He answers, his voice wavering. I love Ray, but sometimes his lack of grit annoys me. He's just a tech guy, never in the line of fire, but fucking get a grip. How hard is it to tell the President no?

"I don't care. Say it again. I am not going back to the states right now." I turn away and head to grab some shitty coffee from our tiny kitchenet. Someone must have gone on a pastry run because there are boxes of donuts and croissants and other French delicacies on the table. I wander over to them trying to decide which one I want.

"Maybe you should go, Xy." Oz says from behind me, his own steaming cup in hand when he comes into view.

"Why?" I ask as I pick up a chocolate croissant.

"This might be a good way for you to figure out what he has planned, what he's doing. I mean, the decoy had to have led to something. And even with Bog there, we don't have that much intel." I set the croissant down and glare at him. We never separate. Ever.

"And if I go, you'll stay here, work with Étienne, keeping Serena safe, and try to track down Raven? All by yourself?" I question before taking a very long sip of my coffee that is in desperate need of creamer.

"I *have* worked alone before, Xyla." I roll my eyes.

"We have too much work to do here." I push, stepping away from him and the table. He catches my arm and holds my gaze. His grip is light but firm, making me clench my jaw.

"Xyla, as your partner, I think this is the one time where us splitting up will be a good idea." I search his muted green eyes behind his red tinted lashes. He's serious and part of me knows he's right but I can't.

I can't leave.

"What if you find her while I am gone?" I whisper, fear lacing my voice. Desperation soaking into every pore in my body as I picture her and him together in Paris while I am stuck in a stupid international meeting. Having a magical little reunion, maybe causing some bloodshed, while I am again in a stupid international summit a world away.

"Then I make sure she stays put until we get her home to see you." He replies. "I won't do anything here without talking it out with you, just as you won't do anything there. The summit is in a couple days, so you'll only be gone a week—max. And then you will be back here to boss everyone around." I suck on my teeth and let my eyes scan the warehouse. I know everyone here would be fine without me, but it feels like I am walking away.

It feels like I am abandoning my post and letting them have all the fun. And it fucking sucks.

"Fine." I say through clenched teeth, because I know I need to go. Something is happening back home, and I need to see what it is. "Jet is coming with me. I'm not trusting one of his men to fly me all the way back to DC. I am not drowning in the ocean. And I'm too hot to be marooned on an island." I scowl and he fights a smile.

Oz releases his hand, but not before giving my bicep a gentle squeeze.

Two hours later I am climbing the stairs to the private jet and collapsing onto one of the cream leather seats. Jet claps me on the shoulder on his way to the cockpit. The doors close and we are off within minutes. The flight itself is long, and I find myself antsy. I spend half the time going through any reports from Radar, sending messages to Serena, or trying to distract myself with the newest episode of The Great British Baking Show, but my mind won't shut down.

I finally drink a glass of champagne and let the alcohol whisk me off to sleep.

When we land in DC, Bog is unsurprisingly waiting for me with one of our SUVs. He gives me a smile, and I see his shoulders droop slightly as if tension is being released. Bog is always tense and always on high alert when he's away from the rest of us. Despite being a killing machine, I think he has a hard time believing we trust him to be in charge. Maybe it's a confidence thing. But I always do my best to make sure he knows he's valued. Even if these men are built for one thing, doesn't mean they don't deserve some praise every once in a while.

"Report." I say with a quizzical look as he falls in line next to me as we walk towards the car.

"You aren't going to believe me." He says softly, opening my door, but I don't climb in. His voice...it's only like that when he's worried about the response.

"What is it?" I push.

"There has been an assassination." My heart drops and I reach for him, as if I could shake the identity of the deceased out of his body.

"My father—" He grabs my hands gently, prying them off his shirt.

"Not him. *Dower.* He was found in his office this morning, while you were in the air. Throat slit, body beaten to hell. Apparently, it looked like a fucking wild beast got at him." He pauses, his mouth opening and shutting before I finally push again.

"What is it?" I ask.

"And a pink ribbon." My mouth drops, blood rushing to my cheeks in—what? Anger? Surprise? Confusion? My face feels hot like I am growing dizzier by the second, and it can't be from the champagne.

Is it dread I am feeling? Or is it almost a sense of relief that I'll get to see her again. That she isn't in Paris waiting for me to come back, that I actually followed her here.

Without even knowing it.

"She's in DC." I say quietly, grabbing the edge of the door to steady myself.

"She is. I already spoke to Osprey." I climb into the car and immediately slip the comm into my ear. A few taps on a tablet later, and I am connected to Osprey back in Paris.

"I'm already coming." He says and I hear rustling as if he's packing a bag.

"No, Oz." I order. "One of us needs to be there for Étienne. And besides, if Raven is here, it doesn't mean Nathan is." He goes quiet again. "Maybe she's alone and I can convince her to come with me. I won't take her to The Nest, not until she's cleared, but this could be a chance to get her away." Silence stretches between us and then I hear him sigh.

"Fine, but you do not go anywhere without Bog and Jet. Do you hear me? I know you can take care of yourself, and we both genuinely believe Raven would never hurt you or let someone hurt you. But there is still the chance she isn't herself. Remember what the decoy said, they don't remember anything they did. Raven could be that way, too. You can take me on a good day, but who knows if you can take her." He orders back, nothing but concern in his voice.

"I know, Oz. I won't go anywhere alone, and I'll try my best not to let a potentially brainwashed Raven kill me." I comply in my usual sarcastic manner, but the act makes him feel good about himself. Like he can protect me all the way in a different country. He speaks to Bog for a few minutes, but I space out, not listening to his orders. After they are done, Bog gives me a tight-lipped smile, and then we are off.

It takes me a minute to realize we aren't going to The Nest when we miss our usual turn off from the airstrip but instead are going to the White House.

"I want to go home first." I tell Bog, but he catches my eyes in the rearview mirror. His jaw is clenched in apprehension, but a quick narrow of my eyes has him spilling.

"Osprey has ordered us to stay at the White House." I groan like a child and lean forward, putting my hand on the center console.

"The bunker is way safer than the White House." I argue. "We still have a chunk of men there, at least a good eighty of them. Besides, Falcon is with my father, so he's protected. I want to go home, shower in my own shower and sleep in my own bed."

"Yes, boss." Bog replies, turning away from the massive black gates and heading towards home.

The building is quieter than usual but considering sixty percent of our men are spread across Europe, it's not at all surprising. The men that are there wave at me as I walk by the dining hall and make my way to the elevator down.

"Have we heard from Miss Dolly?" I ask Bog as he joins me at the elevator? He crosses his arms and nods.

"She said she was going to go to Barcelona. I guess it's someplace her mother always wanted to visit but never could." I smile and my heart clenches. I am thrilled that Miss Dolly is having the time of her life touring the world, but I miss her. I miss having a mother figure.

"Good. I'm glad she's enjoying herself. Make sure the birds keep watch and her bank account stays full." I order, before stepping in and catching his nod before the doors close.

I take a long, hot shower, scrubbing my scalp like I haven't showered in days. I have, but something about flying just makes me feel sticky. I change into my favorite pink capybara pajamas before collapsing on my bed. I have time for a nap before I need to get ready for tonight, so I pull out my cellphone and send a quick text to my father.

*Just got home. See you tonight. X.*

He doesn't respond, but I know he read it. My father has always been good at checking his messages instantly. I like to pretend it is so he doesn't miss anything from me, but I know it's because he gets so many important messages from his administration. I curl up tighter as I plan out the trip home in my head.

I will do dinner tonight at the House, the international summit tomorrow to see what it is my father needs me there for and be back on the plane to Paris the day after. I'll probably take Bog back with me, too, since he currently has Falcon in charge, who is more than capable as long as my father stays at the White House.

But this plan only works if Raven is in Paris...

If Raven really is here in DC, I don't think I could leave. I roll onto my back and stare at the ceiling, my face growing hot again as I think of her. As I think of Raven.

If she is here, then I'll have to stay. Convince her to break free from her brother's grasp. Kill the asshole if I have to. That way she can stay. We can be together.

If she still wants that.

What if she doesn't want me?

# CHAPTER FIFTEEN

## XYLA

The House is filled to the brim with staff as they prepare for dinner, which I am assuming will be filled to the brim with politicians and no doubt Adrina Coral. I scowl.

My red-bottomed stilettos click across the marble floor as I make my way through the halls. I have on a pair of black slacks, a skin-tight black body suit, and a black suit-jacket. My hair is straightened, tucked behind my ears, and I have on my signature red lip. I feel and look menacing as I step into the ballroom where my father is speaking to other suited men. His gaze is less than welcoming when he glances at me, as if I am interrupting him.

He excuses himself nicely before walking over to me, his fists clenched, but he still has the gall to give smiles to all those who he passes.

"Where have you been?" He snaps and I feel Bog step closer behind me, his body heat soaking into my jacket.

"On mission." I say softly glancing around the room, cataloging who I see.

"You have no idea how important this summit is, Xyla. You being here and showing support is just as important." He pushes and I glance up at him, he has a bead of sweat on his temple and he looks unnerved.

"It's just a standard meeting with the other world leaders. It's not like we have anything to worry about. I mean we aren't working with Russia or any other terrorist country, right, *daddy*?" I say the last part with as much innocence as I can muster. His eyes flash, fear making his pupils dilate before he blinks a couple times and clears his throat.

"Of course not, my darling." He plasters a fake smile on his lips before guiding me towards a group of men, his hand on my lower back. "There are a few men I want you to meet." I sigh inwardly before turning my attention to the men before me, used to parading around by now. "Gentlemen, this is my daughter, Xyla." My father introduces me, and I tilt my head as a greeting. A few of them introduce themselves, but I find my gaze shifting to one in particular.

He's attractive, I'll give him that. He gives me the same God-like quality that Kestrel used to give, if he wasn't a complete piece of shit. But a natural radiance about him, perfect skin and white teeth, but there is something...

The room drones out, my pulse pounding in my ears as the deep blue eyes meet mine. Eyes I know. The shape, the shade, the thick lashes. Paired with the dirty blonde hair that has the tiniest wave to it and the sharp jaw—I suck in a breath.

"It's a pleasure to meet you, Miss Bader. My name is Nathan." His suit is well-tailored, pitch black. But he has a single pink silk handkerchief in his pocket, breaking up the monotone look. My eyes freeze on it, the same shade as the ribbons. His hand is hanging in the air, my body refusing to cooperate as I realize I am standing before Raven's dead brother. The Nathan we knew was alive but still had a hard time picturing.

"Mr.?" I reach my hand forward, quickly falling into the mask of the First Daughter. He smiles, revealing pointed canines—just like hers—that poke into his plush lower lip. Lips the shade of a soft rose, like a natural blush.

"Cross. Nathan *Cross*." He responds, his gaze not breaking as he stares at me like he's seeing my soul.

"It's wonderful to meet you, Mr. Cross." I shake his hand, squeezing tightly, plastering an overly fake smile on my face. He responds with the same tightening of his grip before he drops my hand.

"And how do you know my father, Mr. Cross?" I inquire, knowing full well I am not likely to hear the real story. Especially not in a room like this.

My heart is racing as I wait for his answer. I have the urge to search the room to see if she's here, but she wouldn't be. She *couldn't* be. Not out in the open like this. But the need to look around is strong and it takes a lot of focus to keep my attention in Nathan.

"Oh, I do a few things for his administration, mostly intelligence." He waves his hand haphazardly and I narrow my gaze.

"I heard you run the Bader Ballet Company? That is incredible. I also heard they would be performing at the White House Christmas party. I am really looking forward to seeing that. I am sure a former prima ballerina like yourself no doubt trains the next generation of elite dancers."

"Well, Mr. Cross, if you are in town for Halloween, they will also be performing at our Halloween party." I supply, pushing for even a hint of his whereabouts in the next few months.

"Well, if a beautiful woman like you is extending the invitation, how can I say no?" The men around us laugh and I feel the room coming back into focus. His eyes stay focused on mine. A mischievous sort of light fading in as he watches me. I can't tell if his curiosity is faked or if he is truly trying to figure me out.

"I am very happy you two have met, it's an introduction I have been waiting for ages for. I knew you two would get on quite nicely. Now, Nate, if you'll excuse us." My father rests his hand on my lower back before guiding me away, giving everyone else a small nod.

"Father—"

"What did you think of Nathan? He comes from a very wealthy family and has done remarkable work for the nation." I meet my father's gaze, and I see it, the hope. The longing as he raises his eyebrows and smiles slightly.

Oh. My. *God*.

"Are you trying to set me up with him?" I squeak out and my father looks around nervously, seeing if anyone caught my outburst.

"Well, it's been two years, my darling." His hand brushes hair off my shoulder as his tone softens.

"Do you know who he is?" His eyes flash in fear again, and questioning. Wondering what I know, which makes me wonder what *he* knows.

"Whatever do you mean, Xyla?" He plays coy, licking his lips and making a show of checking his watch.

"You don't know, do you?" I step back, searching his face for any sign he's about to lie to me. "You know about the terrorism, that I know for a fact." His eyes widen and he raises his hand as if he was going to clamp it over my mouth.

"Xy—"

"But you don't know whose brother he is." I laugh, covering my own mouth instead.

"What are you talking about?" He looks confused and honestly a little terrified at my laughter, but he steps closer as he speaks, trying to get information.

Information I am fucking ecstatic to share with him.

"Nathan Cross is the older brother of Naomi Cross." He doesn't react to the name, so I keep going. "Naomi Cross is the government name of none other than *Raven*." His mouth drops open, and I see him turn to look at Nathan, who is watching us from across the room. He has a flute of champagne in his hand that is untouched as his gaze stays locked.

"I promise you, Xyla, I did not know that." My father tries to placate but I shake my head.

"But you did know about who he works with, right?" He clamps his lips shut. "He is a terrorist to this country, and you were trying to set me up with him?" I step closer to him, hatred seething off me in waves.

"He is not a terrorist. He has done unspeakable things—yes—but so have *you*!" He snaps and people around us glance nervously. "Nathan has done it on behalf of the administration. What are you doing it for?" I jerk back as if he slapped me.

"How dare you compare me to him. We are not the same. My organization fights *against* people like him." I take another step away and Bog is back at my side. "Ready the car, Bog. I would like to go home." He's gone just as fast.

"Xyla—" I hold up my hand.

"Don't. I will be here for your summit, but after that, I am gone." I turn around, my nails digging into my palms as I storm towards the underground garage.

I tap my ear and hear a familiar, grounding voice.

"I got it all." Oz says, his voice quiet.

"We have a lot of work to do, Oz." I respond, my heart racing.

"I know." I hear a click as he turns his mic off and I push open the door to the garage.

# CHAPTER SIXTEEN

## XYLA

I hear the click of the safety before I feel the press of a gun to my head. My breath evens out and I focus solely on the presence behind me before I move.

I spin around, my elbow knocking into the pistol before I have Raven's Staccato unholstered from my back and pointing directly at—*Raven?*

That even breath dissipates and I am left gaping.

Her hair is slicked back into a low bun, the golden blonde of it lit up by the fluorescent garage lights. She's wearing a black suit, dressed almost exactly like Nathan, as if they were twins. She has bruises on her temple, another on her jaw. She has a cut lip and what looks to be handprints around her neck, the brownish yellow of it showing it's a few days old. My gut clenches as I picture her being tortured, wounded.

"Raven?" I choke out, my throat thick, my heart barely beating. My free hand reaches up to touch the mic in my ear, but her hand slaps it away in a flash. My—her—gun now nearly resting on her shoulder as she appears closer.

"Raven." I say again, her thin fingers gripping my wrist so gently, as if she is afraid to hurt me. "Say something." I plead, begging her to say three words that would make the last two years disappear.

Her eyes search mine, the subtle sheen of tears making them glassy, and I know she's feeling everything I am. She's close enough to smell, gunpowder and leather. Her heat soaking through my jacket, being absorbed by every inch of my body.

"You need to stop looking for me." Her voice is just as thick as mine and I inhale sharply at the sound. The sound of her voice that I have heard every single night since she's left. "He will kill you." I shake my head, finally dropping the gun back to my side as a tear rolls down my cheek.

Her eyes track the movement of my hand, and I can see when she realizes what gun it is. Her eyes go back to mine, wide and red. As if she has been holding onto every single moment between us, too.

"I will never let him hurt you again." I whisper, making that promise to her. "I will never let him touch you again." I holster the gun and reach up to let my fingertips brush her cheek. Her skin is so soft, so smooth and I feel her breath catch. But the moment is gone just as fast.

She wrenches my arm away, spinning me around until my face is pressed against the wall.

"I am not yours to protect, Xyla. Stop *looking*." Her lips brush my ear as she whispers, her chest pressing into my back.

"I will never stop fighting for you, Raven." I say back. Her forehead drops and rests against my shoulder. I hear her sniff as if she's fighting this just as hard as I am. I push off the wall and spin around, making her look at me. "I will not stop. Even if it costs me everything." I surge up on my toes and press my lips to hers. Her body freezes, but then her hands are tangling in my hair and she's shoving me back against the wall.

Her tongue spears through my lips and my hands grip her waist, pulling her even tighter against me. I feel her hot tears as they mix with mine. She pulls at the nap of my neck, forcing my head up. Our lips rip apart, and her teeth are back at my ear, grazing the shell of it.

"I won't warn you again." She pushes off of me, spinning me so I nearly run straight into the wall. When I turn back around, the garage is empty. I stare at the space she stood, my lips throbbing, my core clenched, and tears flowing until the sound of the SUV pulling up jerks me out of my trance.

"You alright, Boss?" Bog asks as he gets out and opens my door, staring at my hair disheveled and my face no doubt red and puffy. "Xyla?" He asks stepping even closer, his face filled with worry. I shake my head, run my hands through my hair and hastily wipe off my tears.

"Yeah, let's just get home." I manage to get out. He closes the door behind me after I climb in, and I rub my fingers around my wrist, still feeling her fingers wrapped so softly around it. But instead of skin, I brush something cool and silky.

I glance down and see the pink ribbon tied tightly around my wrist. My breath catches as I stare at the small gift. The confirmation that it was her all along. And I don't know if it's relief I feel knowing she's been sending us messages, or if it's disbelief that it was her brutally murdering all of those people.

I tap the mic in my ear three times to get to the private channel. The need for comfort and to talk about what just happened overpowering any resolve or strength I have.

"Oz, are you there?" Silence on the other end. "Osprey." I say again, but no answer. Tears prick my eyes again, and I quickly blink them away. *Keep your shit together*, I chastise myself before taking a deep breath

"Osprey, I need you to answer me." I say with a little more force but just get silence.

"Boss?" Bog says softly, his eyes meeting mine in the rearview mirror.

"Have you heard from him?" I ask, averting my gaze.

"Not for about an hour." He answers. I nod and he pulls away, taking us back home.

# CHAPTER SEVENTEEN

## OSPREY

"*What the actual fuck.*" Her voice is sharp, irritated as she stares at the flames shooting out of broken windows, destroying any wall not made of concrete and brick.

"Is everyone out?" Someone says behind me, which prompts a roll call from all of the birds, but I just stare. My mind reeling as I watch our headquarters burn down for the second time, although this match wasn't lit by us. And it's not our home base, which is completely fireproof.

"Isn't this place mostly concrete?" Serena says, her still shrill voice breaking through the haze as she demands my attention.

"Yes, the fire should go out quick. And then we can assess." I respond, my own voice monotone and blank.

"We got a count." Radar says behind me. I give myself one more breath to absorb everything before jumping into action.

"Talk to me." It's Shark that catches up and reports as I walk towards the line of SUVs illuminated a fiery red.

"The explosion started in the basement, in the makeshift barracks. We lost four so far, a few others are injured, one critical. Everyone else got out and is accounted for. We collected as much as we could before we evacuated." He starts.

"Weapons?" The weapon stores were also in the basement next to the barracks. It was the most secure place for them.

"We got what was there, but half were gone already." I stop.

"*What?*" I spin around and stare into Shark's dull, grey eyes, the color of a great white. Fury fuels every single breath as I stare at my interrogations agent.

"Someone got inside. Half our weapons are gone; we are also missing two tablets, a monitor, and three earpieces." His voice wavers slightly and I start a mental checklist of how I am going to torture that waver out of him. Any bit of weakness is getting beaten out. I step closer, towering over him.

"How the fuck did someone get inside with all of us there?" I spit, my face heating. "Someone fucked up. Someone wasn't paying attention and I want names."

"They might have already been inside." Radar adds, his voice equally quiet as Shark's as he keeps his eyes downcast onto his tablet.

My heart plummets.

*Fuck.*

I frantically look up as I search the crowd, looking for one person. One single person with a shrill voice and an unbreakable attitude who was annoying me ten seconds ago.

"Fix." I say loudly. "Rena!" I say even louder as I don't see her unruly mane of coiled, onyx hair that was even more a mess since she had just woken up. "*Serena!*" I scream, my voice borderline a screech. I push through people, knocking them to the ground as I search through the forty men standing around. "Where is she?" I yell, grabbing the closest person to me.

"I-I don't know, sir." The bird stammers and I push off his chest, sending him to the ground.

"*Find her!*" I order, sending everyone running. "Radar!" I push back through the retreating group until I find the barely skin and bones we call our tech wizard.

"I don't see her on any of the cameras. Not a single one." He says, his voice far from even and collected as he taps on his screen viciously

"Her tra—" But I stop. She never got one. I wouldn't allow it. Because I never wanted her to be in the field, be a part of this. Because I didn't want to see her in pain as they cut into her neck to insert it. And because I was so fucking stubborn about keeping her unharmed and safe. Because I tried to force her into a bubble.

Because of all of that, she's missing.

"Check every single tracker of every man we brought with us. Check their whereabouts, their movement history. Find an outlier. Find out who took her." It's Shark that gives Radar the order as he voices what my throat fails to do.

Fury builds first through my chest, adrenaline pounding through every artery and vein, before the deep-rooted nausea and fear takes place. A feral, guttural yell bellows out of my ravaged throat, terrifying the few bodies closest to me, before I send a fist straight through the window of the closest SUV, the bullet proof glass cracking—as do my knuckles.

# CHAPTER EIGHTEEN

## SERENA

Deep breaths. In and out. Nice and slow.

Keep your breath even so your heartrate doesn't elevate. Keep your body loose and relaxed so you don't get cramps. Listen and catalog every sound you hear.

The instructions filter through my head as if Oz is here spouting them. They are the same instructions I hear him give every new recruit before they start torture training.

A chill sends shivers down my limbs as the pajamas I am wearing barely cover my bare skin. I feel a metal grate pressing into my back, my bare legs tied with a rope that feels more like sandpaper, forcing my hips to twist as my knees rest on the ground. A bag is over my head, making each breath feel strained and hot, but I keep them slow. My arms are wrenched behind me, my fisted hands pressing into my lower spine.

Silence around me. No other breaths or hearts beating in what I am assuming is a small space. No other sounds other than dripping water, but even that doesn't sound close.

*Compartmentalize, Serena.* I order myself, forcing my heart to calm as terror sets in. *Keep yourself calm.*

I repeat it over and over again as I recall what I assume was the last hour.

I was talking to Oz, more like yelling at a brick wall because he barely acknowledged me. I was just so shocked and confused at how a brick and concrete building could burn. I was half asleep and freezing. I wasn't paying attention because I didn't think I had to.

We were on the edge of the crowd, closest to the warehouse. I could feel the heat from the flames as we stared. But he walked away, towards the SUVs, and I started to follow him. Someone— someone stopped me.

Brown eyes and hair, not a face I recognized really, but someone I knew was a Bird.

*"Come, miss Serena. We have the SUV ready for you."* He had said. His voice even and calm, and so nonchalant that I didn't question it. I remember nodding before following him towards the SUVs, barely glancing back at Oz. Because why would a bird be a threat? Oz had trained all of them, I didn't even question it.

He led me to an SUV that was running, and I could feel the heater on my skin in anticipation, I was so cold. I remember getting in—and then nothing. Darkness as a bag was put over my head. A small prick in my neck and then I was gone.

I didn't even have time to scream.

I fucking fell for the most basic form of kidnapping and now I am lying somewhere with God knows who. Any bit of training, which was only training I got by listening to Oz and Xyla talking to others, went out the window. Anger spreads through my body like wildfire. Anger in being stupid. Anger that someone even attempted to kidnap me—much less succeed.

Anger that I was never properly fucking trained. They bring me out into the field, albeit sometimes hesitantly, and they never gave me formal training. Not even fighting but fucking tactics to evade people or even things I should look out for. But would I have even let them? They are both stubborn, but fuck, so am I. Did I even give them a chance to say no to bringing me? Have I ever even given them a choice?

I just integrated myself into their business without and invitation and look what it got me.

I am not a mercenary. I am not Xyla.

And I might die because of it.

I bite back a groan of frustration and try to shimmy. I roll my body to the side, dislodging my knuckles from my lower back and relieving some of the tension. The grate that was pressing into my back now presses into my shoulder and hip and I regret my choice of rolling.

The rope moves against my ankles, and I let the groan out this time as I feel the already raw skin get caught in the tendrils sticking out of the rope.

If that scars, I am going to lose my shit.

Or maybe I won't. Maybe I'll finally look badass enough to be inducted as a real bird. Or Oz will lose his mind and force me to get plastic surgery to preserve my scarless body. Or he'll find me repulsive.

*Oz.*

He'll find me. He'll know I'm gone. There is nowhere in the world he wouldn't go to find Xyla, so I have to believe he would do the same for me.

He would, right?

# CHAPTER NINETEEN

## OSPREY

"Boss." Radar calls behind me, and I stop my pacing.

"*Serena?*" I ask stepping into his space.

"No, sir. Xyla." I rip the headset out of his hand.

"Xy—" I start but immediately stop. How can I tell her that Serena is gone? She cuts me off before I can think.

"Oz, she's here." Her voice is rushed and my mind blanks.

"Who?" But I know the answer.

"Raven. She—she held a gun to my back. She acted like she was going to shoot me. But then—"

"There is no way she would harm a single hair on your head." I interrupt her.

"She told me to stop looking. And then she kissed me." I stay silent as she fills me in on her run in with Nathan and her father and then Raven right after. Her wavering voice had steadied, cold calculated reporting replaced it. She ran through every second, not missing a detail before falling silent. "Oz?" She says softly, but I am too busy chewing through the edge of my thumb to answer. "Oz, I need to know what we should do. I don't know what to do right now. I am stuck between panicking and crying and I am not—I don't know what to do." Her voice cracks and I can see her. The beast mask breaking off and revealing the ballerina who loved Raven so fiercely.

That image breaks my stupor. Because there really is only one thing I can ask her to do, and it has nothing to do with Raven.

"Come back to Paris." Her sharp inhale cuts through the earpiece.

"What? And just leave her here?" She yells, her voice a mix of anger and fear. "She is finally here. After two years, and you want me to just walk away? But the kiss—"

"Xyla, listen to me. They are going to come back here; there is no reason they wouldn't. With Étienne and the weapons and—" I stop. The words so hard to get out because I know they will break her.

They are already breaking me.

"And what, Osprey?" Her anger is thick, and I take a deep breath. I have to get it out.

"We have a traitor here. Someone detonated a bomb in the basement, starting a fire and destroying part of the building. We lost half of our weapon stores and some equipment, someone took them. And someone took Serena." Silence. Pure, rage-fueled silence.

"What the fuck did you just say?" She says slowly, enunciating every single word.

"Serena is gone. As of an hour ago. She got out of the building. She was being her usual self and yelling and I was frustrated. I turned away for a second to deal with everything and she was gone." It was my fault, and her silence confirms that.

"I have to choose between Raven and Serena. Is that what you are saying?" She nearly screams at me.

"Yes." And part of me fears she'll choose Raven. Raven is her true love, her soulmate. Her everything. But Serena—Rena is her sister. Her best friend. Her *family*.

And I fucking hope she chooses her.

The silence stretches and I wait with bated breath. I could do this without her, but I don't want to. I need Xyla. I need my partner.

"There isn't a choice, Oz." She pauses. "I'm coming." The breath escapes my lungs in relief, and I smile slightly, fighting back watery eyes.

"See you soon, Beast."

"Right back at you." Her line disconnects and I hand the headset back to Radar.

"Get with Jet and Bog. Xyla is flying out today. Have the rest of Team Black Bird accompany them. We need more men. Have them bring weapons. Leave about twenty or so men at the base, bring another jet if we have too. I don't fucking care. And get us another warehouse, *now*." He types away, and I don't wait for his response before I head back to the fire.

"Shark!" I yell, letting the heat warm my skin.

"Get some trucks here ASAP, get the fire under control. Then empty everything from we can. Every floor needs to be cleared."

"Yes, boss." He responds before disappearing.

First, we need a new base. And then we can find Serena. We won't stop until we find her. I won't stop.

I am not going to go two years without finding someone I love again.

# CHAPTER TWENTY

## XYLA

We landed nine hours later, and every single minute of that flight was spent warring between Raven and Serena. The choice was easy; Serena is my family. My sister. I would always choose Serena over anyone, not a single person would go before her. Raven is the love of my life, but she's safe for now. Serena?

She could be dead.

And whoever had a hand in it would be also, that I can promise.

I take another shot of espresso, the boiling liquid scalding my tongue, before stepping off the plane. It has been thirty-six hours since I have truly slept, and I don't foresee sleep anytime soon.

The mid-afternoon sun is bright, burning my tired eyes as I meet Oz on the tarmac. I don't hesitate and just throw my arms around his neck and hold him tight. His arms go around me, squeezing me even harder before lifting me off the ground.

"I'm sorry." We both say at the exact same time, resulting in us both laughing into the other. He releases me first, dropping my feet back to the ground.

"Let's go find our girl, yeah?" I say, patting his cheek. His eyes are red, his bags a deep purple. He hasn't slept either.

I climb into the front seat, letting Bog and Jet take the back and every single other man take the other SUVs. It'll take them a minute to unload all of the gear we brought with us.

We speed away in silence, and I take the tablet handed to me from the back. I pull up the warehouse footage and fast forward.

The barracks don't have a camera, offering a small bit of privacy, but I watch the door fly off the hinges and people running out of the room covered in soot and blood, rushing up the stairwell.

Fire licks at their backs as the barracks become engulfed, and then the camera goes dead. I switch to the next view, the warehouse floor. I watch as everyone rushes out of the basement, clearing the top of the stairs and not exiting. Laptops, tablets, hard drives, each person grabs something of worth before exiting the warehouse. Osprey and Serena run down the stairs from the observation deck, their hands clasped together.

He keeps her in front of him, his other hand on her lower back as he ushers her outside. Not letting go of her for a second.

I switch to the second view, the front door. I watch them pass under.

I switch again, the entrance. They run out into the pitch-black night. The fire behind them burning brighter as it spreads. I see them standing there, just barely in view. She's yelling something and Oz is just staring. He says something and then turns.

She follows, stepping out of view.

I switch again. My heart racing as I watch her turn away from the crowd, talking to someone out of view. She takes one step, and she's gone.

No other cameras catch her. She stays out of view the entire time, the other person never being shown. I rewind the footage over and over again. I watch her longingly look at Oz right before she follows someone into the dark.

Over and over and over.

"It's someone she knew." I deduce and look up at Oz.

"That's what we figured, but she wasn't close with any of the birds aside from some of us." He inquires, and I can feel the pushing and prodding.

"She's slept around, Oz. There might be someone we don't know about." His jaw clenches and I take a steadying breath. "It doesn't matter. She got away. I am assuming by vehicle, otherwise the birds would have found her once they scattered." I say, watching on-screen Osprey screaming and everyone running as far and as fast as possible.

He looks terrified—petrified more like it. I have never seen him look like that. Ever. I pause the video and stare at his wild eyes, the fire illuminating the muted green into a bright amber.

"We'll find her, Oz."

"How?"

"I think we ask for help." His eyes flick to mine briefly before returning the road.

"You're not saying—"

"Étienne knows every single person in this godforsaken city. He might hear something, know something we don't. We have nothing. She isn't wearing a tracker, and we never saw the other person." I pause. "Is everyone else with a tracker accounted for?" He nods.

"We lost some people, their trackers found by their bodies, or what was left of them. Everyone else is accounted for." I nod.

"Who did we lose?"

"Penn, Bash, Legs, Maverick, and Tell." He says and I make mental notes of each of them. Not any I was particularly close with, and none of which I know Serena slept with. "What are you thinking?"

"And we recovered all five bodies?"

"No—only four for certain. Xy, their remains are pretty gnarly." I stare at him.

"Who did we not recover?" I push.

"We don't know. We can't ID them, only that there were five trackers melted into the concrete.

"It's one of them. The traitor, the person who took Serena. It's one of them."

# CHAPTER TWENTY-ONE

## XYLA

"Okay, let's start." I say from the armchair in our new headquarters. This warehouse is nicer, and closer to downtown. Not as secure, but with the extra men, we are just as safe. We have another observation deck, this one a lot cleaner. It took a few hours, but we got three beds put up here and the bathroom stocked.

"Landon Breggs, also known as Legs, twenty years old. Came to us from Canada. He was a football star in high school, basic family life until his mother and father were murdered when he was 17. He lived on the streets after, until we found him a few years after that. Inducted into the Birds last year and was a part of Radar's team." Oz reads from the tablet, skimming Legs' file.

"What did he do for Radar?" I ask, stretching my leg.

"Surveillance mostly." He adds.

"Put him in the maybe pile." I respond and he nods.

"Dereck Matten, also known as Penn, twenty-seven years old. Grew up in Pennsylvania and attended Penn State. Majored in computer Science. Family is still alive, but not in the picture. Normal family life, no major life altering event in his life. He applied to be in the CIA, but we snagged him last January and added him to the Birds. Radar's team." He says the last part quizzically.

"What did he do for Radar?" I ask, frowning.

"Hacking and coding. Breaking into firewalls, that kind of stuff."

"Hm." I say and then nod, asking him to continue.

"Mason Gury, also known as Maverick, twenty-four years old. Grew up in Texas, right outside Fort Worth. Military family and joined the Marines right out of high school. Showed promise in interrogation and technology, we took him in two years ago. Radar's team." We both sit up a little straighter.

"What did he do?"

"Surveillance."

"The other two?" He scrolls.

"Tell, born David Arsel in Telluride. Surveillance. Bash, born Thomas Sheer in Nashville. Team Black Bird."

"It's him."

"How do you know?" I stand and take the tablet from his hand.

"Four of the men are from Radar's team. Four bodies for sure were found, the fifth possibly just extra destroyed remains." He nods. "Those four must have found something. Found out that Bash was a spy or traitor, found out how he was getting in and out.

Something. They found *something*. So, he made sure they died, and that he appeared dead. It's him, Oz."

I tap the intercom switch on the tablet.

"Radar to observation deck." I say and then switch it off.

"We need—" Osprey starts to say as Radar walks in, cutting him off.

"Boss, boss." He nods to each of us.

"We need you to go through every single thing Tell, Legs, Penn, and Maverick were looking at, doing, investigating—anything from the last week or so. Document anything that seems suspicious, anything that may relate to Bash." Radar's eyes widen as he glances back and forth between us.

"Tell no one what you are doing, Ray." I add, softer. "Not a soul." He nods and quickly backs away before heading down the stairs.

"What now?" I ask, handing Oz the tablet back.

"Not sure we need Étienne now." He says and I chew on my bottom lip. I meet his gaze. "Do you want to talk about Raven?" I shake my head.

"I told you everything that happened. She told me to stop looking. She pointed a gun at me. She kissed me. But, she wasn't herself."

"And you said she was wounded." He adds.

"She looked like she'd been tortured, Oz. She was covered in bruises and cuts. Like she'd been beaten to shit." We stay quiet for another moment.

"I can't believe Lincoln is trying to set you up with Nathan." Oz snorts and I roll my eyes.

"Well, he is hot, but if he wasn't a psychopath or Raven's brother, I still wouldn't. Anyone in politics is a no go." I add.

Silence spreads. The kind of silence that feels comfortable, safe. And I yawn.

"When was the last time you slept?" He asks and I look away.

"The flight to DC."

"Xyla." He warns and I wave him away.

"I'll sleep when you sleep."

# CHAPTER TWENTY-TWO
## SERENA

I don't know how long it's been, but it has to have been hours. Maybe even a full day. My legs are asleep, my hip throbbing from where it is pressed into the metal grate. I have to pee, and I am hungry, and I just want a fucking croissant.

The sound of metal screeching, rubbing against something, echoes through the room and I wish I could cover my ears. It stops and then slams. Must have been a metal door.

"Well, you look a little uncomfortable." The man from last night, the Bird.

"No shit." I say, my voice muffled by the bag.

"I apologize, Serena. We just needed some time." He supplies and I curl my lip, wishing he could see the absolutely terrifying face I was giving him. "And now that the time has come…" I feel fingers trail along my arm, giving me goosebumps.

"Don't fucking touch me." I spit and he chuckles as I try to pull away.

"I think I'll do what I want." He responds, digging his fingers into my forearm and sliding me across the floor. I cry out as the grate rips at my skin, and then I am on concrete. My breathing comes in pants as I try to compartmentalize the pain. I hear the sound of a knife opening and then the press of a cold blade to my thigh.

I freeze. And then it's moving. I hear the sound of fabric being cut and feel the brush of my pajamas as they slide to the floor. The chill returns tenfold as my ass is bared, and then my chest. And within seconds, I am naked.

"Fuck." He whistles. I scream as his boot connects to my left shoulder, forcing me onto my back. My entire arm goes numb, and I can't move my fingers. He dislocated it. "Fuck." He repeats. I hear his knees pop as he bends down and then his hand is between my legs.

"Don't fucking touch me!" I scream again and again as he climbs on top of me. I scream over and over as he spreads my legs and the burning rips through me. I scream it until I hear his final grunt, until I feel his release spill out of me, as I hear him get up and leave the room.

I don't stop repeating it until my voice is hoarse, and exhaustion pulls at me.

Over and over again until the screams turn to sobs and the sobs turn into silence.

Hours pass, maybe a day. I still don't know. I scream as he comes in. I scream as he repeats his earlier torment. I scream and scream until the sobs come.

Again. But the screams barely come, just sobs and pain. Warmth as he spills inside of me. And then chills as his body heat dissipates, leaving me alone.

By the fourth time, by the time I know days have passed, I don't fight. I don't move. I don't cry. I have no more tears to shed. I just feel numb.

I just feel used.

And I take it.

# CHAPTER TWENTY-THREE

## XYLA

"It has been *two* fucking days!" Oz screams, his hand slamming into a monitor, smashing the screen. His hand was already bandaged from where he crushed two knuckles punching bullet proof glass before I got here, because he is a lovesick idiot.

And now the blood is welling up, soaking his white bandages red. Again.

"Would you stop fucking ripping your stitches!" I yell back. "Stitch!" I call out and watch as an exasperated doctor trudges over with the first aid kit to rebandage his wound for the twentieth time. He's going to end up in a cast if he doesn't stop punching things. Oz starts to wave him away, refusing to let Stitch touch him, but I glare at him warningly and he complies. Surprisingly.

I'm watching footage of a black SUV speeding through downtown Paris, nearly taking out tables outside a little café, missing late night pedestrians walking. Driving like a complete asshole. Whoever owned the SUV wanted to make sure it was indistinguishable from ours, which means it had probably been here for a while, and we never knew it. And it was most likely the SUV that had Serena in it, especially with how chaotic they are driving. I chew on the inside of my lip and watch the footage again.

One second it's there, and then it's gone. I replay it,

"Radar!" I yell out, the sound echoing throughout the warehouse as he appears.

"Boss."

"Can you scan this and see if there has been any tampering? Watch this." I play it for him and his brows furrow. He takes the keyboard out from in front of me, and I slide off the chair, giving him space. He watches the same clip I did a few times before he starts typing.

"They've been cloaked. I'll work on it." He answers and I walk away, letting him work.

"Shark, where are we on interrogations?" I ask the stone-faced mercenary leaning back on an armchair next to us.

"Well, I learned that quite a lot of our men don't break under pressure." He says sarcastically. I roll my eyes and turn away from them all, irritation making me pissy.

We have nothing. No leads, no sign of her.

She's just *gone*.

"Oz—" I start and spin around. "What if we ask Étienne?" His eyes widen, the whites of them redder than anything as he ponders. Lack of sleep and ignoring his feelings will do that.

"I am not entirely sure it wasn't him that took her, Xy." He says suspiciously.

"It would still give us something else to go off of." I counter and he crosses his arms.

"Alright, partner. Your call." He gives me a shallow nod, and I nod back.

"Let's make contact with Étienne, set up another meeting." I say to the team, knowing one of them would be on it. I direct the next statement to Oz. "I'm going to take a walk." He opens his mouth to protest but I hold up a hand, silencing him. "I won't go far." I tap the tracker on the back of my neck, and he rolls his eyes with a shake of his head, knowing it's better to not fight me. "I just think some fresh air will help me figure things out." His face hardens, but not in anger, in recognition. He nods once and I know he understands.

I know I shouldn't risk myself, walking around alone. I can handle anyone, but I also know that over-confidence can get me in trouble. But if I just expose myself, go for a walk, maybe the answers will come.

And maybe, just maybe, I won't be the only one who sees them.

The back alleyways are damp, having just rained that morning. The pitch-black sky does little to illuminate the broken cobblestones, but I maneuver around them anyway, using whatever moonlight I can.

I slip my hands into the pockets of my leather jacket, feeling the slight sting of autumn. Back in the states, my father would be having a harvest feast at the house, letting all of the staff enjoy some delicious food with their families. He'd give them all the day off and just have a family day. Same way we would always have grown up, but he brought it into his Presidency also.

Thanksgiving isn't for another month, but since it'll be an exceptionally busy time at the House, he gives them the time now instead. A pre-thanksgiving he calls it. When I was younger, and after he got into politics, we started to do the same thing. It was out favorite first week of October tradition.

Except maybe this year Nathan would be there, and possibly Raven, too. Although I am still convinced my father didn't have anything to do with Raven being alive, he seemed genuinely surprised about the knowledge of Raven and Nathan being siblings. So, they wouldn't be there. At least she wouldn't. Which means she could be here.

And that is the sole reason I am walking around alone. Just in case.

I continue walking until the warehouse is quite a maze of twists and turns away, keeping my pace steady. Making sure I am just far enough away for someone to feel less like they'd be ambushed. And when a second set of footsteps join mine, I keep going. Just until...

The end of the alleyway looms over me with a broken brick wall and a chain link fence, the exact place I wanted to go.

"Cornering yourself, little beast?" Her voice is soft and silky like honey. But the edge of it, the unrestrained hunger or anger—I can't tell—that is what has me taking a deep breath.

"It's not me, I am cornering." I turn around and face her, still startled to see scabs and bruises marring her perfect face. "Your face." I whisper, my voice thick. And then she smiles. Because she hears it too.

Not a normal smile, no. One that is sinister and doesn't meet her eyes. A smile that has never belonged to her. She turns around quickly, spinning on the toe of her boot.

"Osprey." She says and I swear I hear a small catch in her throat as she sees the only man who has never betrayed her for the first time in two years.

Osprey was always hers. She found him. She brought him in. She trained him. Kestrel had his men, his favorites, but Oz was always hers. And when she died, it broke him in a way I never thought possible. I think that's why it took him so long to believe her death could have been a hoax.

That she was alive.

And so, I dangled the fact that if I am alone, she might appear. I knew he'd follow. I knew he would know what I was doing.

I knew he couldn't resist.

"Long time no see, boss." He says, stepping around the corner. The second I tapped the tracker, I knew he'd be on me. Just as I knew she would be waiting.

But knowing everyone's next move is where I draw a blank.

# CHAPTER TWENTY-FOUR
## OSPREY

Xyla is sneaky, I will give her that. She is a plotter and a planner and can see patterns a mile away, so I knew when she tapped her tracker, she was telling me to follow her. I knew what she was telling me.

So, I listened.

For twenty minutes I stayed far behind, letting her guide me through a maze, and it wasn't long before the shadows moved with her and then *she* stepped out.

Her hair was down, waved just to her shoulder blades. She was wearing a black suit jacket, slacks, and steel-toed boots. From behind though, I could see a slight limp in her step, and she was favoring her left size. I couldn't tell if it was her hip or her ribs that were bothering her, but she wasn't well. She *isn't* well.

She didn't see me. She didn't hear me. She was entirely focused on Xy leisurely walking down the alleyway, acting as if she had no care in the world.

Fucking little beast.

For the short time Raven and Xyla were in each other's orbit, because that is exactly what they were, they were each other's gravity. They always found their way to each other, whether they meant to or not. Their focus always on the other, always knowing where the other was. So, it's no surprise to me that Raven was so focused on her, she didn't hear me.

Xyla was her whole world. Now let's hope it's still that way.

This gravity defying orbit was something I thought I had with Serena, until she was taken. Now, I don't know if I will ever see her again. And the ache that is left in my chest has me wanting to scream.

Wanting to punch something.

Xyla stops and looks up, but I stay huddled into a cracked doorway.

"Cornering yourself, little beast?" Raven speaks. Her voice is the same, and it sends a shudder down my spine. The normal smooth tenor, edged with a little sass. The same voice, but is she the same Raven?

"It's not me, I am cornering." Xyla responds, her voice even. I see Raven's shoulders stiffen ever so slightly before she turns around.

"Osprey." She says my voice like it's a prayer, like she's been waiting for years to say it. Because she has. Raven was more than my boss; she was my family. And after two years of believing she was dead, she is standing right here in front of me.

"Long time no see, boss." I say, stepping out of the doorway. Her face is mottled, blooms of purple and blue across her temple, her eye, her jaw. Deep and barely healed slices across her eyebrow and cheek make her usually unmarred skin pale and ghastly, almost illuminating itself in the dark.

She looks—broken.

"*Fuck*." I whisper and she flinches. Xyla doesn't move and part of me doesn't even think she's breathing with how still she's standing.

"You've done well, Oz." Raven compliments and it feels like a punch to the gut. Her voice is slow, determined. As if she is contemplating every single word before she says it.

"You would have done better." I say, smirking. Her mouth twitches and I see her shoulders drop ever so slightly. She would have. And she could. She just needs to come back with us.

Was this what Xyla planned? That we could corner her, and take her home?

"Taking over the Secret Service was brilliant, I don't know if I would have thought of that." She compliments again and I feel like I have been slapped with how casually she says it. As if we are just hanging out, having a normal conversation. This Raven—she seems like she's stalling.

"We were partners, Raven. We would have thought of it together." I take a step forward and she doesn't move. So, I say the words I have wanted to say for years. The words I have never uttered to another being, but ones I mean wholeheartedly. "I miss you."

"I've missed you too, Oz." I take another step and see silver lining her eyes, her brows furrowed and lips turned down as if she is fighting a sob. That I can work with. The old Raven didn't have emotions, so maybe this version of her can be manipulated, convinced.

"We can keep you safe if come back with us." I take another step closer until I can grab her arms. "Come home, Raven. Let's end all of this." She stares into my eyes for a second, and I see the regret pooling. All before it's gone and calculated coolness seeps in.

"I came to say goodbye." She says, ripping herself out of my grip with a wince. It's her ribs, they are probably broken or bruise.

"Ra—" Xyla starts, but Raven cuts her off, almost like she's ignoring her. Or trying to.

"This will be the last time you see me." She pauses and looks at me, a tear sliding down her cheek. "I'm sorry." She says the last part with a broken whisper. As if she does regret what is coming our way. And then her eyes flicker behind me, but I don't have enough time to turn around.

"Well done, little sister." Pain erupts from the back of my head as darkness swells in my vision. I hit the ground, my knees barking as they catch the edges of stone. I hear a gunshot and look up with blurry eyes to see Xyla shooting at someone, her gaze and aim focused. I hear someone grunt and then the sound of a body falling.

Raven's boots spin until she is facing Xyla, facing the end of her gun.

"Raven." Xyla croaks out, almost like a plea. Like she's begging her to not do this. But she doesn't move. They stand, staring at each other, until Raven lifts her arm, a weapon in her hand. Too fat to be a gun, has to be a taser. "Raven." She says again, begging, holding her gun a little tighter as if she'll fire.

But she can't.

And then she is on the ground, twitching.

My vision continues to darken, and I reach forward as best as I can, my hand brushing Raven's boot, a final plea, before it all goes black.

# CHAPTER TWENTY-FIVE
## SERENA

The dark and the cold are welcome. My skin has long since numbed to the brisk, damp air. And my sight being cut off has only heightened my ears. Heightened the other senses as a way to protect myself.

Adapt.

So, I hear when footsteps race through what I am assuming is the hallway outside where I am being held. People shouting, someone laughing.

Something is dragging—no *two* things are being dragged. The sounds of clothes snagging on rocks and debris.

More people?

I stay curled onto my side, arms still wrenched behind my back. I keep as still as possible, hoping they'll believe me to be asleep.

My hot breath cascading over my face as it bounces off the canvas still on my head. They rush past, but they don't go far, and they don't sound muffled.

I don't think there is a wall separating us, it must be bars. It sounds like they are fully in my room, but they aren't, my door didn't open. That I know for sure.

I heard a metal door before I was...touched last time. Which means this is probably some form of cell. An underground prison? Dungeon, considering we are in Europe and there are thousands of miles of underground tunnels and chambers under Paris.

That has to be it.

I hear a body hit the ground, and then another.

"Search them." Someone says—not someone. That's *him*. I grit my teeth as I listen to the sounds of pockets being unzipped and someone's body rolling around, probably checking the back of them.

"Fuck that's a nice gun." Someone else says and then I hear someone get shoved. "Fine, fucking take it." He says and then I hear a chuckle.

Two doors slam, and then the footsteps recede until it's silent.

Alone.

I am alone again.

I listen as best as I can and I hear the subtle sounds of breathing, two sets of breath to be exact.

"Hello?" I say softly. No answer. "Is anyone there?" I say a little louder, but still no answer.

I wait.

For what seems like hours. Counting their breaths, trying to see if someone moves.

And then I hear someone jerk. A limb sliding across the metal grate, and then a deep groan. Silence and then—

"*Xyla?*" *He* says. I hear him crawl, dragging his body and slamming his hands against the bars. "Xy, wake up." He says louder and I hear him groan. Maybe he's reaching for her, but I can't think of anything. I can't even breath because he's *here*.

"Osprey?" I cry out and his shuffling stops.

"Serena?" He says louder and I hear him get to his feet. He's so close. Tears well in my eyes and I start to shake. "Serena, holy shit."

"Oz." I choke out, curling my body in towards itself, trying to cover what little I can of my bare skin.

"I'm right here, I am right here." He repeats as if he's trying to console both of us.

"It's a bird. I don't know his name." I spit out as fast as possible. "He said we were going to another safe house, I didn't think." I try to recount everything. I try to report what I've seen, because that's what he needs. That's what he'll want to hear.

"It was Bash." He grits out and I hear his teeth grinding.

"Do I know who that is?" I ask and I hear him snort, but he doesn't answer. "How long has it been."

"Almost three days, but that isn't important right now. None of it is. I need to get you free." He doesn't want a report. He wants to protect me.

"How close are you?" I ask after a few seconds of silence.

"I can almost reach your bars." I was right. I hear him straining. "Can you shimmy over here and maybe stick your arms through; I might be able to untie them." He doesn't mention anything else and for a moment I feel like maybe he can't tell. Maybe it's so dark he can't see.

"I'm naked, Oz." I say softly. He has to know what that means.

"I know." His voice is strained, halfway between furious and broken.

"It hurts." My voice catches and I fight the shivers running down my body as I recount the last few days.

"I know, baby. I *know*." He sounds just as destroyed as I feel. "Just be strong for a little longer. I need you to sit up. Can you do that for me?" His voice is soft, like he's speaking to a child.

I try to push up on an elbow, but I can't get it under me. One of them is dislocated and the other I just numb.

"I can't." I cry, hating myself for how broken I feel. Tears soak into the canvas, and I feel like I am going to hyperventilate.

"Roll onto your stomach and try to tuck your knees under you." He orders and I take a deep breath. My legs straighten and I feel my knees pop. Pain erupts through my muscles, after being stuck in the same position for days. I roll onto my stomach and bite back a scream as I feel my skin dislodge from between the metal grate that has been slicing its way through me for days.

Fully on my stomach now, I try to pull my knees up under me. Barely formed scabs catch on the grate, and I feel my skin rip as I use every bit of strength I have.

"Fuck, baby. I am so sorry." I hear him say, his voice almost a sob.

My teeth rip through my bottom lip as I bite down to keep from screaming. One final pull and my knees are under me, pressed into my naked breasts.

I slowly sit up and feel my head spin.

"It hurts, Oz." I whimper.

"That's it, you're doing so good. Can you hear where my voice is coming from? To your left." I turn my bagged head his direction and lift a knee, the rope sliding against my calf. I hobble towards his voice, each movement sending slicing pain through my legs. Until I finally feel the bars.

I gasp in pain, nearly passing out as I rest my head against them.

"Can you turn around and put your back to the bars?" I fall to the side as I try to adjust, my head snapping off the concrete. Pain erupts and my head swims. "Fuck, Serena."

"Ow." I whisper as my head pounds. I bend my arms and find a hole in between the bars, shoving them through as best as I can.

"Good job, baby." He says, relief in his voice as I feel his warm fingers brushing my hands.

I start to cry, fully bawling as he unties the ropes from my wrists. One of my arms drops to the ground, and the other stays planted in his hand, his thumb sliding against the sores.

But the feel of his skin on mine makes me want to scream. I'm overstimulated. The pain. The bag. Everything.

I can't breathe.

I am suffocating.

I jerk and pull my arms back through and use the non-injured one to push me up.

And at long last, I pull the bag from my head.

# CHAPTER TWENTY-SIX
## OSPREY

It is taking everything in me to not scream as I stare at her naked body. Dirty, covered in bruises and blood. The ground around the metal grate she was lying on is soaked in dried blood. She looks beat up, but it's the blood between her legs that has my seething. The bruising on her thighs.

I'll fucking murder him.

Her eyes are wild as the canvas is pulled off her head. Her curly mane of hair sticking out in every direction. Dried blood forms a path from the corner of her mouth to her neck. Bruises mar her temple, probably from where it had been resting on the ground.

And nearly every inch of the right side of her body is covered in perfect square shaped cuts, from where she'd been laying on the grate, dripping blood where scabs haven't formed.

Tears pour down her face as she meets my gaze.

"Oz." She chokes out, and I fight my own tears threatening to spill.

"I'm here. I am right here." She reaches a weak arm through her bars towards me, and I meet her halfway. My hand fully covers her as I squeeze.

"It's so cold." She whispers, curling into herself. "My shoulder, I think it's dislocated.

"Here." I let go of her hand and pull off my jacket and the t-shirt underneath. Passing her both through the bars. She takes them and pulls them into her own cage.

After some struggling and wincing, she gets the t-shirt over her head and the jacket around her shoulders. She pulls the bottom of the t-shirt over her legs, curling them into her chest. Tears are pouring down her face, and I want to snap these bars in half to get to her.

To hold her.

But it's my fault she's here.

"I am so sorry, Serena." I start. "I failed you. I never should have let you out of my sight." This could have been avoided if I had just stayed with her. But she was tortured and raped and she'll never get over that. This will stick with her for the rest of her life.

"It's not your fault, Oz. You had an entire operation to command." She says just as defiant as always, but she needs to know she comes first.

"I don't care about them." I care about her.

"They are your people. You had to make sure they were safe." She responds, attempting to make me feel better, but it's her who needs to feel better.

It's her who needs to know how I feel. Why I would risk everything for her. Why Bash is going to be skinned alive.

"*You* are mine. *You* are who I had to make sure was safe, and I failed." My voice cracks. Fuck. No going back now.

"Oz—" She starts but I can't. I have to get it out.

"I love you, Serena. I have long before you moved into The Nest. Long before you left your waste-of-space boyfriend. I have loved you since the day Xyla walked you into the room and ordered me to be nice to you because you were her best friend. And I remember you looked at me, curled your lip and chastised Xyla for being partners with such a brute."

"I—"

"No. Don't say anything." I cut her off. "I fucking love you and I am tired of pretending that you don't belong with me. You do. We belong to each other and I shouldn't have lied. I shouldn't have held back. I should have spent every goddamn second you were in my orbit declaring how much I fucking love you. I never thought I would get the chance after I realized you were gone and I knew I wasted so much time we could have spent together. I love you, Serena. And I will spend every single day of my fucking life proving it to you." I stop my tirade, my head throbbing. Her eyes are wide, rimmed in tears in the watery light. Her lips had parted as she watched my own mouth move.

"You won't want me once you know." She says, nearly a whisper, and my heart fucking shatters.

"I already know." I answer and I see tears pour down her cheeks, leaving tracks in the dirt. "And I don't fucking care. I will spend the rest of your life showing you how you should be treated." I hold her gaze and ever so slowly her hand reaches through the bars.

"I love you, too." She cries out and I feel a weight lifting off my chest as our fingers meet. "All the others, the men. I was trying to erase what I felt for you. I was trying to prevent anything from ruining your partnership with Xyla. I was trying to hide that the second I walked in that room and called you a brute was because the second I saw you I knew that you would be the worst thing that could ever happen to me. But also, the best. And I was terrified. I'm so sorry, Oz." Her voice is weak, broken, and I squeeze her fingers as they lace through mine.

"You don't have anything to apologize for, baby. When we get out of here, things will be different. Everything will be. I will never let you go again. I fucking promise." I give her a small smile, and she rests her head against the bars, holding my gaze.

"I promise, too."

"About fucking time." She jumps as Xyla's voice cuts through, dropping my hand. Xyla's voice sounds gravelly and hoarse, like she just woke up from a coma.

I turn to see her sit up, rubbing her head and looking around the makeshift cells in confusion and then surprise.

"Raven fucking tased me." And I can't help but laugh at the utter disbelief and irritation filling her tiny face.

# CHAPTER TWENTY-SEVEN
## XYLA

I don't bring up Serena's state, or the way her eyes are unfocused and blank, as she stares at the wall. I don't question the fact that she is wearing Osprey's shirt and jacket, how every single sound makes her jump and squeeze her legs against her chest a little tighter.

Because if I think about it, or if I question it, rage fills every vein in my body. Rage at seeing my beautiful, brilliant, and unbelievably strong best friend reduced to a trembling and abused girl. And as I watch Oz watch her, I just pray that whatever God is out there, that we will both get a crack out of skinning the bastard who did this alive.

"Do we have a plan?" Her voice is soft and quiet, like she's afraid to make noise. We've been down here for hours and not a single person has come down. We know Raven and Nathan are involved, but why is the question.

Raven would never hurt me or Serena. At least, the Raven I knew.

But maybe this isn't Raven at all.

Maybe the person we've been tracking is Naomi, and Raven is truly gone.

And if that's the case, would I be able to end her? End *this*?

"Do you remember how often they came down before?" Oz asks her, his hand through the bars and across the damp stone, reaching for her, even if she isn't reaching back. Even though I can tell she wants to, but she doesn't. She stays tightly packed into a ball, unmoving.

Numb.

"At least four times." She whispers, holding her legs even tighter, and I feel the pain emanating off of her. I want to console her, hold her. Run my hands through her unruly hair as she cries and I tell her all will be okay.

But I can't. Instead, I am two cells away, no chance of even touching her. So, I continue to watch. As the horrors pass through her eyes, as she remembers those four times. As she relives them. And every second my eyes search her face; my heart breaks a little more.

"So, twice a day. And I am going to estimate that we have been here for a couple hours." Oz breaks the suffocating silence, and I turn to look at him, forcing myself to stop looking at her.

"Someone will find us. Radar, Shark, Bog. Someone. We have trackers for a reason." I say, trying to be reassuring. Because someone will come. They always will. We always do.

So, we sit in silence. No one daring to speak as we all process. As we all mourn the relative peace we have had the last two years.

As we all realize what our lives are about to become.

Because this is going to be a battle. A blood bath. And I am not convinced we will all make it out alive.

We thought we were looking for someone pretending to be dead of her own volition. But then Nathan became a reality and we realized this is truly a war. A war between two sides of the seedy underbelly of the world. They aren't the heroes, and I wouldn't necessarily say we are either, but we aren't murdering innocents or brainwashing beautiful mercenaries to leave behind everyone they love.

This is going to be the worst few weeks of our lives if this doesn't end soon. And one of us will end up on top.

I just hope it's us and not Nathan.

And as if on cue, the door opens. The relative darkness at the end of the hall next to Serena's cell is briefly illuminated as two figures walk in.

The first is someone I barely recognize but know to be Bash. The traitor. Goose 2.0 if I have a say in renaming him. I see Serena flinch and press herself deeper into the wall as he nears her bars. She winces, her eyes frozen on his.

"Did you miss me?" He whispers before reaching through the bars and caressing her face.

"Don't fucking touch her!" Oz yells, slamming his hands against the bars. A nightmare fueled chuckle comes from the darkness, and I know it. I know the laugh. We heard it just a few nights ago.

Étienne steps in, his face illuminated by the single watery bulb above him. His features are filled with elation, excitement as his eyes scan the room and sees us all caged.

"Ah, *ma chere*, long time no see, yes?" He says as he walks towards me. Oz reaches through the bars, but Étienne skillfully dodges him before smacking his hand with the end of his serpentine cane. I stand as he nears me, my hardened eyes boring into his.

"You betrayed us." I spit.

"I said I needed your aid, *ma chere*. I never said what for." And he's right. He never said what he wanted me for. And he never asked for Oz, just me. He just said he needed a queen. So, what is it he wants?

"What can I do for you, Étienne? You've gone through great trouble to bring us all here. What do you want?" I step closer.

"I already told you what I wanted, to bring Cross down. I offered to exchange his life for that of your bird's, no?" I hold my gaze. So, if Étienne is really going after Nathan, who's side is Bash on? Because he sure as hell isn't on ours.

"So, you bring us here, torture Serena, for what? We already agreed to help you." Oz cuts in. He's standing as close the bars separating our cells as possible, an arm's reach away from me.

"Collateral, I am afraid. You American men are such an unruly bunch. Put one helpless female in their grasp and they cannot control themselves." He shrugs and Oz lunges forward, his face smacking into the bars as he reaches for Étienne. "Now, now." He holds his hands up as if placating a child. "There is someone who wishes to speak with you."

He turns towards the door, where Bash is standing arms crossed, a smug look plastered on his ugly face. And I hear the boots, sound of leather smacking stone. Her presence, her aura is palpable. I can taste it as she steps into the dim light.

She looks the same as she did a few hours ago, her eyes avoiding mine as she looks at Serena. I see the horror in her eyes before it vanishes, merely a second later. I hate to admit how that brief disgust restores a small part of my faith that *my* Raven is still there.

"Do you see what they did to her?" Oz says through gritted teeth. He stares right at Raven, his gaze unflinching. "Do you see how they destroyed her?" Her gaze refuses to look towards Serena, but I know he's getting to her. "Is this who you have become? We used to fucking kill men like him!" He shouts the last part, the noise echoing throughout the chamber. I flinch at the power in it.

"I am here for a reason, Osprey." She says calmly, without emotion, without looking at him.

"Then share with the rest of the fucking class!" It's me who yells this time, fury building beneath my chest, my heart no longer beating. She doesn't look at me either.

"My brother has been controlling President Bader for over four years now. He has every part of the administration eating out his hand. He has developed an unbreakable line between the CIA and Bratva, funneling U.S. intelligence as easily as we breathe. Not a single thing is safe from their grasp." She pauses and looks at Oz again. "I need your help to take him down, as does Étienne."

"Why the fuck would we help you?" Oz cuts in. "Was this part of your plan?" He points at Serena again, and her trembling frame flinches.

"Étienne will release two of you. But I must keep one, otherwise Nathan will know something is amiss. *He* is the one who brought you all here." Her voice is laced with anger, finally breaking a small piece of her shell away as she tries to show she had nothing to do with this. But fuck I will never trust her again.

"I'll stay." The words are out of my mouth before I have a chance to second guess it. Oz whips his head.

"Fuck no, you two go." I shake my head.

"No. I am staying. That is final." I hold his gaze and then tilt my head towards Serena. Understanding crosses his face, and I see his tenses shoulders droop.

"Fine." Raven is watching us, as is Étienne.

"*Chien fidele.*" He whispers to Raven, a laugh bubbling up his throat.

Raven's eyes almost look as if they are filling with tears, but she swallows and looks at Bash.

"These two." She points at Oz and Serena and then steps back as Bash pulls a ring of keys out of his pocket. He goes to Serena first, opening her door and stepping in.

"Don't." Oz spits, slamming his hand on the bars again. Bash hesitates before running his thumb along Serena's lower lip.

"I will let you unlock the beast." He steps out of the cell and hands the keys to Raven, before he quickly disappears up the stairs, running away before Osprey can get a hand on him. Raven holds the key up to Oz's door before pausing.

"Serena was not my doing, Oz. Please believe that. I would never." And I hear it, briefly. The old Raven. Oz takes a second before nodding once and stepping back. She throws open the door and he steps out, coming straight to my bars.

"Do not stop fighting." He reaches through the bars, cupping my face in his hands. I lean forward, and our foreheads touch through the metal rungs.

"I trust you completely." I whisper before looking up. I feel the tears run down my cheeks and watch as he tracks them. "Take care of her."

"With my life." He steps away, his warm hands sliding from my cheek.

He steps into Serena's cell, scoops her up in his arms gently and walks towards Raven.

"I don't think you can be saved at this point, Naomi." He says. His voice is barely above a whisper, but the way she flinched, you'd think he slapped her.

"Étienne." She says, and the don walks towards Oz, ushering him towards the door. I see Serena's eyes, hold onto the warmth in them, as they both disappear up the stairs leaving me alone.

"What will Nathan do with me?" I ask, as soon as it looks like Raven is going to leave.

"He has a fetish for toys, and I fear you may become one." Her voice is cold, restrained.

"Is that what you are to him? A toy to play with?" She doesn't look at me as she makes her way back to the door.

"A toy is loved before it's destroyed. I was destroyed long before I was loved." And I feel my heart break all over again.

# CHAPTER TWENTY-EIGHT
## OSPREY

Étienne's men blindfolded us the second we crossed the threshold. I held onto Serena for dear life, not letting a single gap form between our bodies. Her arms held tightly to my neck, her trembling body cold.

"Just precaution, *fidele.*" He says with a sneer I can hear. I am pushed between the shoulder blades before a different voice speaks.

"Step up." I do and promptly smack my head on what I am assuming is car door. I grunt and duck, settling into the seat. I cradle Serena to my chest and hear as the door closes.

I count the turns, the length between them.

Right, left, left, right, straight for seventy-three seconds. Another right. Another right.

And then I realize they are driving in circles on purpose. Because why wouldn't they? What feels like an hour passes before the car stops and my door is wrenched open. A gloved hand grabs my arm and pulls us out. I stumble, falling to a single knee, but I don't drop Serena.

And then the car is speeding away.

I set her down and rip the blindfold off just in time to see the back of the black SUV, no license plate. Serena pulls her's off and stares at me, her brown eyes watery as she holds onto my arm.

"How will we find her?" She asks, her lip trembling.

"Her tracker. We will get her back, I promise." I rise, pulling her with me, and start walking down the alley, holding her tighter against me so she doesn't get cold.

It takes barely ten minutes before three SUVs race towards us in the alleyway, surrounding us protectively.

Shark and Bog are out in seconds, Stitch close behind.

"Report." Bog says as he reaches us. I fill him in, pausing briefly to place Serena in the open trunk so Stitch can check her. Radar is there, typing away on his tablet before sighing.

"Something is blocking transmission on Beast's tracker." I glance at the map and see Xyla's icon jumping from location to location.

"They have someone on their team blocking it." I surmise and run a hand through my hair. "Let's get back to base." I order and go to sweep Serena back up in my arms. She flinches and shakes her head once. My heart breaks ever so slightly but I nod and give her space.

She doesn't want to be touched. And I can respect that.

She limps to the door I hold open for her and climbs in, settling in one of the back seats. Her eyes are distant, vacant as she stares at the seat next to her. The seat Xyla always takes.

"I promised." I whisper to her. She nods once, still not looking at me. I gesture to Bog to make sure no one sits in that seat and he nods.

I shut the door, climb into the passenger seat, and watch as the alley flies by.

# CHAPTER TWENTY-NINE

## RAVEN

Ice courses through my veins. All I feel is rage and the urge to hurt someone. I climb the stone steps, the sounds of Xyla yelling after me echoes in the corridor. She's yelling my name. Over and over again. Begging for me to come back. But I can't face her.

The betrayal I saw in her eyes almost broke me. Not to mention seeing her shock as I tased her. Her confusion. The jolt through her body as she dropped to the dirty alleyway, lifeless. No part of me is worth redemption, and I am just hoping she'll finally stop trying.

I am exactly like Goose. And I deserve the same ending.

I step through the doorway and Bash is leaning against the wall casually. I walk right up to him and grab him by the collar, making sure to choke him slightly.

"If you fucking touch her, I will rip off your cock and shove it down your throat. And then, when you are almost dead, I'll fucking rip your eyes out and shove them up your ass." His eyes are filled with amusement as he searches mine.

"I thought you had forgotten about the little bird?" He sneers and I shove him against the wall even harder, delighting in the sound of his skull cracking off the stone.

"That was for Serena. And if I hear that you even *visit* Xyla down there, I will kill you." I push off him, letting his weakened body slump to the ground as I walk away in search of my brother.

# CHAPTER THIRTY

## XYLA

The dungeon, because I feel like I am stuck in some stupid fucking fantasy novel, is quiet. I can hear every heartbeat and breath. I can hear every drop of water as it condenses on the stone and then falls straight to the ground. I can hear the scurrying of rats or mice as they search for their next meal.

I stare at the sandwich I was brought. The parchment paper wrapped around it now damp from sitting on the ground. I don't reach for it or eat it. Who knows what they put in it. So, I just watch as a rat nears it, tiny whiskers flinching in recognition of food. I just stay exactly where I am, not moving a muscle.

Silence embeds into my bones. Becomes everything I feel. And so, with nothing else to do, I close my eyes and fall asleep.

I don't know how long it had been, but I eventually wake to the sound of someone's breathing. I fight a jolt of shock as I see Raven leaning against the bars across from me, her brows pinched as she stares.

Watches.

"What is going on between you and Osprey?" My eyes widen and I feel my jaw drop. That is the first question she asks me?

"What?" I stammer out, bewildered as I sit up.

"There is more there than there was before. The way he touches you and looks at you." I pull myself up to my feet and walk towards the bars. Absolutely confused.

"Are you asking if Oz and I are together?" She doesn't meet my gaze and instead averts her eyes down.

"Yes." She says after a few seconds of silence.

"Would it bother you if we were?" I ask and watch her eyes widen.

"I would understand." And instead of curiosity or shock, I feel fucking pissed.

"You would understand? Are you actually fucking kidding me?" I yell and finally her eyes meet mine. "You abandoned me. Made me think you were dead for two years. And you would *understand* if I moved on? Well, I didn't. I fucking pined for you. I searched for you. I made every single move and breath dedicated to finding you. There hasn't been a single fucking person on my mind aside from you for two years."

"Xy—"

"No. Fuck you. You think any of this was easy? I can't even begin to question what you have gone through or done, but I had to do this alone. Oz didn't believe me. Serena didn't believe me. My father sure as hell didn't believe me. Oz only admitted the possibility you were alive a month ago. For the last two years this search has been mine alone." My chest is heaving, and I feel like I am on the brink of completely losing it.

How could she ask such a thing? How could she think I would just move on after she was murdered in front of me. I would never be with another soul for as long as I live. Only her.

"That doesn't answer my question." She says bluntly.

"Oz and I are not together, nor have we ever been. Oz is my partner, my best friend, my rock. He is everything you should have been, aside from the romance. He is my sounding board and my platonic soulmate. I would die for him, and he would die for me. We rebuilt The Nest. We made it bigger and better. It is ours, but we did it for you. Oz is in love with Serena. But me? I am stupidly fucking in love with you. I haven't even looked at another person since you died. And you think I moved on with Oz? Do you even fucking know me?" I can feel my body vibrating with anger, and she just stays perfectly still. Back to the first version I ever met, unbreakable. Unshakeable. Mask always in place.

Always distant.

No emotions.

"And what about you, huh?" She quirks a brow.

"What about me?"

"Have you looked at someone else?" And I know I don't want the answer.

"I have always told you I wasn't the good guy. I am no saint. Never have been." And there goes my heart.

"Wow." I bite my lower lip and nod in disbelief as I back away. "Glad to know how much I meant to you." Her shoulders tense and she shakes her head, as if I am understanding everything wrong.

"You only ever saw things at face value, Xyla. You never saw the bigger picture, and for fucking once, I wish you would. Not everything in life is about love and happiness. Some things are life or death." Her eyes are hard, unflinching as they bore into mine.

"You think I don't know that? Do you know how many men and women I have buried? How many people I have watched die in pursuit of finishing what you started? I see the bigger picture. I see it fucking loud and clear. I just didn't realize you stepped out of frame."

"I didn't step out of frame, Xyla. I am the one holding the camera." I snort.

"So, this is all going according to your plan? We are just being manipulated to fulfill some fucking up check list you have. You're just sitting here plotting how we will ruin everything you built and get ourselves killed. Serena being raped and tortured was on that list too, huh?" I go for the low blow. A test.

"No!" She surges forward, her hands gripping the bars so tight her knuckles turn white. "No. Of course not. I would never." She closes her eyes and shakes her head. "When I came down here last night and saw her, I almost threw up right then and there. And I wanted to rip Bash's head off his fucking neck. I would never, ever, do that. I wouldn't allow that. You have to believe that. I don't care if you think I am a monster and unredeemable, but that you have to believe at least." She looks up then, her eyes lined in silver, and I feel my chest ache.

I step closer and watch her tense, and then slowly I raise my hands, closing them over hers.

"Why are you doing this?" I ask, my voice barely above a whisper.

"I have no choice, Xyla." She whispers back. I can feel her body heat, her breath. And I want to dive in, but I can't. This isn't my Raven, not anymore. "Xyla." Her voice is soft as she tilts her head, as if she wants me to come closer. As if she wants to kiss me.

But I step back, releasing her grip.

I can't kiss her again. Even if I want to.

"I understand if you have a reason. I also understand if you don't wish to share it with me. I hate what has happened to us, but two years have passed, and it was foolish of me to expect the same person who disappeared. Let me go, and I will stop looking. I will stop coming after you." Her eyes widen as her mouth gapes open like a fish.

"Do you find it so hard to believe that I could be the same person?" She asks, her hands tightening even more on the bars.

"Yes. Because the Raven I loved wouldn't have allowed me to be behind bars. The Raven I loved would have killed every single person who stood between us. And you haven't." Her hands drop away and she steps back. "You haven't done a single thing to protect me. And the Raven I loved so fucking much, was never the villain in my story."

And I see it. I see as her heart breaks and the new mask slides into place.

"You're right. I died that night, so maybe you should live your life as if I did."

"Are you letting me go?"

"You're not *my* prisoner, Miss Bader. It is not up to me." Her voice echoes, the coldness chilling my bones, as she turns away and disappears back upstairs.

Leaving me alone.

Again.

# CHAPTER THIRTY-ONE

## OSPREY

My head is reeling as I try and process the words coming out of his mouth. Try to understand the bigger picture of what happened, but all I can see is how she looked laying there with a bag on her head.

Naked.

For days.

"She's asleep right now. She was extremely terrified, too anxious to even let me touch her. I had to sedate her so I could give her a proper exam, which she fought. She didn't want to be put to sleep." Stitch's voice is saddened, low, as he stares at her medical file.

"Why didn't you get me?" I demand, picturing her pleading with him.

"She didn't want me to, and I had to get the exam done." He defends and I suck on my teeth.

"And? What did you find during your exam?" I push.

"Her bones are intact, no fractures or breaks. She is covered in lacerations, but mostly from staying sedentary on the grate. Those will heal fairly quickly; they aren't that deep or in need of stitches. However, the entire right side of her body, including her face, is covered in them. It'll make her sore for a while. It's unlikely she will scar, but if she picks at them or causes anymore trauma to the skin, it might. So, she'll need to keep them clean and covered as best as she can. She has some bruising and swelling on various parts of her body. It looks like she was kicked or hit a few times. But again, her bones are fine, just bruised." He stops for a second when I tense.

Fury radiates off me, and I turn, sending my still-wrapped fist into the wall. Cement wall. I feel the pain surge through me and watch as blood wells up on my bandages.

But it was either the wall or Stitch, and he doesn't deserve that.

"I'm sorry, boss." He says, no doubt worried I'll direct my anger towards him. And I am pretty close to it. Mostly because he sedated her without me present. "There is something else." I close my eyes and nod, fist still resting against the cement wall. "When I did a vaginal exam, there was a lot of trauma. Brusing, swelling, blood. And also, a lot of semen. I loaded her up on antibiotics as well as some medicine that will prevent conception But, she is going to be incredibly sore and tender for a while." Another punch to the wall, this time my hand crunches. My right hand.

My gun hand.

And now it's broken.

I don't even flinch. I just stare at the blood starting to drip down the wall.

"Oz!" Stitch grabs my hand and pulls me into the makeshift hospital suite we set up in the new warehouse. I hear machine beeps and look to see Serena on one of the beds, hooked up to monitors. She's asleep, her body relaxed and I hate seeing her so vulnerable. Unable to protect herself. I just want to cover her up and never let anyone near her. "We will need to x-ray your hand." He demands.

"*Fuck.*" I swear and turn away from her. "Just wrap it." I order and he pauses. "That's an order, Stitch." I snap, my voice growing gravelly as I glare at him.

"Yes, sir." He concedes, although I know he's pissed as fuck. I can see it in how his jaw is tensed.

"Anything else?" I push.

"She will make a full recovery, but I suggest therapy. A lot of it, we can bring someone in or send her out to see someone. She has a long road of recovery ahead of her, physically and mentally." I stay quiet as he wraps my hand in a thicker bandage, holding the bones in place. "I think we should send her back to DC. She needs to focus on recovery, and she can't do that if she's still in the thick of it."

"She won't leave without Xyla." He pauses and stares at me before nodding and conceding. "Thank you." I say after a few seconds of silence, and he quirks a brow. "For taking care of her."

"Of course." He responds, and that is that. We stay quiet the rest of the time he works on my hand. After the bandage is secure, he slips on a brace, further protecting my knuckles. I oblige, knowing I'll end up taking it off later, but figured he'd end up sedating me next if I argued.

I stand and walk towards Serena's bed, sitting in the chair next to it. Her breathing is even, slow, as she sleeps.

"Her sedation will wear off soon, probably within the next couple of hours. I promise to come get you when she wakes." Stitch says, appearing next to me like a ghost.

"Are you kicking me out?" My voice has way less venom than I intended. I just sound exhausted.

"Yes. You need sleep." I glare up at him, but he's unmoving. And right. I rise, placing a soft and gentle kiss on Serena's forehead, her skin cool to the touch and so soft against my lips.

"I will be right in the other room, just knock." I order, turning away from my soul and stepping into the hallway. The room we have set up as our bedroom is two doors down, and after opening it, I step in, passing out the second I hit the lumpy mattress.

I wake to the sound of pounding on the door and am instantly up. It had to be only seconds, but a quick glance at my watch shows that its nearly ten at night and I have been asleep for six hours. I race to the door, throwing it open. I push past Stitch who is staring at me bewildered and I run to the hospital room, panic coursing through my body.

Serena is blinking groggily, her eyes scanning the room as she licks her lips.

"Serena?" I whisper softly, brushing an unruly coil of hair out of her face as she continues to blink rapidly. "When did she wake up?" I snap at Stitch who rolls his eyes.

"Two seconds before I knocked on your door." He says irritated before he disappears into his office. I hear the door close and seconds later, her.

"Oz?" Her voice is hoarse, dry and flinch.

"Let me get you some water." I grab the pitcher and glass from the bedside table and pour her some. When I hand it back to her, she's no longer blinking groggily and just looking down at her body encased in sheets. "Drink." I order and tap the bottom of the glass. She takes a small sip and then hands it back to me.

"How long have I been asleep?" She seems so small. Her pale skin battered and bruised, washed out by the sterile, white sheets and gown.

"Only a few hours." She visibly relaxes and I reach forward again, tucking another curl. She flinches and launches herself back against the pillow. Her eyes are wide with horror, her hands covering her mouth as if suppressing a scream. I freeze and lean back slowly, retreating. Trying my best to show her I'm not a threat. Horror washes over her, and her hands fall away.

"I'm so sorry." She whispers and my heart fucking breaks.

"You have nothing to apologize for, it's okay." I pull the rolling chair over to the side of her bed and sit down. She stares at me, as if terrified I'll reach for her again. "I won't touch you. Not until you ask me to." I say and watch the wheels in her head turn.

"Oz..."

"Not like that." I correct. "I am here. I will be here throughout your recovery, and I won't try to touch you." She seems satisfied with the explanation and relaxes, her shoulders drooping and her head falling back against the pillows.

"Am I okay?" She croaks, her eyes closed.

"Just some cuts and bruises. You'll be just fine." I supply, hoping it'll calm her, but I know what it is she wants to know. I just can't bring it up. I can't. *She* has to.

"And nothing...*permanent*?" She pushes, her eyes fluttering open, looking at me with fear.

"No, Serena. All wounds will be gone in a matter of weeks." Tears pool in her eyes and she slaps her hands over them. No doubt relieved that she won't have to worry about a baby in all of this.

"I'm sorry." She says again, as if her tears are something to be ashamed of.

"Do not apologize to me, Serena. *Never* apologize. We are okay. *You* are okay." She nods, still covering her eyes and I sit there with her. I let her cry, let the sobs make her shoulders shake as she absorbs everything. Absorbs her trauma, her pain.

Absorbs how she is supposed to move on.

And I don't move. I stay as still as possible. Here when she needs me, away when she doesn't.

I keep my body still, my presence known but not intrusive. But all I want to do it pull her onto my lap and hold her. Never let her go.

Never let another person near her.

Because not a single thing that has happened will change the fact that I fucking love her. And I would do anything to make sure she never felt that fear again.

"Xyla?" She asks and when I look up, I see that she's peeking at me through her fingers, red tinged eyes making the blue pop.

"We can't see where she is. Her tracker is being blocked. I wouldn't be surprised if it's something Bash did." She shivers at his name and pulls the blanket higher. "We'll get her back." I add and she nods, the blanket clenched in her fists.

"What's the plan?"

"We don't really have one yet. I have Radar's team watching surveillance and trying to remove whatever shadowing they did to the footage, but if they have the tech to block our GPS, then who knows what they are capable of." I ponder, because we really don't know. Radar is the best of the best, but who knows who they have on their side.

"Doesn't matter, we're better." She speaks my thoughts out loud. I chuckle and run a hand through my hair; the ginger strands longer than they have been in a while. I brush them out of my face and then scratch my jaw, feeling the growth of my beard. "Your hair is a mess."

"Haven't had much time to visit a barber recently." She's snorts once, the singular sound like gold in my ears. A sound that means she is still in there, just temporarily wounded.

"I can cut it." She offers and then clamps her mouth shut. "When I am...better." She adds and I have the urge to squeeze her hand, but I won't.

Not a single touch.

Not until she asks.

"I'd like that."

# CHAPTER THIRTY-TWO

## XYLA

The night is cold, the damp dungeon growing crisp as the darkness continues. And I really wish I had a fucking blanket. I pull my legs up to my chest, resting my chin on my knees as I try to drum up some warmth. But the cold stone floor and the cold stone walls and the cold water dripping from the ceiling are making this stupid place nearly covered in frost.

Because it's really fucking cold.

I groan and rub my hands on my legs, hoping the friction will give me some reprieve. I don't know how Serena survived days down here *naked*.

I still hear nothing, no footsteps or sounds above me. No sounds in a cell nearby. Nobody nearing the door or opening it. Nothing. I have been abandoned. And fuck I am hungry, but I will not eat anything they provide. I don't want to be drugged like the decoy was. Starving is better than becoming Nathan's puppet. Because I don't think Raven would save me. I don't think she'd prevent that from happening.

So here I sit. Alone. I am alone with my thoughts, and that usually ends up dangerous. But I have nothing else to pass the time.

Raven said I am going to end up being Nathan's new toy, something she wasn't. She said it was because toys are loved and she never was, but she couldn't be more wrong. I loved her. I *love* her. And I would never destroy her, but she's letting Nathan burn away everything that made her who she was. Because Nathan apparently gets what he wants. And right now, for some reason, it's me.

With how close he is to my father, and my father's intent on us being together, does that mean this was always his plan? Was it something he and my father had arranged for in the beginning? To destroy everyone and everything and force me to be in Nathan's orbit?

At the dinner, my father seemed pretty hellbent on wanting to know if I liked him. But he also didn't know about Raven. And I have to believe that this is all just a coincidence, because the alternative would change everything. I couldn't imagine that, but I also couldn't imagine a lot of things my father has been doing.

So, knowing the real him, and his real agenda, is just as much of a mystery as knowing the same about Nathan.

About Étienne.

Étienne said he needed a queen, but did he mean he needed one for Nathan? He said Nathan was stealing from him, so he's not on his side, I would assume. He said he'd get rid of him so I could get Raven back, but he's a serpent. A man of twisted truths. Who knows what it is he actually wants at the end of this. He had no qualms about hurting us, imprisoning us, but for what?

What does he want? What does he get out of this?

I don't trust Étienne. Even if he has a good reason, even if he explained everything, he is still the don of an entire mafia that spans three countries. He's a murderer, aids in human trafficking and drugs. He is a monster. Étienne is the type of man we take down. The type we scrub from the Earth with every mission we complete. However, he did release Oz and Ser—Serena.

*Oh god.*

I want nothing more than to know how she's doing. I hope none of her injuries are serious, it didn't look like there were any that would be detrimental, just a lot of bruising and blood.

I just want to be there with her, for her. Hold her, help her through this. But she has Oz and he promised he would take care of her. No one would be able to handle her better and I have to hold on to that knowledge right now. She's safe. She's okay. Oz will make sure of it.

We'll have to sequester ourselves an award-winning therapist to help her through this, though. Not to mention it would probably be beneficial for me too. We could *all* use a heavy dose of psychoanalyzing at this point.

But he'll come for me. Oz will come and get me, just like I would him. Because we would never abandon each other, not when there was still hope. And as long as there is hope on his end that I am not dead yet, then I can believe he won't stop until I am home.

I just need to keep myself safe in the meantime.

My heart aches, matching the pain in my bones from sitting in the same spot for hours. My throat thickens and I feel the sudden urge to cry. To scream. To finally break down after years of holding myself together for the sake of everyone else. To finally, once again, be the girl who had others to protect her. The girl who lived her life so free and fearless. But I am not that girl anymore. And breaking down is not an option. It can't be.

At least not yet.

I have to get home first. I have to see this through. Finish what we started, and then maybe, just maybe, I can revisit what I want in my life. Because I don't think I can do this anymore. I am broken in so many ways. I wanted to keep The Nest alive for Raven. I wanted to find her and keep her safe. I wanted to have the ability and the manpower to do that. And I did. I found her. But she was hiding from me this entire time, and all of that pain I went through feels wasted.

Like it was for nothing.

And I don't know what that means. What that makes me. A child? Immature and naïve to believe I had found someone who loved me? Or is it that she had no choice, and my self-obsessive thoughts are making his about me?

I thread my fingers through my greasy hair and pull at the strands, fighting the urge to scream in agony. Not from pain, but from emotional distress. And that won't do me any good. Not here.

Right now, I need to stay strong and levelheaded. A clear mind is a free mind. A clear mind will know what to do and find a way out of this hell hole.

The old Xyla would have cried, screamed, begged her way out of here. Probably would have willingly slept her way out of here if it had worked. She would have thrown her father's name around, hoping someone could be bought with his endless amounts of dirty money.

But the Xyla I am now wouldn't.

I won't.

No.

I will sit and stay quiet. I won't scream and cry. I won't allow myself to get lost in my thoughts or succumb to any of the emotions fighting for purchase in my mind. I won't do anything that will jeopardize my chances of freedom, or my chances of holding on until Oz gets here with reinforcements.

I'll fight like hell the second I have the opportunity, but the only way out of this is with intelligence. Is with cunning.

I have to manipulate the right people to get that cell to open.

I have to have the right moment. I have to *make* the moment right. But that might mean I'll have to play his game.

Nathan.

Nathan fucking Cross.

Anger surges through me and I groan.

*Focus, Xyla. Compartmentalize.*

I take a slow deep breath and close my eyes.

What do I know? Focus on what I know for a fact.

Raven is *not* dead.

Two years ago, she was taken by either Kes's men, or Nathan. Or maybe a combination of both, they could have been working together all along. Either way, she ended up with her brother and he took her. He headed to Siberia, most likely on that private plane we tracked, and kept her hidden away until he needed her.

After he took her, he must have done *something*. Obviously saved her, but maybe brainwashed her? Psychological conditioning? Would Raven even be impervious to that? She's a fucking brutal monster, the very thing I always wanted to be. She could out-manipulate anyone. But if she was healing from a near-fatal wound, she might not have been as strong. Her mind could have been just as weak as her body.

She had said she couldn't let me out. *Couldn't* be free. So, back to him having something on her.

He *has* something on her.

Or he threatened her, and she's doing this to protect someone.

I shake my head. Nathan's motives are too unknown right now. Who knows what exactly Raven has going on in her life. I only knew her for such a short time. And while I fell quick enough to star in an insta-love Hallmark movie, I didn't know who she was outside of The Nest.

I just assumed she wasn't anyone. That she was just Raven.

*My* Raven.

But Nathan is a completely different breed of monster, and he has his claws in her. And there is a reason we aren't seeing.

What I do know is that he is working with my father and Étienne. He is supplying U.S. intelligence to Russian terrorists, and my father most likely knows about it. He is using Raven to do his dirty work—

The *assassinations*. In all of this, I forgot what it was that she left a trail of.

Bodies.

Dignitaries and senators. Mafia dons, terrorist scum. She was wiping away any competition for Étienne and Nathan.

She was *their* mercenary.

I have to admit that most of them probably deserved it and were men we would have killed at The Nest too. But the connection is there. There has to be a reason those men were targeted specifically.

I have to figure it out.

But that isn't all she left. The Pink God as they called her in Bucharest. She left a silk ribbon. She left a calling card.

And the decoy.

None of this makes sense.

The decoy must have gotten free. She was terrified. She knew she was going to die and so she must have said something. She must have told Dower, and that was why he was killed.

Probably by Nathan.

Or my father.

This all leads back to my father. He knows something. He knows everything. And fuck, I think he might actually be the one in control.

How else would Nathan have just walked into the White House and joined the administration? My father *invited* him. He must have known more about what happened with Kestrel than we thought.

He must have planned it all.

My mother...

Did he plan her death also? There was the fear that he was working with Kestrel originally, but that couldn't have been true.

He never would have hurt me.

Except, I wasn't the target at all. Raven said that over and over again.

I was never the target.

She was. We just couldn't understand how I was connected, how my family was. We thought it had something to do with the Acts passed, the one that ruined the Bratva. But I don't think that was the case.

Raven was Kestrel's target.

But he didn't want her dead, I think her dying, or almost dying, was an accident.

He wanted to control her—or bring her to someone. Bring her to whoever was controlling him. But they had to give her something to lose first.

This was all his plan.

He orchestrated us falling in love. He orchestrated her baring her soul so that she grew attached. He wanted her to have something to lose so she would be easier to control.

It's my father. It was always my father.

*"Oh god."*

# CHAPTER THIRTY-THREE

## XYLA

Hours pass and the horror never fades. The horror that all of this was planned. That nothing in the last few years was started by me or by Oz, but by my father as we assume the role of his puppets.

And he's the mastermind.

So, here I stay. Curled into a ball, knees to chest. Back against the cold stone, soaking through my clothes and chilling my bones. Going through every single thing that has happened and how I could have prevented ending up here.

Here I sit and wait. Because something is coming. Something *always* comes.

I count my own breaths, needing something to pass the time. I keep counting, over and over again. Reaching a grand total of 1,723 before I hear a door open and the sound of leather slapping stone, leading me to believe it's been about two and a half hours. Or longer and I am just delusional. And hungry.

I lean my head back, trying to appear less lost, less broken, as Nathan rounds the corner and comes into view.

His dirty blonde hair is slicked back, the black-out suit he's wearing a stark contrast. He has one hand in his pocket, the other hanging down by his hip, a phone closed in his fist. He smiles when he sees me watching, a sick, serpentine grin that reminds me of Étienne.

"Well look what we have here, the prodigal daughter." He says loudly, his boisterous voice almost making me flinch. "This is a far cry from how you looked the other night." He gestures towards my appearance with the hand holding the phone. "The low cut of the blazer that night, *god* it's like you wore it just for me." He groans and leans his shoulder against the bars to my cell, no doubt soiling his suit. I hope it fucking stains.

"I assure you; I dress for myself." I counter, my voice surprisingly even.

"And undressing?" He pushes, biting his lower lip in a very cringy and not at all hot way.

"Also, for myself." I respond, failing to hide disgust in my voice.

"And my sister I hear." Nathan adds, his eyes gleaming in the darkness as his tongue licks his lower lip. What a fucking pervert.

"On occasion." I pull myself to my feet and he watches me, assesses my every move.

"Given the chance, would you bed my sister again?" He questions, quirking a brow.

"*Bed?* What are you? A lord from the 1800s." I snort and he surprisingly smiles.

"I have heard about your wit, Miss Bader. My sister spoke of you quite often those first few months." I stay quiet, hoping he'll continue speaking. "He spoke about this fiery little ballerina, and all the ways she used her tongue." He winks and I fight a gag. "And then I beat the memories out of her." He adds and I fight the vomit rising in my throat.

The bruises I saw. They were probably from him. He has been beating her this whole time. Oh god, Raven. My heart clenches and I swallow.

"What do you want, Nathan?" I push, crossing my arms.

"I have come to offer you a deal, little beast." *Little beast.* He must have heard that from Raven, or maybe even from Bash.

"Don't call me that." I spit, stepping closer to the bars. He's within arm's reach but grabbing him now wouldn't help me. Wouldn't solve anything. I am still locked in here.

"Play nice, or I'll let you rot in here." He says slowly, a voice that sends shivers down my spine as he tilts his chin and looks down at me.

"What do you want?" I repeat, enunciating every word.

"I will let Raven go. I will release her and let her do as she wishes." He stops, letting me digest. And this tiny flicker of hope ignites deep in my belly but as the seconds pass, it blows out. Leaving nothing but the smoke of realization. Because nothing is ever easy.

"You want me to replace her." He smiles, a wide grin that makes both dimples pop out in his cheeks.

"Your brain should be studied. And I would like the opportunity." He adds and the vomit makes a reappearance.

"Okay, mad scientist." I quip and the wicked gleam comes back.

"I will let Raven go, if you take her place. Become my mercenary but also become *mine*." A look of disgust passes over my face and he catches it. Anger pooling in his eyes.

"Yours? Your property? Your toy?" I spit, stepping up to the bars so I can feel his body heat. Feel how close he is to me, and how quick he'd take his last breath.

"My sister is an asset, but not one I can bed. But you, little beast," He licks his lips before taking a deep, slow breath. "You I can send to the depths of hell to destroy my enemies and chain you to my bed to destroy me."

"I would rather die—" I start but he doesn't let me get far.

"If you say no, I will bring her down her and slit her neck right in front of you." I recoil, horror streaming through my veins.

"What?"

"I will force her to her knees, I will come behind her, and I will slit her neck. I will hold her head up so you have to stare into her eyes as she bleeds out, soaking the floor. And then I will leave her body here to rot while you slowly starve to death right next to her. You can die together; I find that quite poetic." I step back again.

No. He couldn't. That's his sister. Would he really kill her so easily? Just wipe her from the planet? Do I call his bluff?

He isn't giving me a choice.

"But you'll let her go…" I start.

"If you say yes." His voice is even, a little humorous even. Because his plan is working. It all comes down to his plans.

But—

She'll be free. Returned to Osprey and The Nest. Returned to her life. All I have to do is give up mine.

"Her life for mine." I whisper.

"If you love her as much as you think you do, the answer is easy." I stare at him, my eyes burning into his. Because he is right.

Her life for mine.

There isn't an alternate universe or timeline where the answer wouldn't be yes. Orchestrated love, or not.

My heart will always belong to her, and so will my life.

"Yes." He smiles, a bright mega-watt smile that makes tears prick in my eyes. He lifts his phone and taps the screen.

"Your tracker is now active. I want you to hit the button on it that declares you unable to be saved. I want you to hold the button down so they get the notification that you are seconds from death, and they can't save you." Shock barrels through me. That button, that press would be the end.

"How did you—"

"Bash." Of course.

"I want them to think you are lost forever." My hand shakes and I slowly lift it up to the back of my neck. I feel around until I graze the hard metal disk underneath the skin. One press and it'll send an alarm to everyone's phone. It'll preemptively declare my death. Saying that I cannot be saved and no one's life can be risked coming after me.

So, they wouldn't. They would leave me to die.

If I hit this, we have a code. And the code is that there are no exceptions.

Not if it was Oz. Not if it was Jet or Bog or Shark.

Not if it was *me*.

"One press, little beast. One press and she is *free*."

So, I press it. And feel every ounce of my freedom disappear along with the GPS signal that connected me to home.

# CHAPTER THIRTY-FOUR
## SERENA

I hear an alarm, and I jolt awake. My body is shaking, adrenaline flowing through me as I search the makeshift hospital room. No one is in here, the lights dim. The only noise is the sound of the constant, blaring alarm.

It's probably the middle of the night. But the alarm could mean anything. We could be under attack, or someone else is missing.

Oz—

I glance down at the IV in my arm and peel at the bandage. The tape comes off easily and then I slowly slide the needle out of my skin. I wince at the feel of it and then toss it to the ground, ignoring the drops of blood running down my arm. The O2 monitor starts to beep rapidly as I take the thumb clamp off but ignore it.

My feet are bare as they land on the cool cement. I am still in my hospital gown, but thankfully I have shorts on underneath, so I don't have to worry about my bare ass hanging out as I run through the warehouse.

The alarm is still going off; the siren sounds loud and repetitive.

I reach the door and open it to the hallway. The alarm is louder here, blaring. Red lights flash in the hallway, and I find myself starting to panic.

I force myself to take deep breaths and resume my path. The path that leads me to Oz.

I quickly walk to the bedroom door, knocking. I give it a second, but he doesn't answer. I knock again.

Nothing.

I throw open the door and see two bunk beds, with one bed's sheets rumpled and unmade. But no Oz.

I turn towards the stairs but quickly choose the elevator instead, thankful as fuck that this warehouse has one. I don't know if I could go down three flights of stairs right now.

I open it, and step in. One button sends me shooting to the bottom floor. When the elevator doors open, all I see is chaos.

People running around, shouting into phones, the alarm blaring so loud I cover my ears. Red lights flash in corners, and I search the crowd for Oz. I scan the different colors of hair until I spot the floppy orange of him, barely discernible in the light.

I step into the crowd, and thankfully people part as I pass them. I half expected them to barrel into me as they run about. I reach Oz quickly, my hand reaching out for his arm, but I recoil before I make contact. He turns and his eyes widen in disbelief and panic. He glances up and down, searching me for wounds I assume.

"Serena! Why are you out of bed?" He asks and steps closer. I watch his hands and feel both grateful and disappointed he doesn't raise them to touch me, to grab me and hold me to him.

"The alarm. What's happening?" His face is hard, a mask setting into place as I search his muted green eyes. "Oz?"

"It's Xy." He says in a voice I only ever hear when a mission goes sour, but it's edged in something else. In torment and regret.

In blame. But that's not the direction I instantly go. My brain immediately thinks she's home and so I look around as I answer.

"Did her tracker come back online?" I feel the hope bloom in my chest, but his voice tells me I shouldn't feel it. I shouldn't feel that hope. But I hold onto it anyway.

"Yes, but a second later she hit the button." And then it's gone.

"No." The word comes out of my mouth instantly. No chance to think. "No. We are not abandoning her." He searches my eyes as he thinks of what to say, but his mouth just opens and shuts. Because he, too, is lost.

"We have a code." It's Bog who answers, his face solemn. "We have a code she put into place. She all made us promise that there are no exceptions."

"Fuck your code!" I scream and before I can even think, I punch him in the face.

His head snaps back, but he doesn't fall. He quickly covers his bleeding nose and stares at me with wild eyes, eyes that are slightly impressed. My hand aches and I cover my mouth in shock.

"I'm so sorry." I stutter and step back. Shame. That's what I feel. Bog didn't deserve that. He's been nothing but wonderful to me. "I—"

"Serena." I shake my head and turn, but I feel Oz's presence behind me the entire time I walk. I reach the wall and place a hand on it, leaning forward and inhaling as much breath as possible, but it feels like my lungs won't expand. Like air can't fit.

Panic spreads through me. I feel my heart racing, my eyes growing dark. My head is spinning, and I feel like I am going to scream.

I stand upright and face Osprey.

"No." I say with as much malice I can muster. He shakes his head and holds his hands up, placating me.

"Serena—"

"NO!" I scream and hit his chest. I close my fists and hit him over and over and over again and he just takes it. My knuckles burn and exhaustion pulls at my senses, but I keep going. I can't stop. He needs to listen. He needs to hold me.

He lets me punch him until I can't breathe. Until the breath stops coming and I start to hyperventilate. He just stands there as the punching stops and my forehead falls to rests on his chest.

He just stands there.

He doesn't move an inch. He doesn't hug me, or pull me in. He doesn't do anything.

"If you would let me speak." He says, both chastising me and trying to be gentle. "I don't give a fuck what Xyla made us promise, or swear, or agree to. She will *always* be the exception." I lift my head quickly, almost clipping his chin. "As will you."

"You're going to look for her?" I ask, hope returning as I grip his shirt tightly and search his eyes.

"I am going to fucking *find* her."

# CHAPTER THIRTY-FIVE

## XYLA

My neck vibrates and then fades, as the signal stops. I know the alarm that's going through The Nest. The headquarters in D.C. and the warehouse here in Paris will be flashing red, filling the entire space with bright lights that signal a goodbye. It will go on for exactly five minutes before silencing.

And only in those five minutes are people allowed to mourn. It's after those five minutes that we move on. We continue our work, because even if someone dies, the mission doesn't.

That alarm will go off every single time someone hits the button. And news of whose button was pressed will spread like wildfire.

So, news that it is my button, that I am no longer able to be saved, will have reached every person. Osprey will be restructuring chain of command, making Bog his second. Because while we promised no exceptions, we also promised no partners other than each other. We are not replaceable to each other.

Ever.

So, he'll restructure the teams, and most likely move out within an hour. They will head back home to the states, as is protocol during missions. It's how we regroup and figure out how to best proceed with the mission, *if* we proceed at all.

He'll have to tell Serena. He'll have to tell her I am gone and won't come back. He'll have to explain to her why they won't come after me, and she won't get it. She'll hate him and fight him. And probably make his life hell for the foreseeable future. But if anyone can keep her safe and love her, it's him.

And so, I take a deep, shuddering breath, drop my hand, and look at Nathan. He glances at his phone, as if confirming the alarm has been sent, before he looks back up at me. Pleasure curling his lips.

"Well done, beast." He drops the '*little*' and smiles. He pockets his phone and pulls out a key, unlocking the door and throwing it open. "Ready to see your new castle?"

I hesitate only for a moment before stepping out of the cell. His hand falls onto my lower back as he guides me to the stairs, pushing me forward so I go first. I elbow him, forcing his hand off of me, and he shoves me straight into the wall.

My head bounces off the stone, and I gasp in pain as I catch my bearings. His hand returns to my lower back, and he forces me forward to the first step.

I climb them, counting the steps as I go to prevent me from passing out. Seventeen steps and then I am walking into a hallway.

The hallway is open, just an overhang and then a drop off, which he pushes me suspiciously close to. A quick glance over and I see the Siene churning down below, ready to devour me.

We are on the edge of the river. This can't be more than two miles from the birds. We're so close.

His hand stays planted on the bottom of my spine, his thumb caressing me like a lover, as he turns me to the left. A door opens and Raven steps out. Her face is flat as she looks forward at the river, but when she sees movement out of her peripherals, she turns. Her eyes widen and her lips part.

I see her searching, her eyes landing on his hand on me then to the blood I can feel running down the side of my face. The warmth of it startling in the cold air.

"Sister." Nathan calls out and she stands at attention, her face falling neutral. "You are free to go." She flinches and I see panic in her eyes as she looks back at me.

"What?" The question isn't directed towards her brother.

"I am no longer in need of your services." His shoulder rams into hers, sending her flying to the side as we walk by her. I jerk my arm to try and stop him, but his fingers digging into my skin make me hold back.

"Nathan." She says. "Nathan!" Her voice raises in volume and then a hand is ripping his off of my back. "Where are you taking her?" He spins around, his other hand closing around her neck and shoving her into the wall. I dig my nails into my palms and hold her gaze as she looks at me over his shoulder.

And the love I feared was gone, is there. Pooling in her eyes, furrowing her brow, as terror fills her entirely.

"That is no longer your concern." I don't move. A numbness spreading through my mind, through my heart. "Get out of my sight before I kill you." He pushes off of her and walks back to me. Instead of guiding me with his hand on my spine, he threads his fingers through mine.

As he pulls me, my eyes pass over Raven's. I see pain and confusion. My eyes tear up, and I whisper the last word I will probably ever say to her.

"*Live.*"

Nathan continues walking, pulling me through an open doorway and out of Raven's sight.

The door closes behind me, and I take in my surroundings. It's a homebase. Computers sit at desks, men walking around calmly with tablets in their hands. Phones ring and keyboards making clicking noises. Everyone is working, on what, I don't know, but they are calmly working as if this is a standard office.

He pulls me between the desks to another door. It opens to a stone hallway, where he walks to the end, passing by at least ten rooms. He opens the very last door where we are greeted with a suite that's nearly the size of mine back home. It's very French and looks almost Victorian, regal.

A four-poster bed sits in the middle; red linens draped over it. A sitting area sits to the right, a desk and computer to the left. I see a couple more doors, but my gaze is fixed on the bed.

"The bathroom is through that door," He gestures but I am not looking. "I had clothes brought for you, which can be found in the closet. After you have showered and changed, I'll take you to our nurse who will remove the tracker from your neck." I finally turn to look at him, and he is tapping away on his phone, disinterested in this conversation.

"Do you intend to keep me in here like a prisoner?" I ask and he snorts.

"No. I have a job for you, but you smell like dirty water and sweat, and I am not going to introduce my fiancé to my men looking like a sewer rat." He spits, curling his lip in disgust. I gape at him.

"*Fiancé!*" I yell, spinning to face him fully. He looks down at me.

"You agreed, Xyla. And if you pull out at any point, my men will scour the world for Raven and return her corpse to you." His voice is lethal, and I want to fucking stab him in the eye.

"God, you're disgustingly poetic." I murmur, gritting my teeth.

Get through this day. Make a plan. That's what I need to do.

"Would you rather I marry you off to Étienne?" I scrunch my nose, and he gestures again. "Shower. Now." He orders, and I comply, slamming the door behind me.

Now I just wait for the moment I'll fucking skin him alive and go home.

# CHAPTER THIRTY-SIX

## RAVEN

A bag is thrown over my head the second I start to follow after Xyla. He's holding her hand, like she's a prized possession. She was bleeding and her eyes looked bloodshot, which means he hurt her. And fuck I will kill him if he lays his hands on her again. I knew he had plans for her, he wanted to keep her, but letting me go? Just like that?

She exchanged herself for me. I just know it.

I fight against the arms holding onto me, kicking out as best as I can. Grips tighten and I find myself wincing as my arms are wrenched in an unnatural angle. I'm dragged only a few feet before they let go. I spin around, reaching for the bag to rip it off.

Bash and two other men are standing there, smirks plastered to their face. That fucking traitor. Always serving whoever is on top. The birds, Étienne, my brother.

"Can birds swim?" Bash asks and then his foot is hitting me square in the chest, sending my flying into the Siene.

The water is ice cold and slams into my back like concrete. The current is strong, pulling me down and to the left. I kick out, forcing my body to rise, but the current keeps sucking me under. I finally break through the surface and inhale, seeing that I have already travelled a dozen feet from where they kicked me in.

I start to swim towards the edge, but then the shots ring out. One hits the water right next to me and I gasp. Another shot rings out and clips my shoulder.

I cry out in pain and force myself to go under. Bullet after bullet flies through the dark, dirty water, barely visible. Another hits me in the same shoulder, a few inches down. I kick, swimming with the current, until the shots stop and I can finally come up again.

I inhale desperately, my lungs burning, and glance around. I am alone. I kick towards the edge of the stone until my hands can grip the rough rocks. It's about five feet up to the edge and I groan as I pull myself up onto the boulders and rocks below the wall. It takes a few minutes, but I finally feel steady enough to grab the top edge and pull myself up.

I scream as pain lances through my arm. I pull myself over the edge and collapse on the stone floor. I am a good fifty feet from where I started, but I am still alone. The hallway bare and all the doors to Nathan's hideout closed.

I bring myself to my feet, cradling my arm to my chest and spin on my heel.

I won't survive if I go in now. I need reinforcements.

I need Oz.

# CHAPTER THIRTY-SEVEN
## XYLA

The clothes Nathan laid out for me, make my chest ache with the familiarity of them. All black, down to the fresh pair of boots on the floor. Exactly what Raven always wears.

A thin camisole, a bulletproof vest, a bomber jacket, leggings, holsters—but no weapons. Which, I don't blame him. I would probably shoot him on sight. I dress quickly, leaving my hair towel dried and down.

One deep breath later, and I step into the hallway.

There are men on either side of the path to the front area, dressed in all black as well. They both look exactly like Bash, which is to say absolutely unremarkable and forgettable.

I pass by them with my chin held high and walk through the door to what I am assuming is the main room since that is where everyone is working. Still the same scene consisting of people typing away, some men standing by a wall probably watching paint dry.

There has to be less than fifteen men, which means his operations aren't as large as he wants everyone to believe. I debate counting them, committing each face to memory, but I don't.

My gaze fixes solely on Nathan.

"*Little beast*." He calls out as if I am a dog being ordered around. I narrow my eyes, push my shoulders back, and reluctantly walk towards him. "I have an assignment for you."

He's going to let me out. This soon? It's been like three hours since I was locked behind bars. Is he fucking stupid?

"And Bash will accompany you." Of course not. He's sending a babysitter.

"The fuck he will!" I yell and immediately feel the sharp sting of a slap across my face and then I am being thrown across the desk. I gasp at the feel of my body slamming into a hard surface. Nathan's hand tightens on my throat, holding me against the hard wood. A keyboard presses into my spine, a broken monitor slicing through my jacket and into my elbow, but I just stare up at his cloudy blue eyes. My hands go around his wrist, trying to lessen the weight on my throat, but it does nothing. So, I hold my breath, which is far better than gasping for air in his presence.

"You will do what you are fucking told. No exceptions." I grit my teeth to bite back a retort, because I have a sneaking suspicion this fucker would snap my neck in a heartbeat if I proved anything but useful, but then he'd have to deal with the aftermath.

There has to be a reason besides my ability to be fucked, that we he would choose me over Raven.

Could it always all lead back to my father?

I feel the lack of oxygen start to burn my chest just as he pushes off of me and straightens his suit jacket. I rise slowly, brushing non-existent dust off the front of my shirt and glare at him, letting my desperate need for breath calm into a smooth inhale.

"Your target's name is Lucas Monvoi. He is the son of La Morsure's right hand man, Deluca. You have 24 hours to dispatch." He shoves a file at me, and I scramble to catch it, losing whatever edge I had.

"Yes, sir." Bash says smugly to my right, and I elbow him—hard. He grunts and raises a hand to retaliate but drops it with a snarl. I turn on my heel, temporarily satisfied, heading for the door before a hand snakes out to grab me, ripping me back into a hard chest.

"Do not make me regret letting you out of your cage, *beast*." Nathan sneers into my ear. I lean away from him, tossing a saccharine sweet smile at him.

"Wouldn't dream of it, *Crow*."

# CHAPTER THIRTY-EIGHT
## RAVEN

My shoulder is aching, the pain radiating through every nerve as I stumble down the alleyway. The sun is starting to come up, which should hopefully warm the air up, but not fast enough. Right now, during the first week of October, being soaked to the bone in the crisp, cold air, does nothing but make me even more miserable.

Blood mixes with the dirty Siene water as it drips off my fingers, landing on the broken cobblestones. I don't know how much longer I can last.

So close.

I tell myself, over and over again.

I have to be close to The Nest. Which means they should see me on their cameras. Which means—

The roar of an SUV's tires careening over the stone has my head snapping up. Lights blind me as it comes into view, stopping a foot away from me and I feel relief.

"Hands up!" Someone yells. I hold my hand up to block the light, trying to see who the voice belongs to. It's not Oz. "I said put your fucking hands up!" He yells again, and I comply. A cry wrenches from my throat as I lift my arm. My knee gets kicked and I fall the ground. Before my hands can catch me to prevent a not-so-glamorous faceplant, my elbows are wrenched behind me, something tying them in place and I scream in pain.

"I need to see Oz." I say, my voice hoarse.

"What?"

"Take me to Osprey." I say with a little more force. I am pulled to my feet and shoved towards the SUV. I let them push me into a seat. The door closes and I see there are three people. One in the driver seat, one in the back with me, and one climbing into the passenger seat. Another bag is pulled over my head, and I silently curse. Everyone and their theatrics, goddamn.

The SUV lurches forward and my stomach pitches. I feel us make a sharp U-turn before we are speeding along the bumpy road. It only takes a minute or two before we slam on the brakes. My body shoots forward and I smack my face straight into the passenger seat in front of me.

"What the fuck." I mutter. My luck is so non-existent right now. I need to be in a bubble.

The door opens and I am pulled out. I trip, because of course, and land on my knees.

"Can you stop treating me like a ragdoll?" I yell and hear a familiar chuckle. "Osprey, Goddamnit." I yell and the bag is ripped off my head.

Oz is standing in front of me, illuminated by the SUV's headlights, and I see we aren't at the warehouse. We are in some abandoned parking lot.

His ginger hair is slicked back. He's wearing a black t-shirt and jeans, his usual lace-up boots. He looks like every stereotypical mercenary, and I want to kick him in the balls, even if I am the one who made him this way.

"Is this necessary?" I ask, trying my best to roll my screaming shoulder.

"Well, considering you haven't been on the right side the last two years, yeah I'd say it is." I roll my eyes.

"I have always been on the right side, Oz. You just don't know the full story." I retort, pain turning every thought muddled and irritated.

"Enlighten me then." He sneers.

"Not yet. We need to talk. Nathan has Xyla." I say the last part slowly and see the hurt flash across his eyes.

"I know that." He spits out.

"No, you don't. She isn't locked up anymore. He kicked me out, claiming he didn't need me anymore. He plans to use Xyla as he did me, except Xyla he can actually use in more ways." My voice trails off. "He plans to marry her."

And Oz being Oz, busts out in a cold, uncontrolled laugh. His eyes squint and his dimples pop out. He puts his hands on his knees, leaning forward to catch his breath.

"Do you think I am fucking joking?" I yell, patience growing thin. What the fuck is his deal?

"The Xyla you left is not the Xyla that remains, Raven." He says cryptically and I stare up at him. "She is a fine-tuned weapon. She is everything you could have been. If he has let her out of her cell, he is going to wish he killed her. We call her Beast for a reason. She's who goes in when nothing else has worked. She is our hidden secret." He gets down onto a knee, leaning closer to me. "She is a monster."

"*You* turned her into a monster." My heart breaks as I think of my sassy and sweet ballerina. The woman who was so strong-willed but needed me. Needed all of us.

"No, *you* did Raven. You turned her into this when you left." He rises and nods towards the man behind me. "Let her go, Bog." He orders and I hear something being cut roughly, nicking me in the process.

"What now?" I ask as I pull myself up and cradle my bleeding shoulder.

"I don't know what you're going to do, but I am going home." He sighs and turns around.

"Home? To DC?" I ask, stepping forward. Another person blocks my path, and I go to knee him, but he's quicker, throwing his arm around my neck and spinning me until I am face down on the ground.

"No, to our safe house." He says with attitude.

"What about me?" I yell out.

"You're on your own." I hear their footsteps dissipate and I start to panic.

"Don't leave me, Oz." He looks back over at me, splayed out on the dirty ground. His eyes soften and I see the pain in them.

"You're the one who left, Raven." That's all he says before he climbs into the SUV, and I watch them all drive off.

I stay on the damp pavement for what seems like hours, watching the sun rise, turning the sky a muted orange. My breathing grows shallow and I realize I am bleeding out.

Oz left me to bleed out and die.

Because it's what I deserve.

An elderly woman pops into my field of view, her face concerned. I try to speak, but my throat is closed off and dry. I feel dizzy, out of it. I turn slightly and see the blood soaked into the pavement. I look back up at her and let the tears building finally spill.

Seconds pass and I hear the sirens. More people come into my field of view, and I stay frozen, heartbroken. Shattered into a million pieces. I let them load me on a stretcher, putting me in the back of the ambulance.

And when they ask me my name, I tell them Naomi.

# CHAPTER THIRTY-NINE

## OSPREY

Two weeks have passed since I left Raven bleeding out. Radar hacked into their system and found out someone was brought into the local hospital, so I know she got medical care. But what surprised me was seeing that she wasn't checked in as a Jane Doe.

She was checked in as Naomi Cross.

She was discharged a few days ago, after two surgeries and a lot of post-op care, but she didn't make an appearance, even though I figured she would.

I hated leaving her like that, but who would I be if I just gave in and let her back into our operations? I saw the pain in her eyes, and I know what she spoke was true, but the risk is too great. She could be another mole.

But I should have let her explain, tell the whole story. She tried, but I stopped her. How would I know whether it was the truth, or just another lie to add to the list? So, I left her, bleeding out from a wound on her arm or shoulder, I couldn't really tell.

But I left her. And I would be a liar if I said I didn't do it as revenge. Payback for her leaving us. I let myself walk away this time.

Movement to my right has me spinning around, gun poised. Serena is standing in the doorway of the makeshift office, her hands raised. I quickly drop and holster my weapon and sigh.

"I'm sorry." I whisper. She offers me a soft smile.

"I know better than to sneak up on you, Oz." She comes forward to lean against my desk. "Any news?" She asks, glancing at my screen.

Her skin has healed nicely, the scabs across her face and body finally in the last stages of healing. She is almost back to normal—aside from the touching. She still gets nervous around everyone. But she's doing so much better, and I can't help but feel my heart swell at the sight of her doing so well. She'll brush her hand on my arm, or pat my cheek, but she hasn't asked me to touch her yet, so I stay distant. I give her all the charm I have vocally, but my hands won't touch her skin until she begs.

"Not yet." I say quietly.

We haven't seen any movement from Xyla since we were released. She has to be working for him, killing for him, but no bodies have been found. No word has spread of a new murderer on the loose. None.

So where is she? No planes have taken off, and all eyes that have been on their HQ have reported no movement either. There are people there, but Nathan and Xyla haven't been spotted. Bash has, multiple times, but not her.

"Where could she have gone?" Serena asks.

"They have to be getting in and out a different way, a tunnel of some sort. There is no way they are staying couped up in there this entire time." I ponder; my eyes focused on the surveillance feed.

"If only there was someone we could ask." She sarcastically offers, giving me a wry smile at the same time.

"Don't." I warn.

"Come on, Oz. Do you really think she would come to you unless she was free? That she would trap you ag—"

"Again? Like she did last time?" I cut her off and her face falls.

"That was different. She wasn't hurt and begging." She tries to appeal to my tender heart, but I don't have one. Any tenderness I have is for her.

"So, we should believe her because she was bleeding?"

"No, you should believe her because you love her." I hold her gaze.

"Any familial love I had for Raven disappeared the second I saw you in that cell." Horror fills her eyes, and I watch as they line in silver. Her mouth falls open slightly and I almost feel guilty for bringing it up, but it's the truth. "She allowed that to happen. She was complicit in your torture, and I can never forgive that." Her eyes close and she takes a slow breath before opening them again, fire pooling in the bright blue eyes.

"Blame Nathan. Blame B—" She chokes on his name. "Blame *him*. But don't blame Raven. I forgive her. Why can't you?"

A tear escapes her eye, and I fight the urge to wipe it away. One day she'll ask me to touch her, one day.

I have to keep telling myself that.

"You forgive her?" I ask, searching for any hint of deception in her gaze.

"I do. It wasn't her fault, and I saw the horror and disgust in her face when she came down and saw me. She didn't know. And what little I know about her from Xyla, she never would have let it happen if she knew." Her voice is so soft, so sure of the words she speaks.

"That Raven doesn't exist anymore." I cut her off and push out of the chair, pacing.

"How do you know?"

"I *know*." I raise my voice and instantly regret it. I see anger fill her face as she slides off the table and looks at me.

"You won't even give her the chance to apologize, to start over. How could you possibly even know who she is anymore if you won't talk to her?" She questions, forever fighting me. On everything.

"I will not allow her near you!" I spit out getting in her face. She flinches slightly and panic seizes me. I step back, putting as much distance between us as possible.

"I am not yours to control. Some pain-induced proclamation of love does *not* mean you own me!" Her voice is laced with pain, not anger and once again, I fight the urge to grab her and never let go.

"Serena." My voice cracks on her name.

"Xyla is missing, possibly enduring worse than I did. Raven could be the answer to saving her, to ending this. Are you willing to risk Xyla's life because of your personal relationship, or lack thereof, with Raven? Because I wouldn't. Even if she was complicit in what he did to me, I would still turn to her. Because she is the only key we have, the only *lead*. And I know when to set aside my own vendettas for the greater good." Her speech hits me right in the gut and I swallow.

She's right. My hesitance to work with Raven is because *I* am hurt. I am mad. I need to set it aside for the chance to fucking end this. Serena is right, and she'll never let me forget it.

"Alright." I say in finality, my shoulders dropping. "We will contact her."

She visibly relaxes and walks over to me. Her hand rests on my arm, giving it a little squeeze, before she walks back to the door.

"Thank you." She says over her shoulder before leaving.

I slump back into the chair and tap the comm in my ear.

"Radar. Establish connection with Raven."

"*Yes, boss.*" He says in return, and I stare up at the ceiling.

I am going to fucking regret this.

# CHAPTER FORTY

## RAVEN

I wrap the jacket tighter around me as I exit the hotel lobby. Nathan may have kicked me out, but my bank account was left full. After my release from the hospital, I checked into a five-star hotel in downtown, figuring if anyone came looking for me, they would find me.

They'd know where I was.

I didn't use Raven or Naomi, though. I checked in under Ana Bader, Xyla's dead mother. Why? Because I needed to get their attention. I needed to make a statement, and maybe it worked, because right across the street stands a well-dressed man in all black. His eyes focus on me and then quickly scan the street. He pulls out his phone, probably trying to seem distracted, but I know the signs.

The steel toed boots, the slight darkness in his left ear from the hidden comm, the thickness of his chest from where a plate is hidden under his shirt, the loose fit of his suit jacket to conceal holstered weapons. The dodgy look in his eyes as he pretends to not be watching me.

I wonder which one of the birds this one is. It's not the one Oz called Bog, that one deserves a punch in the face.

I cross the street and pass right by him, giving him a sidelong glance. I hear his footsteps behind me, leading him into an alley next to a coffee shop. Steam billows from vents in the road, making the area smell like burnt espresso beans and sewer. I turn down a second alley, getting further away from the main street. His footsteps pick up, and I spin around, shoving the end of my pistol underneath his chin.

"Good morning." I say with a smile.

"Raven." He responds, holding his hands up in defeat.

"Who do you belong to?" I ask. I know he's one of Oz's, but always best to check.

"A little birdie." He says with a smile, revealing pointed canines. I scoff and release him, holstering my weapon.

"What can I do for you?" I cross my arms, pleased that the sting of the dissolving stitches lessens each day.

"Someone wants to meet with you." I suck on my upper teeth and contemplate.

"Didn't seem that way when I was left to die in an abandoned parking lot."

"You seemed to survive." He shrugs.

"Who trained you?" I question, stepping closer.

"Beast." I flinch at her call sign.

"Before she was a beast, she was the beauty." I counter and he smiles again.

"She is still the beauty, but she bites." His smiles pisses me off, so naturally, I punch him. His head shoots back and then he quickly covers his nose. "*Bitch*!" He yells, taking another step forward. A short whistle sounds and we both turn towards the alley entrance.

Another bird is standing there, this one taller and slimmer. He has a little bit more of a superiority air to him.

"And you are?" I ask, crossing my arms again.

"My name is Jet, and the person you just punched is Shark." His voice is crisp, commanding.

"Interesting names." I muse.

"Your presence has been requested." Jet says, his voice even and calm. I like him. He's probably good under pressure. Shark on the other hand has a short fuse.

"When and where?" I ask. Stepping around Shark but still keeping him in my peripherals.

"Eleven tonight. He'll find you." Jet answers, turning on his heel. "Shark." He orders and I feel his shoulder slam into mine as he walks past me. I grit my teeth at the pain that lances through me but hold back.

He wants to meet. That's a step.

A very important step to getting my life back.

# CHAPTER FORTY-ONE

## SERENA

I can feel how tense Oz is as we stand in the main room of the warehouse. People are buzzing around, their energy palpable. Word spread fast that Oz and Raven were going to meet, and with some convincing, I am going too. So here we stand as Oz debriefs Bog and Shark on protocol.

The warehouse will go on lockdown as soon as we leave. No one in and no one out. Oz wants to make sure that everything here stays safe if something happens to us, which I have tried to assure him won't happen. I don't think Raven is a threat, not from what I saw in the dungeon.

So, I just wait for him to finish.

"Keep an eye on our trackers." He orders Radar. I finally convinced him to let me get one after my abduction. It took a lot of pushing, but before I was released from Stitch's care, I got one implanted in my thigh. He didn't want it in my neck, said that location is too well known. So, mine is hidden in my inner thigh. And let me say, that shit hurt more than the birth control implant in my arm, but I feel a sort of reassurance every time I touch it.

Knowing Oz will always come.

"Yes, boss." Radar answers.

"You're in charge." Oz tells Bog who takes a deep breath and nods. He has quickly risen in the ranks here at The Nest and Osprey and Xyla trust him immensely. "If anything happens, this is all you."

"You got this, Boggie." I whisper and he winks at me.

"Thanks, Fix." He whispers back.

"Alright. We are leaving." Oz doesn't touch me, but his hand hovers by my lower back, the heat of his presence enough to guide me forward. He hasn't touched me once. I don't know whether I should feel grateful or disappointed.

He said he'd wait until I asked and every fucking time we are alone I want to do more than ask.

I want to beg.

And then I picture what it would feel like, his rough skin touching mine, and my heart hurts. Because I know I'd enjoy it, I would love it, but it would feel too much like *him*.

We reach the main barn doors and step through. I turn and look over my shoulder and watch as the steel door is slid shut before a loud *clank* sounds, symbolizing being locked out, which feels a little terrifying.

There is an idling SUV, and I climb into the open passenger door Oz holds for me. He shuts it and then climbs in the driver side. He takes one deep breath. Then another, as if he's stalling.

"Let's go, Oz." I glance at the clock and see it is almost eleven. He nods, switches the gear to drive and then we are off.

The drive to Raven's hotel is quick. We park right in front, the street nearly deserted. Oz opens my door and leads me straight into the lobby.

"What room?" I ask Oz as we walk towards the shiny silver elevator doors.

"1411." He says quietly. The elevator attendant dips his chin at us before calling the elevator. We step in once it opens and another attendant smiles at us. Damn, this is fancy.

"What floor?" He asks in a thick accent.

"Fourteen." Oz responds and the man nods. Within seconds we are shooting up to the fourteenth floor. The elevator sings and the doors slide open silently.

Red and gold carpet greets us, it's demask pattern a little busy for my taste. I follow Oz down the hallway, our footsteps silenced by the thick carpet. We pause in front of her room and I feel his apprehension.

"Just knock." I groan and he looks over his shoulder at me, his eye narrowed but playful. His hand lifts and a single sharp knock echoes. Silence passes and then the sounds of the door unlocking.

The door opens and there stands Raven in all her glory. She looks a little hesitant, as does Oz. They just stare at each other.

"Raven." I step around Oz and hold out my hand. "We've met but I don't think we have every been properly introduced. My name is Serena. I am Xyla's sister for all intents and purposes." I smile as she stares at my hand. "I promise I don't bite." A smile breaks through her tight lips, and she takes my hand, gently shaking it.

"I am glad we are meeting under better circumstances." She offers me a soft furrow of her brow with her smile, and I nod slightly.

"Agreed." I release her hand and elbow Oz, who chokes.

"Can we come in?"

"Why not?" She opens the door wider to her room and we walk in. It's a rather large room, but still only consists of a bed, desk, table, TV, and bathroom. The room is fashioned in various shades of red and gold, matching the carpet that spreads to the rooms as well. The door shuts and Oz stiffens next to me, as if he could be any tenser. I walk straight to the small table that has four chairs, dropping down into one. Oz stays by the door, but Raven joins me.

"We have some questions." Oz starts, crossing his arms and leaning against the door frame.

"I figured. Ask anything you want." Raven responds, her shoulders relaxing.

"Why did you use Ana's name for your reservation?" It's me who asks the first question and Raven whips her head towards me.

"I wanted to attract your attention, but most of all I wanted to attract Xyla's. She's out there somewhere, and I wanted her to feel like she could come to me." I bite my lower lip, surprisingly satisfied with her answer.

"Is there another exit besides the three doors bordering the hallway next to the Siene?" She looks back towards the door.

"There are a series of tunnels that lead to other warehouses and even an abandoned church along the Siene. You have been to one of them, the night you met Étienne in what I believe was an abandoned wine cellar." Oz frowns, his gaze growing distant.

"Are you working for Nathan, or Étienne?" Oz asks.

"No one right now."

"But before?" He counters.

"Both. Nathan was the one who controlled me, but I did things for Étienne that undermined Nathan, such as releasing the two of you." Her response is vague, and it irritates me.

"What did you do for Étienne?" I ask. She takes a deep breath, chewing on the inside of her lip.

"I sabotaged certain missions I was sent on, didn't kill the targets. I would claim they never showed or were hidden by someone. I also funneled money from Nathan's secret accounts in Étienne's."

"Why?" Oz pushes off the door and steps closer. "Why would you help a literal mafia don who deals in human and weapon trafficking?"

"Because he promised to kill Nathan." Her answer is short, succinct, but important.

"So, you were working for Nathan but also sabotaging him for Étienne in the hopes that he would kill Nathan for you." Oz summarizes.

"Yes. Nathan is unstable. He's a grenade with his pin caught. He'll explode and take a whole crime syndicate with him."

"And that's a bad thing because?" I push.

"It's not. That's what I am getting at. Nathan thinks he controls La Morsure. He thinks he controls President Bader. But he has no control. Every sector of his operation is under scrutiny; he kills more of his men than he ordered me to kill. When he goes, the whole operation goes." She tries to explain but I just still don't get it.

"Start from the beginning." Oz's voice is tight as he sits on the edge of the bed facing us. Raven's face falls and I see pain in her eyes.

"When Kestrel shot me, I took my last breath. I died in Xyla's arms. I was ready to go because I saved the woman I loved. And I thought that was a valiant way to go. But then I woke up. I was in so much pain, it felt like I was electrocuted. And when I opened my eyes, I was on a plane. Masked doctors and nurses were performing surgery on me in the air, but they didn't sedate me. I felt every slice and cut. I felt each bullet they took out of me. I screamed and screamed, but they had me restrained, so I couldn't move. I endured all the pain, and eventually they stopped." She pauses.

"When the darkness creeping along my vision finally cleared, I looked around as best as I could. And there, on a sofa in the jet, was my brother. My big brother would I had believed was dead for years. The brother I mourned. The brother whose death made my parents disown me. The person responsible for every single thing I had become. He was there." Her fists tighten on the table, and I see her knuckles turn white.

"There was this sense of overwhelming relief and pain that surged through me, and I cried. For the first time in a long time, I cried so hard I could barely breathe. He unlocked my restraints, climbed onto the blood-soaked operation table, and held me. I cried for hours and eventually he picked me up, carried me to the couch, and laid me down. I fell asleep with my head in my brother's lap. I had never felt so conflicted in my life, but also so relieved. But when I woke up again, He wasn't comforting me. He was sitting across from me with a gun pointed at my head."

# CHAPTER FORTY-TWO

## RAVEN

I swallow, hard. The memories flowing through me as if it just happened. The callousness and detachment in his face.

"The Nathan sitting there wasn't the one who soothed me to sleep. I sat up and he threw a stack of papers at me. They were ballots. Thousands of them. Ballots with Lincoln Bader's name on it."

*"What is this?" I asked, my gaze flitting across all of the papers.*

*"Lincoln Bader is going to win the election in a few months. He will win by a landslide, making him the youngest U.S. President in history." Nathan said, his voice rough and cold.*

*"You are rigging the election?" My voice came out as a shout and his hand tightened on his gun.*

*"Yes. And when he wins, he will appointment me into his administration."*

*"As?" I asked, incredulous and confused.*

*"Special intelligence." He answered and I just stared at him.*

*"If what I have observed is correct we have some friends in common. Lincoln Bader is the father of your girlfriend, correct?" I nodded. "Good. Then you will prove very useful."*

*"How?" I threw the papers on the ground and he smiled.*

*"I will murder Lincoln Bader in front of his daughter, the last family she has. I will torture and skin him alive and then force her to listen to his death rattle before I take her as my own and destroy her too. All while you watch." My face paled, nausea coiled in my stomach.*

*"What do you want, Nathan?" His smile will forever be engrained in my mind.*

*"I need an assassin. I need someone to do my dirty work, and your extensive work history has proven you are the perfect person. Work for me and I will let Xyla and Lincoln live the rest of their lives unharmed."*

*"What's the catch?"*

*"The whole world will believe that you are dead."*

"Jesus." Serena says under her breath to my right.

"You just took him at his word?" Oz questions, and I can see how pissed off he is. "You didn't even test him to see whether it was a bluff?"

"Over the next few days, while I healed, he would show me pictures of Xyla and of her father. He had men following her. One of the pictures was of Xyla asleep in her bed, and someone was holding a knife to her throat. The next day, the same picture but Miss Dolly. And then again, with Lincoln. I knew he had his ways."

"And if he was able to stay hidden for all these years." Serena adds and fuck I like her. She has been validating everything I've said. I smile at her.

"Exactly. He had the resources. He took me Siberia, where we met up with Bratva. I had the unfortunate opportunity to meet some of Kestrel's comrades, all of whom Nathan granted time alone with me." My eyes flick down to the table, and I pick at the wood. A cool hand grasps mine and I look up at Serena.

"You did not deserve what happened to you." I can see Oz staring at our hands from the corner of my eye. I squeeze her hand back.

"Neither did you." Her smile is soft and doesn't meet her eyes.

"Then what happened?" Oz pushes. Serena pulls away and I put my hands on my lap.

"We travelled a lot. I was given names, occupations, locations. We jumped from Siberia to Paris to Bucharest, over and over again. And I soon realized that some of the men I was killing were U.S. agents undercover. The others of course actually deserved it; they were horrible people who murdered others and tortured women. Men that were a part of a mafia or crime family. But the U.S. agents were all people who questioned the election or questioned Nathan's involvement. Or even people Nathan was scared would get too close. I started to relocate some of them, not all, but some."

"Where are they now?" Oz asks.

"A safe house in Scotland." My voice breaks and I swallow.

"Why the pink ribbon?" Serena questions.

"No one could know I was alive, no one. Any picture of me was scrubbed. I couldn't exist, but I had to find a way to make sure you knew I was alive." I look at Osprey. "I wanted you to know." He doesn't meet my gaze. "I got the ribbons from Repetto, Xyla's favorite pointe shoe company in Paris. They are the exact same ones she uses. I bought the ribbons in bulk, and with enough money, they didn't ask questions. I started leaving them on the bodies. At first Nathan was pissed, and definitely took it out on me, but when he saw that people were calling me the Pink God, another serial killer, her started to claim it was his idea, that way no blame would ever be shifted to him. I was a lone wolf."

"If you got caught, there would be no evidence tying you to anyone." Oz adds, finally meeting my gaze.

"Exactly."

"So, all these years, you have been just killing for him? How did you get caught up with Étienne?" Oz asks.

"About a year ago, I was sent to kill someone from La Morsure. The right-hand man's son. Étienne was waiting for me and gave me a proposition. See he knew Nathan was coming. They had been working together for years apparently and the man I was sent to kill had evidence Nathan, and I, were stealing weapon shipments from him. So, Étienne sent the man away so he wouldn't be killed. He provided me with a body for me to mark, and I accepted his proposition. From that point on, I worked for both. I saw my way out." I shrug, because I'm not ashamed. I did what I had to do.

"And what happened to that man? The one you were sent to kill?" Serena asks.

"He was found dead two weeks ago. It seems Nathan found out he was never killed, so he had Xyla do it."

"Xyla killed an innocent man?" Serena whispers, and I hear her heartbreaking.

"Lucas was not innocent by any means, but he didn't deserve to die. At the end of the day, he is a part of La Morsure, but he was born into it, it wasn't his choice. I felt sorry for him. He was never given a chance to be anything other than this." My heart clenches.

"You are not working for either of them now?" Oz asks.

"No. I have ties to no one." I admit. Because I don't. I'm alone.

"What would you get out of helping us?" Oz pushes.

"My life back. I want this over."

"What makes you think you would be welcome back in The Nest? Or that Xyla would ever welcome you back?" Oz pushes even further.

"I don't think she would, but being free from Nathan and Étienne means there is a chance. I will fight every day of my life just for the *chance* that one day she will look at me the way she used to again."

Silence spreads across the room, but I don't break my hold on Oz's gaze. His muted green with my bloodshot blue. We just stare, the way we used to when we needed to talk silently.

"Okay."

"Okay?" I parrot.

"We need your help. We need it to get Xyla back and to end all of this. For good. But after it's over, Xyla makes the call. Xyla gets to choose what involvement you have in our lives." Relief washes through me.

I'm getting my chance. That's all I can hope for.

"Deal."

# CHAPTER FORTY-THREE

## OSPREY

Having Raven back in my orbit is...different. Her presence used to be craved—sought after. I used to dream of having her back at The Nest, in charge, but now things have changed.

She is subdued, quiet. Where she used to be fierce and take charge of everything, she's silent and watchful.

"We don't have a clear-cut plan." I start, staring at the conflagration of birds. I'm standing against the back wall, Serena to my right, and Bog to my left. Raven, instead of standing with the others, is off to the side. Her shoulder pressed into the concrete of the outer wall; her gaze focused on me.

"What is *she* doing here?" Someone says in the back of the crowd.

"She is on our side, Cliff." Bog says, silencing the shit-starter.

"Raven has been inside Nathan's ranks for two years; she knows the ins and outs. She knows where they are located and where they are going next. Believe it or not, we need her in order to bring Beast back." Murmurs erupt.

"But protocol?" Someone else chimes in.

"Fuck protocol. This is *Beast*." Serena says, anger seething off of her. My crossed arms flinch with the urge to hold her back, but if she wants to pummel someone, I will gladly watch. "Xyla has never once abandoned any of you. She picked most of you off the street, gave you a home and a family. Do you know how many times she has gotten the alarm from one of the Birds and *still* went after you?" I glance over at Raven and see her brow furrow; she doesn't know about the alarms. Or that Xyla triggered hers.

"Trigg." Bog calls out. A wide shouldered, skinny legged man raises his hand. His boyish face looks scared at being called on. "You hit your alarm last December. You and two others were on a recon mission. You were the last alive and you knew you weren't going to make it. You hit your alarm, telling us to not look for you." Trigg nods. "And who rescued you less than three hours later by herself?"

"Beast." He answers, his nervousness turning into a grin of pride.

"She snuck out, telling no one, and came back with you. *Unharmed*." Bog continued, making a point.

"She saved my life." Trigg responds, eliciting more murmurs.

"Gopher." Serena says this time, calling for another Bird. "You have a similar story, don't you?" A stout, overly tanned man steps through the crowd, making his way to the front.

"Yes, ma'am." His voice is all sharp angles and diplomacy. "I was on a solo mission in Bucharest last year, when we were searching for Blackbird. My chopper went down and I was ambushed. I was tortured for two days before I realized I wouldn't be let go and hit my alarm. Beast and Jet arrived within hours with a fresh chopper and an M230. I heard the concussing sound of the building being demolished, and five minutes later, she was dropping from a line, landing in front of my chair, and hauling me back up. It was the first and only time I have ever cried." Gopher finishes and silence spreads.

"Beast is our boss, our number one." I step forward. "She has never once let you go. She always devises a plan and executes it. She has saved almost every single alarm ringer we've had. The only exceptions are if she was not in the country. Despite my orders and protests, my partner is *resilient*. She takes no orders but her own and her orders have always been to put her Birds first. Are you going to stand by and let her die?"

Loud cheers of agreeance echo around. Some shouting plans, some shouting ideas. I hate to admit it warmed my cold little heart.

"Now, I need the same teams as before. The Blackbird mission is over. Mission Mother Bird begins. I need Radar's team on surveillance, intelligence transmissions, communications. Everything. Go." I order, and part of the crowd disperse. "Team Jet. I need you working with Team Radar to make sure we have all available airspace. We need choppers and jets in the air aiding surveillance. We need visuals and we need getaway birds on standby. Go." Team Jet departs, heading towards the back right corner. I glance at Bog and nod, letting him instruct his men.

"Team Blackbird, you are now Team Mother Bird. You will be a part of extraction and the front lines for either negotiations or war. I need you training, cataloging inventory, making sure weapons are hot and ready. Go." Bog's team disperses and then he glances at Stitch. "Team Stitch. All aircrafts fitted with first aid and trauma kits. Ensure every bird will have a trauma kit on their belt. Go." Everyone disperses except for a select few.

"Team Shark." I finish up. I need you getting an interrogation room set up and outfitted. Make sure a quick change from talking to torture is streamlined. I will need quick information out of everyone we bring in. Make sure cells are fashioned." Half of the remaining dissipate.

"Lastly, Team Oz." My arms, as I call them. Team Mother Bird is technically our main team, with Bog overseeing it. But Team Oz is what keeps us safe. "Checkpoints secure, set a two-mile radius around HQ. Report anything that isn't a rat. Go." The rest of the men dissipate and all that leaves is Serena, me, and a surprised looking Raven. She pushes off the wall and walks over to us.

"Wow." Was all she said.

"Anything you'd like to say?"

"What are the alarms?" I knew that question was coming.

"Every single one of us are outfitted with a tracker, an invention we stole from Kestrel. However, we don't have them set to murder our birds. Instead, we added a button right up against the skin that can be pressed. This alerts the team that there is no hope for the bird and that all rescue attempts should cease to prevent a greater loss of life." I explain.

"And Xyla, she never left an alarm unanswered?" I shake my head.

"If she could help it. I always protested, but she would sneak out. At some point, I stopped trying or offering to help. She wouldn't take it. I think it was something she had to do herself." A dangerous, stupid thing, but that was Xyla.

"She was doing it because of you, Raven." Serena pipes in, and Raven's head whips in her direction. "You never came home. It destroyed her. She didn't want anyone else to feel what she did. She fought every day to prevent any unnecessary death so no one would hurt like her." Serena's voice was both tender and sharp. As if she was trying to be gentle, but her anger peeked through.

"I stayed away to keep her safe." Raven responds, her voice thick.

"We know that now, but she doesn't." I cut in.

"And she hit her alarm?" She asks, hesitance in her voice.

"She did. And then her tracker went down." Raven's face crumples.

"He's taken control of her."

"He has, and she has killed a nice chunk of Étienne's men the last couple weeks." Bog says as he walks back up to us.

"I know." Raven says solemnly. "I saw Étienne the other day, he was trying to get me to go in and kill Nathan to avenge Lucas, but I can't. I don't have the manpower." I sigh and cross my arms.

"Well, you do now."

# CHAPTER FORTY-FOUR

## XYLA

The smell of his aftershave makes me want to vomit. I am sitting on the settee with a thick blanket wrapped around me. Nathan is in bed, pouting like a child because I refuse to lay in it with him.

"Xyla." He chastises.

"You'll have to brainwash me on top of kidnapping me in order for me to do anything but kill you if given the chance." He snorts.

"My fiancé ladies and gentlemen." He theatrically declares.

"I am not your fuckin' fiancé!" I yell, spinning in the settee to glare at him.

"You are." He declares exhausted.

"I will never be anything but your captive and your bloodhound. I will never love you or touch you. I will not marry you. And I will never fucking roll over and be complacent. I am doing my duty. I am killing whoever you ask me too, but I will do nothing else." I spit before fluffing my pillow and plopping my head down.

"God you're more exhausting than my sister was." He groans.

"A sister you threatened to kill unless I became your new slave." I mutter.

"Collateral." He says and I see red. I throw myself off the cushion and storm over to the end of the canopied bed.

"She worshipped you. She talked about you all the time. How you were her favorite person in the entire world. How you gave her the callsign Raven because you were Crow. And ravens always think they are better, something to do with a superiority complex. She credits you for the creation of The Nest. She believed you hung the fucking moon and lit the sun every morning from beyond the grave." He has the audacity to actually look shocked.

"She—" I cut him off.

"And then when you died, your parents disowned her. They cut off all communication, moved without telling her where or when. They disappeared off the face of the Earth because they blamed her. They said it was her fault you died in the line of duty. It ruined her life and threw her into the arms of Kestrel who would beat her every chance he got." He stays silent. "You are the sole cause for every bad thing in my life, Nathan Cross. You connected Kestrel and Raven, which resulted in him murdering my mother and then attempting to murder me. You are the villain in this story and forcing me to share a bed with you will never change that." My chest is heaving and his lips part with shock.

"I didn't know about our parents." He finally says after a few moments of silence.

"But you knew about the rest?" I demand and he, surprisingly, nods.

"I rigged the votes so your father would win the election." It's my turn to stare at him shocked. My knees wobble and I step back, collapsing onto the cushion. "I'm surprised my sister hasn't told you all of this." I stare at him dumfounded.

"We haven't had a chance to talk." I retort.

"Well, I guess it's up to me to fill you in. You're always the last to know everything, aren't you?" He scoffs and I feel my stomach drop, because he's right. I am always the last to know. "I don't know how much you know but Kestrel was never in charge. It was me all along. I have known Lincoln for years, and his plan to run for President was my idea. I pushed him to do it." I stop breathing. "He is what he is because of me."

"Was Kestrel killing my mother ever part of the plan?"

"It *was* the plan; it was your father's in fact." I feel dinner surge up my throat with the horror and I vomit. All over Nathan's stupid Parisian rug.

"You're lying." I choke out.

"Well, I had suggested you, but when we spoke of our plan to bring Raven in, well, we decided on killing your mother instead. That way you could seduce my sister and give her something to lose." I feel another surge of vomit.

"You fabricated our relationship? We fell right into your hand. And Kestrel killing Raven, was that part of your plan too?" I yell through my dry heaving.

"No, that was a little lover's quarrel. See, little beast, you think you have been making the rules, but it's actually my game you are playing. Right now, Raven is with your Birds, no doubt planning on how to rescue you. Another thing I predicted, planned for, and set into motion. Nothing that is going to happen hasn't been my exact goal. I am controlling every step they make, and they have yet to know it." His voice is stern, calm as he sits up to stare at me. His bare chest mottled with scars as the blanket slides to his waist.

"What do you want?!" I yell, clutching my stomach as another wave of nausea hits me.

"Well, if I tell you that, where would the fun be?"

# CHAPTER FORTY-FIVE

## RAVEN

Seeing how Osprey controls the new version of The Nest gave me an overwhelming sense of pride. Oz was my right hand, and I had chosen well. I thought him taking over The Nest would be enough, and that he would do it perfectly, but seeing how engrained Xyla is in everything, breaks my heart.

I never wanted this for her. I wanted her life to be one filled with love and dance, and I hoped that is what she would return to after I died. I heard about the Bader Dance Company opening and how she was singlehandedly training a new prima ballerina. I heard about the Bader Real Estate company she opened in DC, the office close to The White House. I learned of everything she did. I followed her life. I saw her in news broadcasts and papers, standing with her father. The pride that shone in her eyes as she stared at him.

But now I know that was all a front.

She may own the dance company and real estate firm, but she didn't run them. She probably never even went to those buildings. She had been running The Nest with Osprey this entire time. And not just running it, she was becoming their matriarch. Their rock, like she had been mine. They don't just obey her, they love her. And it's clear in her actions that she loved them.

That Oz loves her. Xyla had said that Oz was her other half, and I can see it now. How similar they are, yet balance each other out. But I still can't help but picture the Xyla I knew, not the beast they keep calling her. She said she was the last one sent in, and I didn't believe it. But hearing the stories of how she singlehandedly saved all those men after they declared themselves unreachable, is borderline insane.

She did that.

Not the girl I loved Xyla.

But the *new* Xyla.

Probably the version of herself that she was almost meant to be. And me dying set that into motion.

Me dying was the best thing that ever happened to her.

I'm leaning against the wall by Radar, Osprey's tech guy. He's typing away, and I am just watching everything. All the men and women fighting in the training ring. The tech team pulling up surveillance and mapping out routes with Jet's team. This whole operation is a well-oiled machine, which is impressive given how many people they have versus how many I had.

This version of The Nest is the best it has ever been. This is everything I had planned and hoped for, and they made it happen. Not me, *them*.

And while that should make me feel sad or detached, feeling like I didn't leave behind a legacy, all it does is make me feel proud.

"Got something, boss!" Radar yells and Oz's head pops up from where he was talking to Bog.

"Coming." He responds and I step over to Radar. I lean over his chair, and I see him look over his shoulder. I see a lot of code and images, but I can't make anything out.

"What is this?" I ask, and he ignores me. I roll my eyes and stand up straight as Oz walks over.

"Report." He orders and Radar starts to type again.

"I have been trying to hack into Nathan's surveillance system, because they have to have one."

"They do." I interject and Radar sends me a glare. The fuck is up with this kid.

"It's been hard, they have some good tech and clearly have a someone on their side who knows a bit about security and firewalls." He continues.

"Ahh, but my guy is better." Oz says, clapping him on the shoulder.

"Look here." He points at his screen and we both lean in. It's a string of code with numbers and symbols, but between that all...

"*The nine gates.*" Osprey reads.

"What does that mean?" I ask.

"I don't know. But I took that and dove deeper, and I found this." We stare as another screen pops up, showing a list. "The reformer, helper, achiever, individualist, investigator, loyalist, enthusiast, challenger, and the peacemaker." He reads aloud.

"I don't understand." Osprey says putting his hands on his hips.

"There are nine gates to get into his system. Nine steps one must take to get into in order to take him down." Radar explains, excitement in his voice.

"What is this? Some kind of mystery novel?" I exclaim, irritated. Oz is just staring and staring, his eyes focused.

"*Shit*." He says under his breath.

"What?" I ask glancing back at the screen.

"Click on the top one, the reformer." Radar complies and a question pops up. "What is the cost of perfection?" Oz reads. "They are riddles."

We stare at the screen longer and a fresh set of code pops up, filling the box below the question. Radar starts typing immediately.

"It's code. I'm going to unscramble it." It only takes him a second, the first gate quick to unlock. "Purity."

"It's not just riddles or gates, they are people." It's me who speaks.

"What?" Oz asks.

"Purity. Someone who is kind and selfless, but in order to achieve perfection, you give that up. You are no longer pure hearted." I add.

"That doesn't answer my question." He says flatly.

"It's Xyla's mother, Ana. She was charitable, perfect in every way possible. That's what Xyla always said. That she was pure hearted, but she gave up her purity in order to save Xyla's life. She gave up herself."

"I don't think that's it." Oz interjects and I meet his gaze.

"Who else would it be?" I ask.

"Ana didn't strive to reach perfection by getting rid of her purity. She was considered perfect already."

"Okay what if it wasn't saving Xyla. What if it was accepting her husbands' awful path in life, the fact that he was complicit in terrorism and planned to—"

"That's it!" Oz exclaims.

"Alright, I wasn't talking or anything." I mutter.

"You said that Lincoln and Nathan are working together. They stuffed the ballots, so he'd win. What if they did that to make him Senator, and Ana knew. She must have known all along what her husband was up to. So, she sacrificed her purity in order to achieve that perfect family front." He's right.

"So, each of these gates are people. And Ana started it all." We stare back at the screen. A text box is flashing and after a second, Radar types in Ana Bader. The gate disappears.

"Click on the next one." Oz orders and clicks on The Helper. Another text box pops up. *Surrendering to achieve.* Instead of a code box, an upload button pops up.

"We have to give the firewall something in order to move forward."

"We are not giving Nathan anything." Oz retorts, sitting back up. I sigh, realizing we are at a temporary standstill. "Radar, work on the others and see what we can do to unlock—"

"Sacrifice." I interject. "He wants you to sacrifice something."

"I get that, but—"

"Goose. He sacrificed Goose. He knew he'd be killed once he was outed. Kestrel and Nathan sacrificed *Goose*." I stare into Oz's eyes and see the pain flow in. The pain of knowing he is the one who pulled the trigger.

"They are all people." He says quietly, affirming everything I said. I nod and he gives me a small smile. "Welcome back." He says and I feel my heart swell.

# CHAPTER FORTY-SIX

## SERENA

The cold glass under my forehead feels so good, my body sweating despite the frigid temperature outside. I trained a little bit with Bog, trying my best to not really make myself a formidable opponent, but to learn enough to protect myself long enough for help to arrive. I have no desire to be on the forefront like Xyla, but I want to be safe.

I don't want what happened to me to ever happen again.

My eyes stay focused on Raven and Oz as they talk with Radar. I can see their bodies stand tense, their shoulders rigid and spine straight, but something passes between them, and their relaxation is almost dramatic. I see their posture relax and their firm faces dissipate.

I don't know how I feel about it. I don't trust Raven; I don't trust that she won't betray us. The only thing I can guarantee is that she will help us save Xyla, but at what cost? Will she sacrifice Osprey to do it?

Would I?

I truly believe that Xyla would sacrifice Osprey for me, and I would like to think I would do that same. But I don't know. Two halves of my heart are warring, and I just hope that I never have to find out.

Osprey steps away from Raven and I see him make his way to the stairs. I avert my gaze from Raven, just as her head lifts up to look at me. I keep my eyes focused on other parts of the room, failing at any chance of looking nonchalant.

"You okay, Serena?" Osprey asks as he enters the room.

"Yeah, just hot. The glass feels cold." His thundering steps grow closer and then I see him in my peripherals.

"Do you have a fever? Do I need to get Stitch?" I smile and shake my head.

"No, I was training with Bog." His shoulders return to their neutral state, and I lean away from the glass, turning to look at him. "I see you and Raven are feeling a little more comfortable with each other." I observe and he gives me a sheepish grin.

"Working with Raven has always been second nature, and doing it again after all this time, it felt like coming home." My chest tightens and I look down, why do I feel like this? I have no reason to be jealous—especially not of Raven. I loosen my tightening fists and look up at Oz.

"I am really happy for you. I hope this works out, for your sake and for Xy's." I offer him a smile, and his returning one has a hint of confusion. "So, what's the next step?"

"Radar found a way into Nathan's security system. A list of nine 'gates' that correspond to a riddle and a word. And we have a suspicion that each gate and word corresponds to a person. So far, we have purity connected to Ana, and sacrifice connected to Goose." He explains, running a hand through his smooth hair.

"What are the others?" I ask.

"We don't know yet. We have to sacrifice something in order to move on to the next gate I am pretty sure. I have Radar looking into the others to see if we can tackle any of them, but I have a feeling Nathan isn't going to make it easy." He sighs.

"I think we should talk to Raven. She's told us Nathan's motives and threats, but she hasn't told us his grand plan. What is he even going for? World dominance? I want to know his connection to Kestrel and the Bratva. I feel like there is still so much more we don't know." I push, my brain spinning.

"I know, but I am learning pretty quickly that Raven doesn't know as much as we thought she did. She knows the ins and outs of the operations, but I don't think Nathan disclosed much of his plan. I am getting the impression that she truly was just the hired gun, and Nathan didn't trust her as well as she probably thought." He surmises and I chew on my lip.

"It would make sense. He had to know she would abandon him for Xyla eventually. She only stayed because of the threat on Xyla's life."

"Threats don't really inspire true loyalty." He says softly.

"No. Loyalty is bred from shared trust and faith in the other person and their goals. That is why everyone is so loyal to you." His cheeks redden and he looks away. The urge to reach out and touch his warmed cheek, to feel his lips on mine—but I can't. I can't. Even thinking about his weight on me makes me start to sweat, and not in arousal. In fear. Because I know it won't feel like Oz, it'll feel like Bash.

"You never answered my question." He cuts through my thoughts, and I quirk a brow.

"What question?"

"Are you alright?" I did not hear him ask that at all. I shrug. "I'm fine."

"Serena." He starts and I hold up a hand.

"I am coping, alright? Stitch has me on some anxiety medication to help, and I think it has been. I am working on it."

"Is there anything I can do?"

"Just be here Oz and save my best friend. And…" I trail off. This next request is something I have no right to ask, but I have too. I need this, and I think both of them do too.

"And?" He pushes.

"When Nathan is dead and we get all of this cleaned up, be done. Be done with this life, the risk. Be done with the endless fighting and fear. Just step away. Both of you. Start over." His eyes widen and he stares at me.

"You want Xyla and I to leave The Nest?" He says, barely a whisper.

"Yes." I respond quickly. "You both have almost died a countless amount of times. You are losing the ones you love. And I want you both to walk away." He stays quiet, no response or even gesture to provide.

"It won't be that easy." He throws his hands up. "We have a team of people, what are we supposed to do? Abandon them? Just walk away from the mission and purpose of this place?" His voice rises in volume and I flinch. His eyes flare and his arms drop. "Serena, I'm sorry for yelling. I am just—" He cuts off. "This has been my life for nearly a decade. I don't know who I am without this." His voice sounds so broken and small. He truly believes this is all he is. Just a weapon.

"You are more than what you were made to be." I step forward, my hand rising to rest on his chest. I feel his breath, hot on my face as I look up at him. I want to tell him, I want to ask him to touch me, but I don't. "There is a whole life out there for you. You are so young, so damn young. You can be anything you want."

"I don't know what I want."

"Then we can figure it out together."

# CHAPTER FORTY-SEVEN

## XYLA

My mind is numb. After Nathan's revelation about my mother and my fa—father. I can't believe it. He chose to have my mother murdered to kickstart some sort of game.

I want to say he would never, but that isn't the truth.

During his campaigning, he leaned so heavily on the murder of my mother. How the loss of his wife ruined him, and how he would never be the same. How he wanted to focus on crime rates and gun violence. How he vowed to do everything he could to prevent another baseless death like my mother's.

How Ana Bader wouldn't die in vain.

He was right about that last part. She wouldn't die in vain because her death gave him his freedom.

Gave him his power.

My entire body shakes as the trembles run down my arms, my spine. I feel the nausea roiling up and then it comes out. Right into the trash can Nathan not so kindly threw at me last night. I curl up into a smaller ball, letting the thick fleece wrap around me like a tourniquet.

Stop the bleeding. Tighten the straps.

Prolong the suffering until the paramedics come.

But no one was coming. I told them not to. I ordered them. And I did this to myself. But I did this for her. For Raven. Everything I have done the last two years has been for Raven. And what did that get me?

Nothing.

I'm just going to bleed out.

She was alive, free to see me if she wanted. Free to tell me she was alive, but she never did. She let me suffer. She let Oz suffer. While she killed and murdered without recourse. While she became what The Nest always despised.

And fuck it I despise her.

I *hate* her.

Nathan may have put this all in motion, but *she* is the villain in *my* story. Her presence preludes death and it's only a matter of time before that death is mine.

I throw the blanket off, fury radiating off of me, fueling the coldness seeping into my heart.

I dress quickly, strapping myself with weapons.

Nathan is the enemy, but so is she.

And she can't control me anymore.

I am not *living* for her. I am living for my *mother*.

I storm out of Nathan's room, stomping down the hallway, and then throwing open the door to the control room. Surprised glances from men I refuse to familiarize myself with. And then Nathan. I stride up to him, anger mixing with confidence.

"Give me a target." I order and his eyes search mine, looking for the catch. "Give me a fucking target." I say again and he rewards me with a sadistic grin.

"Damiano Trevoli." I nod once and then take the file off the table. "Bash." He orders and I feel his heat on my back, following me out.

I'll get Damiano. He's dead.

But so is Bash.

# CHAPTER FORTY-EIGHT

## OSPREY

"Any luck?" I ask, leaning over Radar's table.

"I can't get into gates three through nine without sacrificing something to gate two." He replies, frowning as lines of code fly through his screen.

"What can we give him that is of no consequence?" Raven says from my side.

"That's the thing. Look," He points to a long list being typed out in front of us. "He has specifications. Must be involving U.S. Intelligence. Must be something he doesn't already know. Must be in the form of a pdf."

"Is that really one of his specifications?" I snort, staring at the words.

"If it's something he doesn't already know, how will he be able to prove it's fake?" Raven presses, getting closer to the screen.

"I'm sure he has his ways."

"What if he doesn't like what we give him?" Radar turns from the screen and looks up at me.

"Then the gates are destroyed, and so is our way in." Shit.

"I don't like this. It feels like one of his games. He wouldn't let us in this easy." Raven ponders, dropping into a chair. "He has to get something out of this.

"I think he's giving us a chance to see who his next mark is, but we have to put ourselves at risk to do it. That's where the sacrifice comes in." I counter and she watches me. I see her mind spinning, the wheels turning as the old Raven slowly resurfaces. The Raven that would know what to do.

"U.S. Intelligence can be any secret pertaining to the President, right?" I nod.

"What are you getting at?"

"He has another daughter." Serena makes us all jump as she appears out of nowhere. I spin around.

"What?"

"Lincoln has a five-year-old daughter named Mira." My heart drops to my stomach as I see the guilt eating away at her.

"Does Xyla..." Her eyes flick to Raven and she shakes her head.

"Mira was born from an affair. I found out about it from Dower, who didn't know what he was discovering. It was a house in Atlanta owned by Lincoln. A small, modest family home. The second name on the deed was Mira Bader. Dower didn't question it, like the idiot he is. So, I looked her up. Mira Bader is a five-year-old little girl. Her mother's name is Marina Alvarez, former secretary to Lincoln. Mira looks just like Xyla, just a little tanner. Same cheekbones and chestnut hair with strands of gold." Tears prick in her eyes.

"Xyla has a little sister, and you kept it from her." My voice is thick, and I feel almost a form of resentment towards her. How could she keep such an important secret from her best friend?

From me?

"Xyla is a part of a world that can get her killed any second. So is Lincoln. So are we. Why would I subject a little girl to that life? If Xyla knew, she wouldn't leave it alone, and you know that. She'd want to be in her life. She would endanger her."

"But you are endangering her now!" Raven rises and steps forwards towards Serena. Surprisingly, she doesn't shrink away. Rena steels herself, narrowing her eyes and straightening her spine.

"This is no longer about the safety of a little girl. This is about taking down a terrorist organization." She responds and I have to agree with her.

"We can protect her. We can send any remaining DC birds to Atlanta, get Mira and her mother to safety." I interject, stepping in front of Raven so she's not leering over Serena.

"And we can use that as our sacrifice."

"We are risking the life of a child, here." Raven says louder and I snap.

"It is between Mira or Xyla right now."

"And she would never forgive you if you got her little sister murdered!" Raven screams in my face.

"You don't fucking know her!"

"The Xyla I loved wouldn't be okay with this." She steps back, her head shaking, before she turns on her heel and storms out of the warehouse.

"Oz." Serena whispers, her hand firm on my shoulder.

"If we do this, we have to be prepared for Xyla's anger." I say without looking at her. I instead look at Radar, who has been watching this entire thing. "Do it." He nods once and then gets to typing.

"Bog, get men sent to the Bader residence in Atlanta. Make sure they are safe." He nods from my left and disappears.

Silence aside from the sound of Radar's keyboard.

And then...

"Show me who you pretend to be." He says.

"What?" I stare at the screen. That's the phrase. I read it again and again and then the screen goes black.

We all stare for a second and then we see ourselves. The camera moves around, tracking our features, before stopping on me.

"Radar." I order and he starts typing. The camera zooms in on my face, the furrowed brows and messy hair. I watch as part of it distorts. My brows unfurrow, my eyes open and wide. I see any signs of aging disappear until I am looking at a twenty-year old version of myself. I open and close my mouth, the younger version of me doing the same.

"What is going on?" Serena whispers, getting closer to the screen.

I watch in horror as a black eye appears and then a split lip. My cheek grows red. And then I see my cheeks squish as if someone is grabbing them.

Because they are.

It's my father.

When I was a child, up until I got into the military, he beat me. He would rough me up every time I misbehaved, treated me like I was unwanted. The burnt-out cigarettes on the back of my hands, the ribs he broke time and time again.

"Osprey?" Serena whispers and I realize only then I have a tear rolling down my cheek.

"I killed him."

"What?"

"My father. Right before I left for the marines, I killed my father. He did that to me." I gesture towards the screen and watch in terror as the younger me gets more and more bloody.

*"Who you pretend to be is not who you are."*

A robotic voice sounds from the computer and then the screen goes dark. The command screen pops back up with a text box, a lime green cursor blinking in tune with my heart beats.

"What now?" Serena asks.

"Joshua. The answer is Joshua." Radar hesitates before typing it in. The text box disappears, and gate three has been cleared.

"You're the third person."

# CHAPTER FORTY-NINE
## RAVEN

My steps are quick, borderline jogging, as I pass through cobblestone alleyway after alleyway. I hear kids laughing and people talking the closer I get to downtown. I smell fresh bread and burnt coffee. I feel cool air as October rages on.

I feel

Like I am being watched.

I stop in my tracks, my eyes scanning the surroundings. I wait with bated breath before a sharp kick hits me straight in the spine.

I fall to my knees, but I am back up just as quickly. I spin around, gun in hand, pointed straight at Xyla's face.

"Xyla?" My elbow dips and the gun drops. Her eyes are narrowed, her jaw taught as she stares at me with hatred. "Xyla?

What happened to you?" She rears back and sends her fist flying straight into my nose. My head snaps back and I barely correct my balance before I can fall. I holster my gun and sweep my leg out, hitting her ankle and sending her to the ground. I straddle her, tying her hands up above her head.

"Get the fuck off me." She spits. Like actually spits. I flinch as the wet saliva smacks me in the eye. Her knee goes up, twisting around my hip, before she successfully gets a foot planted against my rib. She kicks out and sends me flying.

Before I can get up, she kicks me again. I cough out, and reach for her ankle, pulling it out from under her. She hits the ground hard but immediately starts crawling away. I pull her, dragging her body against the cobblestones.

She reaches down and unholsters her gun right before whipping me across the face with it.

I'm stunned, my breath coming in shallow pants.

"Every single person who is dead in my life is because of you and your fucking brother!" She screams, climbing on top of me. She goes to punch me, and I grab her wrist, halting her.

"What the fuck!" I scream before rolling her under me. She tries to wiggle her knee in again, but I don't let her.

I look down and only then do I realize she soaked in blood. Not all mine. Definitely not hers.

"Whose blood is this?" I ask. She spits again, but I dodge. "Why are you covered in blood!?" I yell louder and she relaxes slightly.

"It's Bash's." She says proudly and I loosen my hold.

"Why are you attacking me?"

"Because you are the enemy. You ruined my life. You ruined all of our lives. And I fucking hate you for it." My heart cracks in two as I stare down at her.

"I did everything I could to protect you, Xyla. Everything."

"You're a liar!"

"Do you know why I was being held for so long? Because Nathan said he would skin your father alive and make you watch if I disobeyed him."

"I don't care! Your brother and my father killed my mother, and I am going to kill them both." She screams, the ferocious little cat I fell in love with right here in front of me. My eyes soften and surprise crosses her face.

"And then what?"

"I'm going to kill you."

"And after that?" I push and her face falls.

"I'll kill myself." Those three words feel like a gut punch.

"Xyla, no."

"I can't do this anymore, Raven." All the fight drains from her as tears fill her eyes. She stares up at me with so much desperation, so much fear and exhaustion. "I can't do this." Her eyes close and a tear drips out, rolling to the ground. I release her arms and lean back but still stay on top of her.

"I know." I whisper and her eyes open to find mine.

"When my father brought you in to protect me, I thought all would be well. And when you died, everyone thought I would continue unchanged. But I couldn't. I changed my whole life so I could find you, track you down. Part of me always feared I would find an unmarked grave, but at least I would have something to mourn. But you were here, all this time. Flying around the world. You became what you swore to destroy, and I can never forgive you for that." Her words tear me to shreds and I slide off of her, landing on my butt.

"You're right." She doesn't say anything in response. "I thought if I stayed away, it would protect you, but I think it made things worse."

"It did." She agreed, sitting up. "I will never forgive you, Raven. I will never forgive you for what you did to me, but most of all for what you did to Oz. He lost his best friend, his sister, and he has never been the same. When all of this is over, if it ever is, I never want to see you again." It's my turn for tears to pool in my eyes and spill over. I watch as she rises.

"What did Nathan threaten you with?" I call after her.

"He threatened to kill you." My heart swells, hope filling it, right before she crushes it. Her fingertips brush my cheekbone and then my jaw, before she drops her arm. "And if anyone is going to pull that trigger, it's going to be me." And with that, she walks away, leaving me bloodied and abandoned.

A position I seem to find myself in quite often.

# CHAPTER FIFTY

## OSPREY

"Stitch!" I yell as Raven stumbles in. Her teeth are stained red with blood, a huge gash along her cheek. She's clutching her ribs, and I barely get her in a chair before he legs give out.

Stitch rushes over and immediately starts checking her.

"What the fuck happened?" I question, holding her upright.

"Xyla." She gasps out, and fear consumes me.

"Is she okay? Did you find her?" The words come out in a rush.

"She found *me*." She coughs out, covering Stitch's face in blood. He stares at her in disgust but continues working.

"Did she do this to you?" I say slowly and softly. Raven looks up at me with pity and a small bit of humor, and nods.

And I cannot help the fact that I burst out laughing. My back aches, my chest throbbing from the uncontrollable cackle pouring out of my mouth. To my surprise, Raven starts laughing too. Her lips lopsided and swelling starts to take shape, which makes me laugh harder.

"Did she pistol whip you?" I ask and she nods, starting up a whole new round of laughter. "My god, I love her." I release her and she slumps forward a little bit.

"I deserved it." She gets out with a groan of pain as Stitch prods her ribs.

"Yeah, you did." We sit in silence for a second. "Did she look okay?" Raven lifts her head slowly.

"She did. She was covered in Bash's blood, but something tells me he didn't get a hit in."

"Atta girl." I say with a smile. "Stitch?" He is busying himself with pushing on Raven's ribs and feeling around.

"Nothing broken, just a hell of a lot of bruising. You are going to feel like shit tomorrow." He quips.

"I feel like shit right now." But despite the wounds, she looks almost relieved. Relieved that Xyla beat the shit out of her.

"Why are you so smiley?" I ask as Stitch cleans her cheek.

"I saw her. I saw the old Xyla a little, but I guess new and improved. But she said that the only thing Nathan was holding over her, was me. She did this to keep him from killing me." She ends the sentence with a hopeful furrow of her brows.

"Probably so she can kill you herself." I joke and her face falls.

"She said that too." I stare at her and she holds my gaze.

"Nothing is going to go back the way it was. That life is gone, Raven. And if she chooses to love you and trust you again, it will not be the same. Not just in feelings but the power dynamic. She was weak when she met you. She wasn't who she is now. And if you want to fix things and be with her, you have to love today's Xyla, not the ballerina from two years ago." She rolls her eyes, a defense mechanism.

"When did you become the relationship expert?" She snarks.

"I've always been wise." I say defensively.

"And a certain lawyer had nothing to do with it?" I stare at her.

"We have something, but she won't let herself. And I won't push. Not after..." My voice trails off, and I see the realization flash in her eyes.

"I said this before, Oz, but I will keep saying it. If I had known she was down there and Bash was...well doing what he was doing, I would have stopped it. I never would have let that happen."

"I know Raven. Despite the years and the fact that I don't know who you are anymore, that is one thing that will never change. You will never let someone be defenseless." I see the appreciation in her eyes, and she surprisingly reaches her hand out. I grip her fingers tightly and look down.

This whole thing. This whole situation.

It just feels weird.

Like something is going on that we don't know about. Like this is all just some elaborate trap.

# CHAPTER FIFTY-ONE

## XYLA

Walking away from Raven was the hardest thing I have done so far. From being torn between slitting her throat her professing my never-ending love for the mercenary that changed my life, my conflicted heart feels heavy. Broken.

I run through the alleyways, tracking my way back to where I left Bash. His body is still, blood still pouring profusely from the back of his skull from where it slammed onto the edge of the cobblestone beneath him.

I approach slowly, and his eyes flutter open. His breathing is shallow, strained and I fight against the smile on my lips.

"He...will kill..." He starts to choke out, and I smile before bending down and placing a blood-soaked finger on his lips.

"Shh, it's okay. Save your strength." He tries to lift his hand to push me away, but the fact that his elbow is bent in the wrong direction on his left arm, and his right is out of its shoulder socket, that isn't really possible.

We left on our mission, the one given to us by Nathan. And it started out like every other one over the last couple weeks. We find our target, we eliminate our target, we bring back a souvenir. Despite Bash being the biggest piece of shit on this planet, we have worked well together. Until today.

We walked away from the decapitated body left in another alleyway not too far from here, liberating the corpse of its wallet, and Bash had the fucking audacity to call us a team. A pair. So, I snapped. Finally, after wanting to kill him since the second I saw Serena.

I roundhouse kicked the back of his leg, sending him flying into the street. He got onto his knees quickly, I'll give him that, but the resounding pop of his shoulder as I ripped his arm backwards and twisted nearly made me groan. He screamed like the pussy he is and then fell on his face. I grabbed his other arm, stepped on his elbow, and then yanked it up. I felt all of the bones crush under my boot, heard every single snap of tendon and bone.

His scream will echo in my ears for years to come, but not out of trauma, out of *satisfaction*. And then I hauled him up to his feet, listened as he blubbered on and on about sparing him and how he'll never tell Nathan it was me. So, I sent a heeled boot into his neck and watched as his body flung to the ground. The back of his skull hit the cobblestones and he lay still. Not a single movement.

I checked, and he had a pulse, so I figured I would take a little walk.

And there she was.

Her golden hair shining in what little moonlight peeked through the late October clouds.

And now here I am, back in hell.

Bash's skin is pale, sickly, and I briefly sympathized with what he was probably feeling. Knowing you are going to die is probably one of the most terrifying feelings. Aside from not knowing when your abuser was going to come rape you again.

So, fuck him.

"I hope your last breath takes forever and that when you finally die, you know that it could have been prevented. All of this was for Serena. And I can't wait to tell her what a worthless, weak, piece of shit you were in the end." I smile, tilting my head as his eyes widen ever so slightly.

"Don't…" He starts to speak again.

"I'm sure someone will come for you, darlin'. But it'll be too late I'm afraid." His chest shudders and his breath comes in panicked pants. "Bye now." I rise, blow him a kiss, and turn to head back to my cage.

Being scared of Nathan has never even occurred to me. He was a tool. A person who used money and other people to do his dirty work.

I step into the room and his eyes narrow on me instantly. I don't know if it was the droplets of blood on my face, or the fact that Bash wasn't standing right next to me, but his face reddened and his jaw clenched.

"Where is he?" He asks, throwing a file down on one of the desks as he passes it, heading straight to me.

"Seconds away from his last breath half a mile from here." I say nonchalantly, picking a piece of non-existent dust off the sleeve of my jacket. His hand whips out, striking me across the face. I bite my cheek to keep from saying something stupid, before turning back to look at him.

"How fucking dare you—"

"Do you not agree that he deserved it? Do you truly believe Bash was a valued member of your esteem business?" I ask, titling my head. And as the words leave my mouth, the voice that comes out isn't mine. The cold, sharp twang of it. The lack of emotion, of heart.

And I realize I am slowly losing myself.

I told Raven that the Xyla she knew died along with her, but this version of me, I don't like her.

This isn't the version I ever wanted to exist.

But I swallow the fear and stare up at him, those stupid blue eyes making my heart ache for Raven.

"Pack whatever shit you have. We leave for D.C. in an hour." He spits at me, before pushing past and exiting. No doubt off to see what remained of Bash. I take a slow deep breath, wink at the man to my left who is staring at the blood caked to my hands with horror and then head to my room to grab whatever I have.

Which is absolutely nothing.

# CHAPTER FIFTY-TWO

## OSPREY

"Boss!" Radar yells from across the room. I step away from the chair Raven is occupying as Stitch still checks her out. "We have movement." I peer over his shoulder as I see a jet is on the move from the private airfield a mile from us.

"Who is it?"

"It's them." I clench my fists. "Destination is D.C." I slam my hand on the desk and then run it through my hair.

"Jet!" I yell and he appears at my side. "Ready the plane. Small crew."

"Yes, boss." He nods once and then turns back around.

"How close are you on the gates, Radar?" Raven appears next to me.

"We are on gate four, since boss was gate three." He responds, pulling up the black screen with a single line of text. *Passing means facing it without denial.* I read, my brow furrowing in confusion.

"What the fuck does that mean?" I spit, standing upright.

"It's a riddle. You have face something without denial." He responds as if I couldn't fucking read. Which I start to open my mouth to say, and Raven touches my arm, shaking her head slightly.

"Pack up, bring it all with us." I say instead, pulling away from Raven in search of Serena. "Wheels up in twenty!" I yell to the room. I'll leave it to Bog to coordinate with Jet on who's coming. I climb the wrought iron stairs two at a time as I head to the room we use as a bedroom. Serena is lying on one of the bunks, her headphones in as she types away on her phone.

"Rena." I say softly and her eyes flash to me.

"Is it Xyla?" Her voice is filled with panic as she rips her headphones out and rushes over to me.

"She's on the move, headed to D.C. We are leaving right now." Her shoulders relax slightly.

"I wonder what for?" She questions as she slips her headphones back in the case. "I'm coming." She says over her shoulder.

"That's why I came up here. Grab your stuff."

"Why do you think they are leaving?" She asks.

"I don't know, but my guess is they are headed to see her father." Her face falls.

"I can't wrap my head around the fact that Lincoln is a part of all of this. And that Xyla is with them, right now. I just want to slap the shit out of her." She says the last part with a frustrated sigh.

"There is still a lot we don't know, Serena. A lot. Some of it Raven probably knows, the rest we would need Xyla and Nathan to fill in the pieces. But right now, we just need to be at least in the same country as them, especially if we want any chance to end this once and for all." She steps close to me, her hand reaching up to brush hair out of my face.

"Thank you." She says, a smile playing at the edge of her lips.

"For what?"

"You have been so patient with me, with my recovery."

"Serena, it's been a couple weeks. I would wait years for you to heal." I add, my throat thick. Her eyes widen slightly.

"You would, wouldn't you?" She whispers. I nod, unable to speak as she leans up and places a kiss at the corner of my mouth. "Thank you." Her hand slides from my cheek to my chest and then she's gone, throwing stuff into her duffel. "I am going to pack Xyla's stuff too, just in case we don't come back here." She adds as if the last two seconds didn't happen.

"Good idea." I respond, clearing my throat. "I'll send one of the birds to grab everything. Be downstairs in five." I turn on my heel and quickly run down, almost straight into Raven.

"Calm down, Romeo. Where's the fire?" She jokes as she pats my shoulder. "Radar is packed up and Bog collected a few men from his team to accompany us. The rest are staying here, if that's alright with you, boss." She added the last word with a hint of sarcasm, and I roll my eyes.

"Perfect. Thanks. Let's get the fuck out of Paris."

# CHAPTER FIFTY-THREE

## XYLA

We return to DC while Halloween festivities are in full swing. The Secret Service met us at the tarmac, and I nodded at the few I recognized. I climbed into the SUV and watched the Halloween lights pass by as we drove to the White House.

My father and Adrina Coral met us in the foyer, his arms pulling me into a bear hug. I didn't return it and when he pulled back, I let him see the anger simmering in my eyes. He plastered a fake smile on his face, shook Nathan's hand, and then started talking.

"The annual Halloween ball will be tomorrow night. I have already gotten in touch with Dalton," he says glancing at me over his shoulder, "And your company is prepared to be the entertainment." Leave it to my father to arrange a private performance with my ballerinas while I am gone. It was already planned that they would perform on Halloween, but the specifics were never arranged. I don't meet his gaze. "It will be a masquerade ball, so Adrina has gotten with a few designers and ensured a dress was made for you, my love." He says to me. The lead us to the residential wing of the house and I blindly follow as he leads me to the guest room that has unofficially been mine since his first day here.

"All black attire for everyone. Nathan, there is a suit for you in the room next door." He stops and smiles, looking between us. "I am so happy to see the two of you together." He looks like a proud matchmaker and I roll my eyes.

"I am nothing more than his captive, daddy." I respond and Adrina quirks a brow. My father and Nathan laugh it off, and to add to the show, Nathan pulls me into his side and kisses the top of my head.

"This one, I swear." He squeezes my arm tighter, no doubt leaving bruises. I plaster a fake smile on and direct it towards Adrina. She relaxes and smiles in return.

"Alright, I will leave you to get settled." My father touches the small of Adrina's back as he leads her away and I fight the urge to throw her down the stairs. I elbow Nathan, slip out of his grasp, and into my room. Flashing him a devilish grin before slamming the door.

I collapse onto the four-poster canopy bed and groan.

What the hell has become my life? I want to go home. I am less than a mile from my room, from my entire life, and here I am, stuck in a fucking nightmare that won't end. I curl up in a ball, letting exhaustion finally pull at me. It's after midnight, so I only have a few hours before I'll need to start getting ready for the party, so I let my eyes close and sleep wash over me.

Despite the atrocity of her name, she does have good taste. The dress Adrina had made for me is a little scandalous for a presidential affair, but she probably saw what I normally wear and figured she'd appeal to my style. The bodice is pure black lace with a corset underneath. Pannels on the edge of the corset expose my bare skin. The dress flows to the floor with lace that looks like spiderwebs. It's thick, offering just the smallest peek of my legs through the fabric. There is no slip, just a pair of very short shorts, that leave nothing to the imagination.

The mask is made out of blackened steel. Small diamonds are encrusted in thin legs that brush across my cheek and into my hair. The body of a spider sits over my right eye, with the left covered in thin strands of spider web made out of the same steel. It's a delicate little piece that looks fierce, intense. I smile at it.

I also smile at the pair of sleek black stilettoes with blood red bottoms sitting next to the full-length mirror. At least I get expensive shoes with this ridiculous endeavor.

I leave my room and am immediately greeted with a suited man. He's one of the service members, but not one of mine. I give him a tight-lipped smile, and he just stares at me.

"I am off to see my father. Care to join?" I ask, putting on my best flirting. He quirks a brow and then nods, holding an arm out. I scrunch my nose and wink as I head down the hallway to the stairs leading down to the Oval Office.

My father is in a white button up, the sleeves rolled up. His brown hair is gelled back, keeping it out of his face. He's furiously typing away at his computer, but smiles when I walk in.

"My sweet, how are you today?" He asks as I round his desk and lean down to kiss his cheek.

"Slept like a baby." I add. I glance up at the service member standing by the door. My father follows my gaze and nods at the man, telling him to leave.

"What is it?" He asks, leaning back in his chair and crossing his arms.

"Oh, nothing, daddy. Just had a nice long chat with Nathan about our shared history." He looks at me skeptically, and I give him a sweet smile.

"Alright?" He says, questioningly.

"I heard a fun little tale of a puppet and a puppet master. How easy it is to control someone's life and plan for their end. It made me realize how much we have in common." I sigh and lean against the mahogany wood.

"You and Nathan?"

"You and me, daddy." My hand flattens on his desk before tightening into a fist. The cold metal of the fancy ballpoint pen kissing my palm. His eyes widen as he realizes what I mean and then my hand is slamming into his leg. I reel back, the pen sticking out.

"Fucking hell." He curses quietly as he rips it out, covering the wound with a handkerchief.

"Not going to call for your men?" I ask and he glares at me. "That was for mama." I walk back around the desk. "And one day, as you take your last breath, I'll make you feel what she did." With that, I exit the prestigious room, now soaked in my father's blood, and take a drive to my ballet company.

# CHAPTER FIFTY-FOUR

## XYLA

After six hours of training and practice with Dalton, I was caught up to speed with the choreography of tonight's performance. It's one dance to Dark Academia by Gabriel Saban. And while Loreen was set to be the star of the performance, I have taken her place.

It's a group dance meant to feel witchy and gothic, with a lot of black lace. Thankfully, I already have the perfect dress.

As I slip on the red-bottom heels, I stare at my reflection. My hair has been straightened, tucked behind my ears. Deep blood red lips, like always. Winged liner and mauve cheeks. The mask covers the rest of my face, and I am thankful as that meant less makeup to apply.

The dress falls around me like sticky webs, the lace fine quality with a small metallic sheen. I spin in the mirror, getting a feel for how it falls before the dance tonight. A satisfied nod, and I am opening my bedroom door.

Nathan is standing there in a webbed mask, black suit, and a tie covered in the same lace as my dress. I look him up and down before scowling. He holds his hand out, and I take it, knowing how little choice I actually have.

When we step into the ballroom, we are transported to a Halloween store. Fake webs and purple lights cover the ceiling. Actors and performers walk through the crowds, scaring old men and overly botoxed women. I frown, but when the first group sees me, I plaster on my fake smile.

"Let's get through this night without bloodshed." Nathan whispers into my ear, his lips brushing the shell of it. I take a slow deep breath to fight the urge to flinch away.

"Yes, sir." I say through gritted teeth, and then he is leading me through the crowds.

# CHAPTER FIFTY-FIVE

## RAVEN

The White House is an obscene shade of purple with the lights that look like they came from the dollar store. I'm sure they had expensive designers working on the decorations, but I could have done better and I fucking hate design.

I'm in a black suit, my blond hair slicked back into a bun. I have on a simple black mask, covering the top half of my face. I step into the main ballroom unnoticed, grab a flute of champagne, and pretend to fit in.

I haven't spotted Xyla yet, but I am assuming she's here. Radar found the correspondence between Dalton and Adrina Coral about the performance, so I figured she'd be here, especially after we watched her on the surveillance cameras at the ballet studio today.

Serena and Oz are making the rounds, people already knowing them. Once Bader realizes they are here, he can't do too much about it without drawing attention. Serena is his bonus daughter and is well-loved, and Osprey is the head of his Secret Service. Their absence from this party would draw more questions than their presence. So, Nathan and Lincoln will have no choice but to let them stay.

Serena is wearing all red, dressed like a vampire beetle she said. The glossy texture of her dress makes her shine like a beacon as it hugs her skin and strategically covers every healing wound she has. Oz is wearing a matching suit to mine, letting us blend in with the agents on the floor.

I push deeper into the ballroom, looking for golden laced chestnut hair, when I see her out of the corner of my eye. Her arm is through Nathan's as she's laughing at something he said. Her dress is sheer in all the right places, showcasing her lean legs and toned stomach. She's dress like a spider, and a peak at the underside of her heels, makes me realize she's a black widow. All black with red on the underside.

She looks beautiful, her silhouette like a goddess.

Nathan leans down and whispers something in her ear and her face falls slightly before she plants a false smile to her lips. When he straightens, his eyes lock onto mine. I raise my glass to him before taking a sip and disappearing back into the crowd.

"She's here." I tap my ear.

"Location?" Oz says back.

"Back corner, black dress, with Nathan."

"Heard." He replies.

The lights dim and when I look back, they are both gone.

The loud sound of a violin fills the room, and I see everyone vacating the dance floor.

It's time.

# CHAPTER FIFTY-SIX

## XYLA

Darkness spills across the marble like ink, swallowing the last remnants of chatter as I slip onto the dance floor. Cloaks whisper, masks shift, and jeweled silhouettes turn, all their excited murmurs silencing.

The bold violin cuts through the silence. Its cry slices the air cleanly, and I step into the center of the room as if summoned. My heart pulses in time. The warm, sure hand of my dance partner lands lightly on my stomach, guiding me into position. We breathe once, together.

Piano trickles in like water over stone. A heartbeat later, drums thrum in the deep. And then—blinding white—the ballroom lights blaze to life, tinted amethyst.

We move instantly.

He pivots me, and I spin, spiderweb skirts flaring like spilled smoke. My stilettos are long gone; black pointe shoes lace my feet, letting me float just above the ground. We glide like a current weaving through the crowd. The company of dancers behind us, mirroring our every move. Pirouettes melting into a fractured waltz, sharp accents followed by breathless stillness.

It's effortless. *Too* effortless.

We move as though forged for one another, though we only rehearsed for a few hours that morning that I was able to get away from Nathan. His frame is tight, lean, steady as he lifts me high above the floor. I feel the room tilt with the spin, feel the air split around us, and when I look down into his eyes—I freeze.

Not him.

Her.

*Raven.*

My breath catches, and for a heartbeat my body forgets the choreography. But she doesn't. Raven sets me down cleanly, spinning me out so my landing is precise, toes pointed like knives. I jump, jeté across polished tile, and land inside a turning pirouette. Her hand snakes around my waist the moment I complete it, twisting me into her, our bodies aligning as the crescendo barrels toward us.

Drums. Piano. Violin. Bass. Cello.

A full storm converging.

The final move is supposed to end with him throwing me into the air.

She.

*Fuck.*

I rip away from the sequence we practiced, adjusting, adapting—falling into the ten-part fouetté with the other ballerinas as if this had always been part of the plan. The room blurs as I whip around, and then I break free, sprinting straight to Raven.

Her dark eyes catch mine. No apology. No explanation. Only that wicked, knowing smile.

She opens her hands.

Braces herself.

I leap.

Her grip locks around my waist, and the momentum of my run launches me upward. The world flips as I twist midair so my back arches above her head. Arms stretched, ribs expanding with the music, I feel her turn beneath me—then suddenly, she lets go.

I drop.

But she catches me again, one hand at my waist, the other gripping my leg as she releases the rest of my weight. I spill forward toward the floor, rolling out of her hold—only to stop an inch from the marble, her hand a barrier between me and the impact.

The music cuts.

Silence snaps tight. Then comes the explosion.

The ballroom erupts into cheers, roaring applause bouncing off the vaulted ceiling. Raven pulls me upright, her touch unexpectedly gentle, and I find myself curtsying, bowing, lungs burning, heart stampeding.

The lights dim.

And suddenly a mouth crashes onto mine.

We're moving—stumbling—being pulled through the discreet door behind us. Her fingers thread through my hair as her tongue parts my lips with infuriating ease. I shove her chest, but she holds fast, relentless, consuming.

So, I give in.

I fucking give in.

My hands clutch the lapels of her jacket, dragging her closer as the kiss deepens. One of her hands slides lower, to my spine, guiding me against her in a way that steals the last of my restraint.

Then a shift of air behind me has me stiffen.

A presence I know better than my own.

I pull back sharply, breath uneven, and a cloth clamps over my mouth.

Raven's eyes widen—something I don't have time to decode. They're the last thing I see before the world folds in on itself and darkness claims me just as it did the ballroom.

# CHAPTER FIFTY-SEVEN

## RAVEN

The taste of her tongue was like coming home. Her lithe body in my grip as we danced. As I practiced the choreography Radar got off of the surveillance of the theatre. I spent almost ten hours, all night, learning this piece in the off chance she takes over for the lead today.

And I was right.

Thank God. I never want to dance again.

And then I guided her into the room, our mouths fused as I led her into a trap.

Her eyes filled with betrayal as she felt the cloth fall over her lips. Her hand tightened on my lapels in panic and then I watched the light fade from her as she fell into Osprey's arms.

He hoisted her up and then we were sprinting. Serena was already in the SUV, Oz and Bog slipped her out during the dance. I pushed open a door and ran straight into my brother's chest.

"I knew you'd make an appearance sister." He says, his voice cool and collected.

"Move, Nathan." I spit, stepping back so I am in front Of Oz and Xyla.

"Return my fiancé, and I'll let you leave."

"Your fiancé?" I yell in disbelief. "She'd sooner die than marry you."

"I think she'd actually say that about you." His words hit straight into my heart and I furrow my brows. "Her and I have come to an understanding." He says with a sickening smile.

"Fuck off, Crow." Oz says behind me.

"I'm not letting you leave with her."

"And we aren't letting you leave." The click of a gun echoes as Bog appears, the gun pointed directly at Nathan's head.

"Pull the trigger, Bog." I say and he doesn't glance in my direction. "Do it!" I yell and step forward. Nathan grabs me and shoves me towards Bog, knocking his arm down. Bog tries to raise his arm again, but Nathan grabs the gun and wraps his arm around Bog's throat, the gun pressed to his temple.

"Fucking move and *I'll* pull the trigger." I feel myself pale. He'll kill Bog. Oz's right hand. I glance at Oz and see no hint of regret in his face as he stares at Bog. Bog's own gaze is locked on Oz's, and an understanding passes between them.

I can see it. The way the communicate is the same way we used to.

He's sacrificing himself.

"Oz—" I start, but he doesn't look at me.

"Brother." He says softly and Bog relaxes, a smirk plastering to his face.

"See you in Scotland." Bog says and it hits me right in the chest. Scotland. The last words I said to Xyla.

And if Bog is saying them, that means—

That means Xyla held onto those words and has said them to everyone who has died. It became a saying. A hope for the future, exactly what it always was for us.

It became peace.

"See you in Scotland." I repeat and Bog's eyes shut.

We get through one hallway before we hear the gunshot. I flinch but push forward, letting Oz go first so I can cover his back.

And when we get to the SUV, we face another obstacle.

Lincoln is standing next to Serena; a gun pressed into her ribs.

# CHAPTER FIFTY-EIGHT

## SERENA

"Let me come with you!" I push back as Oz shoves me into the SUV, the first time his hands have touched me.

"No. I am not risking you. We only came for her." He says, his face close to mine.

"You're risking yourself. Nathan won't let you take her without recourse. Not all of you will come back." My voice cracks and I grip his face. Bog steps away, giving us some privacy.

"Serena." He starts.

"I can feel it." A tear drips down my cheek and he follows its path.

"We will all be right back, I promise." The muffled music through the walls is reaching its peak, we only have another minute.

"Oz—" I start and my eyes go to his lips. Panic and fear gripping me as tight as possible. The fear that I won't ever see him again. The fear that this is goodbye if he walks back in there.

"Serena." He says again.

"Kiss me." His eyes widen and he leans back slightly, pulling my hands with him. And then hunger pools into the depths of his gaze and his lips are slamming into mine. They are desperate, starving, possessive. His hands stay planted on the door frame, not touching me, as his lips claim me.

Steel my very breath.

My hands thread into his hair, pulling him closer as I taste him. Devour him as he is me. And then he pulls back.

"Don't die." I whisper against his lips.

"I promise, baby." He says, and then he's gone. The tears pour freely as the door back inside slams shut. I close the SUV door and kick off my heels. I count to pass the time, knowing they should only be gone a couple minutes.

And when the music stops and the door opens again, relief washes over me.

I open the SUV door and jump out, ready to hold him again, but it's not Oz standing there.

And I didn't look before I jumped.

Like always.

Instead, it's Lincoln. A pistol in his hand pointed directly at me.

"You told Nathan about Mira." He says and I freeze.

"She's safe, Lincoln." I say, knowing with my whole heart, that she is.

"Who told you?" He yells and I flinch.

"Dower found her." I say slowly.

"Goddamnit!" He yells and I bite my lip to keep from jumping. He runs his hands through his hair, disrupting the gel. I take a step forward and he raises the gun again. "Don't move!" I hold my hands up, my fingers trembling.

We both jump as a muffled gunshot echoes through the abandoned garage. I look at the door, pain ripping through me.

"No!" I cry out and run towards the door. Lincoln grabs me and shoves me back against the SUV, the gun pressed to my temple.

"They got what's coming to them." He spits; his hot breath laced with bourbon.

"That's your daughter." I cry out, looking into his wild eyes.

"Xyla won't be harmed." He says adamantly.

"Do you even know what Nathan has done to her? To me?" His glare falters slightly, before returning.

"We had a deal. She will be unharmed." He says again.

"He broke your deal." I whisper. He stares at me and then turns around, pressing the gun into my chest as we both face the door as it opens and Osprey steps out. Xyla in his arms, Raven behind, but no Bog.

*Bog*.

# CHAPTER FIFTY-NINE

## OSPREY

"Don't make me shoot you, Bader." I say as I hand Xyla to Raven, slipping the gun out of my holster.

"Give me Xyla and Serena lives." The President says callously and I freeze. Because this is the choice I never wanted to make.

Between Xyla and Serena.

"He's bluffing." Serena says and Lincoln presses the gun harder into her. "He won't fucking do it!" She spits in his face and he gets closer.

"You don't know me, child." He says softly before looking back at us. My hand tightens on the gun as I watch Serena. Her eyes are hard, not at all scared, and then I realize she's assessing.

I know that look. She's assessing his grip on her, her likelihood of getting free.

It's what we all do.

"Serena." I start, warning her not to risk it, but she takes that as a sign to move. She shoves an elbow up, throwing his arm into the air. The gun goes off and cement rains down on us as the bullet lodges in the ceiling. I run forward just as Serena kicks Bader between the legs. He falls forward and I kick out, getting him in the forehead and knocking him out.

We stare at him for a second before Serena runs forward and throws her arms around me.

"Touch me." She whispers and then my arms are going around her. I tighten my grip as much as I can without hurting her, attempting to mold her body to mine.

"You're okay." I whisper. Mostly to myself. She pulls back, tear-filled eyes meeting mine before she kisses me.

"Let's go, guys." Raven says from behind.

Serena moves aside as we slide Xyla in the back of the SUV, before we shut the door and drive off.

"Bog?" Serena asks after we pass through the gates. I meet her eyes in the rearview mirror and shake my head. She slumps in her seat, and I see Raven watching me from the passenger seat.

"He saved us." She starts. "He chose Xyla's life over his own." I nod, not deigning to respond. "We will never forget."

# CHAPTER SIXTY

## OSPREY

We get to the compound within ten minutes, and I am cursing myself at how close it is to the White House, but we never expected this. The only good thing is that this place is so secure, Nathan could never get in. I carry Xyla in and use my handprint to open the elevator.

We get to the bottom floor, and I carry Xyla to Stitch's wing. He came back on the plane with us and was prepared for this. I set her on the hospital bed and Stitch hooks up an IV to her for fluids. I step away and meet the others in the hallway. Jet is standing there talking to Radar and Raven.

"They cracked the others."

"What?"

"The other gates." I follow them back upstairs as Radar opens up his computer.

"Gate four, sorrow. Someone who experiences immense sorrow. This gate is meant to enact some sort of feeling of despair. So far, we have Ana as purity, Goose as sacrifice, Osprey as pretender, and now we need someone as sorrow."

"And who do we know has experienced the most sorrow anyone could handle?"

"Xyla." Raven says and Radar nods.

"Xyla was gate four." Radar finishes.

"Gate five?" I ask.

"Knowledge. It gave us a riddle and the answer was knowledge. *I am the first truth, the last question. I am older than memory and younger than thought. Name me and you claim nothing, understand me and you claim everything.* And who is Nathan using for knowledge?" He asks.

"Lincoln." He nods. "Gate six?"

"The loyalist, who do you trust when nothing is certain?" My first thought is Xyla, but she was already sorrow.

"Not someone you trust to fix things, but someone you trust for information. Back to knowledge. It's you." I surmise and Radar nods. "He knows who we all are."

"Ready for the rest?" I nod again, my fists balling. "Next was the enthusiast, a maze of illusions that are used as distractions meant to tempt you. Which we determined was actually Raven." I turn and look at her.

"All of this is a game to him. He planned everything down to Kes telling Bader about me. I was the distraction. The temptation for Xyla. I am gate seven." My mind spins and I nod.

"Gate eight is the challenger, the power. And believe it or not, the answer was Étienne." I roll my eyes; because of course he sees him as the power, he uses Étienne for his own gain.

"That leaves the last gate." I say and the three of them pause, glancing around. "What?"

"Gate nine is the peacemaker."

My whole world shifts.

"Serena."

The screen goes dark before a maniacal chuckle sounds through the speakers.

"What is this?" Raven asks and then everything goes dark. All of our laptops and hard drives shut off, and even the mechanical sound of our system shutting down echoes through the floor.

"Fix it, Radar. Now." I demand and he gets into action. We all stand and watch as he types in codes until finally the screens turn back on. One screen staying black with a lime green button saying *enter*. It's me who reaches forward and clicks the button.

And all we receive after the nine gates of hell, is security footage of Serena's assault. It's stuck on a loop, with no way to turn it off. It just plays and plays. The sounds of her screaming, of him slamming into her over and over again. The whimpers and cries for help. I can see it all.

"Oh god." Raven whispers. "It was all just a game, a distraction, it wasn't for us to actually get into his system. It was nothing." A feral growl sounds out of me as I lunge forward sending my fist through the screen, stopping the video and the accompanied sound.

It was all just a game to him. A distraction.

There was no purpose to this other than to rattle us and get us to divulge secrets.

Now we have nothing.

Except we finally have Xyla.

# CHAPTER SIXTY-ONE

## RAVEN

"We are under the assumption that all of these people and gates are who will die. Who he wants to kill. People he'll sacrifice."

"We don't know that for sure." Jet interjects. "It just so happens the first two are dead." He shrugs and I roll my eyes.

"Why Serena, why did they all lead to Serena?" His voice grows in volume, and I raise my hand to calm him.

"Serena is your weak point. And Xyla's. Get to her and you two would do anything to save her. He knows that. She's the peacemaker. The lawyer. She's his key to domination." He kicks at a chair with a yell, and it goes flying against a desk.

"He won't get her again."

"I don't think that's what he's saying." I retort. He looks at me. "Nathan wants knowledge and power. He wants to be in control. And by orchestrating deaths and relationships, orchestrating political maneuvers, he thinks he is. He thinks he is in control of everyone and everything, but he is forgetting one basic thing. The most important thing every person has."

"What?"

"Free will. He doesn't account for free will."

"I don't get it." It's Jet that answers.

"He expects everyone to do certain things. Steal Xyla back, attack him. Rebel. But what if we don't. He expects it because it's what we always do so he thinks he can manipulate how we do it. So, let's just *not*."

"Not fight back?"

"Exactly. It'll throw him off." Oz stares at me for a few beats before he smiles and nods.

"Jet call back every agent. Bring them home." Jet nods and steps away, heading to his own desk. "You better be right."

"I am." He claps my shoulder and heads back to the elevator. "This place is incredible." I say as I follow him.

"It really is. You didn't get to see much this morning. I'll take you to Xyla's room." I pause before climbing onto the elevator with him.

"Are you sure that's alright?" I ask, hesitantly.

"Yeah, I think it is." He smiles, a relaxed and easy smile, before I step in after him.

He's quiet as he unlocks his door with his handprint. Only certain doors can be unlocked with certain biometric meters. And

Oz and Xyla can open every single door, naturally. I also like how close their suites are to the make-shift hospital. Just a few steps away, it keeps the wounded safe.

The door opens and I am greeted with a plush blue rug in front of the door. I toe off my boots and step in, my feet sinking into the cushion. My eyes have a hard time finding something to focus on. Splashes of yellow and blue, pinks and greens. A bright couch covered in thick blankets, a kitchen with a blue Smeg fridge. Straight ahead on a blank wall I see a couple shadow boxes. I step forward, walking around the couch to the glass.

Inside sit paperwork from my time in the Marines. A few of my accolades, and some other paraphernalia. My heart clenches.

"Where did she get this?" I ask with a thick voice.

"It arrived shortly after you went missing. We never knew who sent it." It had to have been Nathan. My fingers graze the shattered glass of the empty box. "Your gun was in here." I stay silent.

To my left there is an open door, and to the right, two closed doors. I go for the open door.

I nudge the door further and stare in shock. It's Xyla's office, fit with a black wooden desk, a comfy leather chair and bright pops of color that showcase her personality. But it's the corkboard covered in photos and red lines that has me freezing.

Pictures of bodies, flight manifests, plane tickets, polaroids of people who kind of look like me but aren't. Names and places. Red strings and black strings. And finally, a blood-soaked silk ribbon.

It's a physical representation of her tracking me the last two years.

"I ruined her life, Oz." I whisper, my voice catching. I grip the back of her desk chair and stare, my eyes watering.

"We both did. But we also gave her something." I look at him over my shoulder. "A family."

We hold our gazes before his vision shifts and then he taps his ear.

"She's awake."

# CHAPTER SIXTY-TWO

## XYLA

My head is throbbing and I try to sit up, but I'm handcuffed to the hospital bed. Stitch is leaning over me, watching my every move.

"Is this necessary?" I sneer and he smiles.

"Precaution, in case you lost your shit." Osprey says from the doorway. I peer over Stitch's shoulder and relax at seeing him.

"I'm home. I think this is the one time I won't lose my shit." I laugh, but he doesn't join me.

"Stitch, can you give us the room?" Stitch nods and walks out, patting my foot on the way. My pulse quickens as I stare at Oz, the pain in his eyes.

"Oz?" I push and he joins me by my bedside. He sits down slowly before looking me in the eyes. "Oz." I repeat.

"After we chloroformed you, we were taking you out of the house, but we were stopped. By Nathan." Tears pool in my eyes. Oh my god, it's Raven, isn't it? Raven is dead. Or Serena—

"Who?" I ask through a closed off throat.

"We had a choice to make, and Nathan didn't think we'd choose you, for some reason." He stalls, grabbing my hand and squeezing it.

"Oz, who?" I push and he finally meets my gaze again.

"Bog." He takes a deep breath. The world comes crashing down around me. I didn't even think him an option. Sweet and strong Bog. The person we'd hand The Nest over to when we were done. Our right hand. Our number one.

"How?" I ask, not wanting to know, but needing to.

"Nathan had a gun to his head and had us choose between you and him. It wasn't a choice, and Bog knew that. He was okay with that. He said he'd see us in Scotland." I shut my eyes and lean further into the pillow. God, he was one of the few who knew about Scotland and what it meant to us.

It was his way of saying he loved us.

"That's not all."

And then I spent the next hour hearing everything. To learning about my little sister and the nine gates of hell. To hearing how my father almost killed Serena. To hearing everything that has happened in the last month since we have been a part.

And when he was done, it was my turn. I filled him in on what Nathan said about ballot stuffing, which he learned from Raven already, to how he and my father orchestrated my mother's death.

After we were both done and our reports were complete, I cried. He cried. And we sat in silence. He unlocked the cuffs and climbed in the bed with me, holding me until the tears dried and I could finally take a deep breath.

"What do we even do from here, Oz?" I ask, clutching his arms as they sit wrapped around me. I feel him shrug and I sigh. "You said we should stop fighting. Stop all of this with Nathan, does that mean we just go back to our normal jobs? Getting rid of those who deserve it?"

"I think so. Radar has some people lined up who have been trying to get in contact with us. I say we take a day to recuperate and figure out how our lives will be for now, until we have our chance to take down Nathan. And then we accept a mission." I nod, but neither of us get up to move, finding comfort in one another.

After some time has passed, we both rise, and I head to my room for a shower. My bare feet sink into my rug, and I take a deep breath, relishing in the feeling of being home. This is my home. The best home I have ever had.

I throw my pointe shoes onto the carpet and head straight for my bedroom. I open the door and go straight to the bathroom, turning on the shower.

I drown myself in scalding water, letting it wash away any lingering pain and tears. And once I was done, I took a deep breath, slipped on my capybara pajamas, and stepped back into my bedroom.

And only then did I realize I wasn't alone. Raven was in my bed, her breathing even and shallow as she slept deeply. Her mouth open slightly, the baggy t-shirt she took from me, too short so I can see the very tops of her thighs from where she lay on top of the covers.

Her hair is messy and wavy, as if she slept on it wet.

I step closer, letting my fingers brush the unruly strands away, and still she slept. So, I cross the room to the other side of the bed, climb in, and fall asleep.

# CHAPTER SIXTY-THREE

## SERENA

It took ages for Osprey to return to his room, where he was surprised to find me waiting. I had showered, changed into one of his shirts and his eyes slowly slide across my body down to my bare legs, where I could feel his gaze like a caress.

"I thought you would be asleep in your room." He says softly, guarded. I watch his throat as he works a swallow.

"Should I go?" I ask, cocking my head to the side. He drops his jacket on the floor and walks towards me.

"You may do as you wish." He whispers, his breath cascading over me. I lift my chin, my heart racing in tune with his uneven breath.

"Touch me." I whisper back. He hesitates before his hand goes to cup my cheek, his thumb caressing my jaw. "More." I say.

And he shoves my head back and chin up, his grip firm. Rough. I close my eyes as he leans in, his nose running down my throat. "More." I repeat and he nips at the skin between my neck and shoulder. His forehead falls against me, and I grab his shoulders to stay upright.

"Serena." He warns, but I'm having none of it. I grab his free hand, bringing it directly to my thigh. I guide his fingertips up the bare skin until it brushes the hem of the shirt. I bring his hand even further up until he brushes my tracker. I feel a spike of pleasure straight to my core at the sensitivity. I keep ahold of his hand until I move further up, until his hand is against the apex of my thighs.

Until he feels how wet I am for him.

"Touch me." I whisper again. He leans back, his eyes blazing, holding my gaze as he slips one finger inside of me. His other hand presses into my lower back and I grip his shoulders again. My mouth falls open and my brows furrow as I feel the stretch of skin. He slowly pulls out and I shake as he puts in a second one. I whimper, holding his fiery gaze, not letting him look away. "Oz." I whisper and his lips are on mine.

He bends down, scooping my legs up so I can wrap them around his waist. I can feel his erection pressing against his jeans, rubbing the perfect spot. I groan as I dive into his mouth, our tongues tangling in tandem. He pushes a door open and then I am being thrown on the bed. I bounce on the mattress, and a surprised giggle comes out of my mouth.

He smiles as he rips his own shirt off, unbuckling his belt and kicking his jeans off, but leaving his boxers. He grabs my ankles and drags me down to the edge of the bed.

"You're wearing my shirt." He says, his breath fanning the inside of my thighs.

"Should I grab someone else's?" I say breathlessly. His answering growl is all the warning I get before he's on me. His tongue is soft and expertly skilled as he sucks and bites every inch of me. My breath is coming in shallow pants as his teeth nick my clit and I cry out. His fingers return, slamming inside of me over and over again. Every time he pulls out, he hooks them, scraping them along the perfect spot inside of me.

I can feel my legs shaking, my climax coming as he picks up his pace.

"Fuck, you taste so good." He says against me and I come undone. I slap a hand over my mouth as I orgasm, a scream tearing through my throat. I'm left boneless and breathless as he kisses me softly on the inner thigh before standing.

He towers over me and I stare up at him as if I'm being look down at by a God.

"Touch me." I whisper again and then he's crawling on the bed. He hooks an arm under my waist, sliding me higher up on the bed as he crawls. I grab his face, bringing his lips to mine. I taste him and me, mingled together. He grips the hem of the shirt, pulling it up and helping me take it off.

I slide my fingers under the waistband of his boxers and he shivers. My fingers glide further down until I feel his hard length, the pulsing in tune with his heart. I slide a sharp nail down his cock and he bites my lip.

He's ignited as he kicks his boxers off and lifts my hips up, ready and angled for him.

"Are you sure?" He asks, searching my eyes. I hold his gaze, trying to send whatever silent communication I can to him. This is all I have ever wanted. You.

I lift my hips until I feel the tip of him pressing into me. I lift even further until he slides in, just a little bit. His lips part, mimicking mine as he slowly tilts his own hips, sliding in further.

And fuck is he big.

I feel the stretch of my skin, my mouth falling more and more open as I hold my breath.

"Oz." I whimper and then he slides the rest of the way in.

"Fuck." He curses as he searches my face. "Baby?" He asks and I nod, encouraging him. He slides out a few inches before slowly sliding back in. Soft, and tender. Slow but so fucking good. I pull his head down, my lips brushing the shell of his ear.

"More." I whisper. And he moves. He slams into me hard and I cry out. "Again." I say and he complies, except this time he doesn't stop.

My body is on fire, the good kind, as he fucks me the way I deserve. As he kisses me and holds my naked body the way a man holds the one he loves.

He doesn't stop moving until we are both shaking, sweating, panting, begging the other to not stop. And when his lips silence my screams, he cums inside me, pumping over and over again to brand me. To fill me.

To make me *his*.

And as we both come down and he holds me against his chest, I feel like I am finally home.

# CHAPTER SIXTY-FOUR

## XYLA

I feel someone staring at me, so it's no surprise that when I wake up, I find that Raven and I are facing each other on the bed. Her eyes are searching for my face and so it takes her a second to realize mine are open.

"Hi." She says softly, her cheeks reddening.

"Hi." I reply. Her hand twitches and she slides it a half inch closer to me.

"Still want to kill me?" She asks playfully and my eyes soften.

"Yeah." I admit and she smiles even harder.

"Well, little beast, I won't make it easy for you." And with her simple nickname for me, I find myself smiling. But the silence returns, as does the sadness.

"I dreamed about this moment for years." I whisper. "You, alive. Waking up on a random day to you here in our bed. I wanted this for so long." I fight the tears as the threaten to form.

"It's not too late." She whispers back, her voice just as hopeful.

"Yes, it is, Raven." Her hand moves across the space, gripping mine tightly.

"No, it's not. I love you. I am so in love with you and none of that has changed. I did everything I could to tell you I was alive without putting you in danger. I tried so hard to keep you and your father safe." I tense.

"My father doesn't deserve your protection."

"But you did. And I will always choose you, over anyone." She means it, too. But I can't let that be the case.

"I need you to promise me something."

"Xyla—"

"No. I need you to listen. If it ever came down to me or Oz or me and Serena, let me go." She pulls back, but I tighten my grip. "Let me go. I can't live in a world without them. Let me go."

"I will never let you die if it could be prevented, even if you hated me for the rest of your life." I smile and release her hand, reaching forward to rest it on her cheek.

"I will always hate you, Raven. Always. But there is a very thin line between love and hate and our paths are forever stuck in both." She searches my eyes and for once, I see a tear escape her baby blues. "Let me go if it comes down to it." She doesn't respond, she just closes her eyes and nods. "I'm really tired of the death, Raven." I whisper, closing my own eyes.

"Me, too, Beauty." She whispers back, and I fall back asleep with my hand on her cheek.

"Alright, report." I say, holding the mug of coffee to my chest tightly as we sit in the third-floor conference room. Raven is sitting to my left, wearing her usual black. Serena is to my right, in a black hoodie and jeans. Osprey is across the table, eyes focused solely on Serena, wearing the same thing. Me, on the other hand, I am wearing knee high knit socks, leggings, and an off the shoulder jumper with a capybara on it.

We're home, so I am taking advantage of the comfy clothes. I am also not wearing shoes, so being curled up on the chair like I am, is exceptionally comfortable.

Raven smirked when I came out of the closet, no doubt enjoying that I haven't forgotten my capy obsession. She chucked my chin, offered me a smile, and then stole clothes from my closet. I abandoned her, as she proclaimed, as I went to the main floor for breakfast with the team. And after ten minutes she found her way there.

After we ate, the three of us went back down to Stitch and he installed a tracker into her. Although, she opted for her inner thigh as well, which makes sense since the tracker Kestrel had in her neck left a nasty scar. She probably didn't want to relive that.

I got a fresh one put in, also, since Nathan had mine removed. Inner thigh. I think that'll end up being the new place.

Now, we are sitting in the conference room with Jet, Radar, and Shark waiting for an update on our newest target.

"Antonio Becerra lives in Baja, California and on top of drug smuggling, he deals in sex trafficking. A very wealthy man lost his daughter to one of their parties, and he never saw her again. He believes her to be dead and has paid us to kill Antonio and see about possibly rescuing his daughter if she is there." Radar reads off the report, and I chew on the inside of my lip.

"Drug lords are an easy day's work. And I'm sure we can find information on his daughter." I say, sipping the latte in my hands.

"Arabella Daniels was quite a party girl, and there are photos of her at Becerra's mansion the night she disappeared. Several other girls photographed with her are also missing."

"So, like I said, easy day's work." I say again. Why does everyone look so skeptical. "What am I missing?" I glance at Osprey who looks just as confused as I am.

"Someone fucking speak." Oz demands and Radar jumps, poor guy.

"The Becerra drug lords have a tie to Étienne." I roll my eyes and slam the mug down, spilling it.

"Of course they do." Raven mutters.

"So, we don't do it?" Serena answers this time.

"No, we still are. It has nothing to do with Étienne. This man is a piece of shit and that's what we do. We take out the trash."

"How cliché of a phrase." Serena says with a chuckle and I laugh back.

"It really is, huh?" I respond and we start laughing.

"Are you two done yet?" Oz snaps and it makes us laugh harder, so much so that Raven even looks concerned for our mental well-being.

"Do they do this a lot?" She asks, gesturing towards Oz, sending us into another raging fit.

"Yeah, usually just to piss me off."

With us laughing and all sitting around the conference table, it almost feels like everything will be okay again. And that is enough to give me hope.

Hope to continue.

Hope that we will finish this.

# CHAPTER SIXTY-FIVE

## RAVEN

The flight to Baja is short, and we land on a stormy beach by the end of the day. We rented out a beach house on the water, because Xyla said she was done with warehouses. So, we step into beautiful Mexico and enter La Mansion Ensenada, a huge multi-million-dollar estate that's about to become our front.

"Jesus, this is huge." I mutter and Xyla smiles next to me.

"It has over twenty bedrooms!" She exclaims, clapping like she won the lottery." She hooks arms with Serena as they watch two Birds enter the house to clear it before we move in.

The first jet of men came from Paris this morning. They had a mere hour to clean up before two jets headed here. The rest of the birds should be landing in D.C. any minute now, effectively abandoning all of The Nest outposts across Europe.

As a newly reinstated member of The Nest, it feels weird to enter such a world of high-tech luxury. We had it easy and good when I was in charge, but with Xyla's money, The Nest became something I never dreamed it could reach.

Serena is wrapped up in Oz's arms as they wait for the all clear and my heart hurts. Xyla is standing next to them; her arm still hooked around Serena. And I feel like such an outsider. But is that because of them pushing me out, or because I am not allowing myself to integrate?

I shake my head and walk forward so I am standing next to Xyla. She peers up at me through thick lashes ad gives me a small smile.

"You alright?" She asks and I nod.

"Just adjusting." I reply softly.

"Adjusting?" She questions.

"To the idea that you still want to kill me." I smirk and she smiles.

"You think you don't deserve it?" She slips her arm out of Serena's and faces me.

"Oh, I definitely do. I am just curious on how you're going to do it." I tease and she sucks on her upper teeth.

"Well, I remember a particularly sensitive spot right—" She steps closer and her fingers lightly brush my thigh, sliding up until— "Here." She presses into the apex of my thighs with her thumb and my knees buckle.

"*Xyla*." I start, grabbing her arm to steady myself and looking around noting that we are surrounded by people.

"I think I could get away with anything after that." My mouth falls open and I realize she's *flirting* with me.

"Even without that, I'd let you do anything you want to me." Her eyes flutter a half second as I surprise her.

"Promise?" She whispers and I nearly fall to my knees at the sound. A sharp whistle sounds and Xyla's smile returns. "Yay! Let's explore!" She grabs Serena's hand and rips her out of Oz's grasp as they run towards the mansion.

"What are you doing, Raven?" Oz says to my right.

"Trying to get my life back." I say, taken aback by his hostility.

"Don't reel her in if you don't plan on staying." He warns. I turn to face him, stepping so close until we are almost nose to nose, so he understands every word that comes out of my mouth.

"I am not going anywhere. Not until she asks me, too. I will fight for her until my last fucking breath. Same as you would for Serena. So don't act all high and mighty. You got your girl, now let me try and get mine." He searches my eyes, his stony gaze matching mine. And then he nods. A single nod that means he'll step aside.

And he does.

So, I walk right past him and into the gorgeous, yet ostentatious mansion, that will house us for the next few days.

The house came with a chef, so the second I walk in I smell an abundance of foods, which makes my mouth water. I'm the first to the kitchen and immediately grab a corn tortilla off the plate and pile chunks of carne asada into it. A little sprinkle of white onion and cilantro and I am diving in.

It melts in my mouth with a combination of spice and buttery meat. I groan and shove the rest in.

"Delicious?" Xyla says from behind me.

"Yes, you need to eat one." I shove a taco in her hand and she takes a bite, her eyes widening.

"Oh my god." She groans and I see juice drip from the corner of her mouth and down her chin. I smile and bite my lip. "What?" I gesture towards her mouth and she wipes at it, missing it completely. I step closer and grab her chin.

"Let me." I say and she stills. I lean down, the tip of my tongue starting at the edge of her jaw, sliding up to the corner of her mouth. She stays frozen as I finish, and then I step back, make myself another taco, and walk away.

Once I am out of earshot I exhale loudly.

# CHAPTER SIXTY-SIX

## XYLA

Breakfast was laid out before we even woke, and despite a chef being on the property, I have yet to see another person. But the birds scoped the place out, so I assume all is well.

I pile eggs, beans, rice, and salsa onto my plate and dive in while sipping on some black coffee. Wish I had a latte right now, but the coffee is surprisingly good.

Radar joins me first, his hair kind of messy like it usually is early in the mornings. He pours himself coffee and slumps into a chair across from me.

"Morning, boss." He mutters and I smirk.

"Are we all set to head out this morning?" I ask and he nods.

"Jet has the SUVs packed and ready. Still think it's kind of risky going during the day." He adds.

"We are just scoping out. Not going in. He has a party tonight, that's when we go in." He nods but still looks wary. "Is this about Bog?" Bog and Radar were close, almost like me and Oz. Good friends, partners, so losing him has to hurt if it's this painful for me.

"Yeah. He always came back." He whispers, sipping his coffee.

"We'll all come back this time, Radar. I promise." I reach for his hand and grip it, giving him a reassuring smile. He gives me a forced one in return, and I decide to give him some time alone.

I leave the kitchen, heading the one of the living rooms. Oz is lounging on the sofa, socked feet resting in Serena's lap as she reads. Osprey is watching the news, all in Spanish of course, and I plop down next to him.

"Radar says we are set to leave whenever." I say, watching a car crash replay over and over again on screen. "He's still shaken about Bog." I add and Oz glances at me.

"We all are." I leave it at that and relax deeper into the sofa. "Have you seen Raven yet today?" He asks and I shake my head. "Weird."

"Spit it out." I snap and he smirks in my direction. Serena peeks over her book at us, her eyes revealing that she is also smiling behind there. "What?"

"Well, I just figured she'd be in your bed last night."

"She has her own room, Osprey." I spit and cross my arms.

"Just be careful, Xy." He warns and my irritation fades.

"Why? I plan on killing her anyway."

"Sure." Serena adds returning to her book. I roll my eyes and hastily climb off the very comfortable sofa.

"I'll go find her then I guess." I start to step out, and as if on cue, she appears a little out of breath.

"Alrighty, I have good news and bad news." The three of us stare at her flabbergasted and she stares back confused. "Well pick one." She pushes and I sigh.

"Good news I guess."

"I found Arabella." My eyes widen and Oz shoots off of the couch.

"You what?" He yells stalking over.

"What is the bad news?" I interject, holding Oz back.

"Antonio saw me."

"Okay, you can kill her now." Osprey says nonchalantly and throws his arms up.

"I couldn't sleep!" She yells, defending herself. "So, I went to the Becerra mansion and I saw Antonio. He was talking with a bunch of people and after some snooping around, I found a stairwell leading down. After living with Nathan, I knew psychos like basements, so I went down. After a very long tunnel, I found a door that led to another room that was filled with girls. A minimum of twenty. Bruised, bloodied, and every single one of them naked." She explains.

"And how did you know it was Arabella?" I question and she looks at me like I'm stupid. Me. Not the one who walked into a drug lord's den by herself.

"I asked, obviously." She retorts. "I called out her name, and a girl held her hand up. I told her we'd be back."

"Jesus fucking Christ, Raven. You act like being a mercenary wasn't your job for years with this newbie type shit." Oz loses it.

"And let me guess, Antonio saw you when you were leaving." She nods and I groan.

"Okay, game plan?" Serena pipes in from the couch. "How do we move forward? I'm sure this isn't the only time someone has fucked up a mission." Raven sends her a scathing look and I snort.

"I say we proceed as planned. Raven already did recon, so we don't have to. She can give everyone the lay of the land and let us know where to go. We go tonight during the party, kill Antonio, save the girls. Have a margarita." Everyone nods along until I get to the last part and then all eyes are on me. "We're in Mexico, I want to enjoy it a little bit." I shrug.

"How do we even get invited to the party?" Serena asks and I give her a knowing smirk.

"I already have that covered."

Two hours later and Serena and I are golden, glowing, and in some very expensive bikinis as we roll up to the beach club Antonio owns with Osprey posing as our security. Because I am somewhat of a celebrity, the bouncer pales when he sees me, calling someone on his earpiece.

"Miss Bader, it's an honor to have the President's daughter here." I give him a sultry stare and flip my hair over my shoulder.

"Well, I heard this was the best beach club, and well my best friend over here is going through a terrible break up, so I figured getting drunk in Mexico was the best cure." I thread my fingers through hers and she gives me her most sad face.

"By all means." He unhooks the velvet rope and gestures for us to enter.

"I hope you don't mind, but Agent Osprey must accompany us. International security and whatnot." I say haphazardly, flicking my hand as if it's an annoyance, and the bouncer glances at him.

"Of course not, Miss Bader." He says with hesitance as Oz enters behind us. He's dressed in a black polo and black swim trunks, but with the sunglasses and giant earpiece, he looks the part of a rich girl's bodyguard.

The beach club itself is basic. Tiki torches, servers wearing basically nothing, comfy lawn chairs, a heated pool, and then obviously the beach. The sky is a little overcast, which I am thankful for because burning is not on my agenda for the day.

Serena and I settle into chairs facing the main bar that also houses what looks to be an office building. I see one man, who looks like another bouncer, gesture towards us to someone hidden behind the bar. I rest my head back, close my eyes, and wait for the show to begin.

# CHAPTER SIXTY-SEVEN

## SERENA

I may have the curves, but Xyla has the face and the name. Everyone is staring at us, more importantly *her*, to the point that I feel a little uncomfortable. I feign a chill and drape a towel around my shoulders, attempting to cover up.

Oz is close, close enough I can feel his presence. He's glancing around the beach club, gathering intel no doubt. Xyla on the other hand, has her eyes closed, glasses on, and looks like she's taking a nap.

I know she's not, but the feigned unaware act still puts me on edge. I see a group of men, all dressed like the bouncer, staring at us and I avert my eyes. They look menacing, a little violent based on the scars and cuts scattered across their visible skin. They are probably some of Antonio's henchman. Out of the corner of my eye

I see someone approach and I glance at them as if their presence bothers me.

Approaching is an incredibly gorgeous, deeply tanned man with slicked back hair, a white button up polo half undone, and bright pink swim trunks that actually look great against his complexion. His smooth skin and dimple meet blacked out sunglasses that hide his eyes and where he's looking.

Oz appears behind us, his hands ready as he gets closer.

"Ladies! I heard we had some special guests today." He claps his hands and beams at us. Xyla slides her glasses down the tip of her nose and gives him a once over.

"We aren't interested, thanks." She says dismissively and then slides her glasses back on while holding his gaze. Surprisingly, the very attractive man just laughs.

"I'm not here to sell you anything, Miss Bader, although there is quite a lot I'd give you for free." He winks and I fight the look of disgust. He may be hot, but that was cringey. "My name is Antonio and I wanted to invite you to a little gathering at my villa tonight. It would be an honor to host the First Daughter."

Xyla sits up then, interest piqued.

"*You* are Antonio?" She says with a quirked brow. Antonio runs his hands through his gelled hair or attempts to I should say.

"Well, Antonio Jr. to be exact." He says sheepishly.

"So, this is your father's place? And the villa you invited us to, is also your fathers, not yours?" She teases. At first it sounds vicious, cold, but the playful look in her eyes tells a different story. He shifts, probably growing uncomfortable in his nether regions based on how he adjusts his shorts.

"Yes." He says under his breath, eyes focused solely on her toned body completely exposed in her thin bikini.

"Well, Junior, I'd be happy to attend your little soiree." She leans back again, bending a leg to expose her inner thighs.

"I'll have a car pick you up at your mansion at six." He says, giving us a final wink and disappearing.

"He already knows where we are?" I hiss at Xyla as she relaxes in the gloomy heat.

"Of course. I rented out the most expensive mansion available and put it under my name so his father would know we were here. I wanted to make an entrance, and I did." She shrugs and then lifts her hand and snaps. I flinch and a man appears with a tray and two very fruity drinks. "Drink." She says, handing one to me and I take it.

"Don't we have to keep our minds sharp?" I whisper behind the glass.

"If we don't drink anything it'll be more suspicious. Oz will keep an eye out. Enjoy yourself for the next two hours."

And I do. We end up having about three drinks each, Oz watching us like hawks. We dance, we swim, we get hit on, and I hate to admit it feels a little like old times, back when we were in college. We are having the first bit of carefree fun in years and I don't want it to end, but the two-hour mark comes and Oz herds us back to the SUV.

He helps us both in, mostly because we are too busy giggling and tripping over one another to walk properly, and by time we are on our way back to our rental, he's rolling his eyes at us.

Honestly, he should be used to us by now.

# CHAPTER SIXTY-EIGHT

## RAVEN

I'm half asleep on the couch watching a show I can't understand when Oz walks in with a girl thrown over each shoulder. It literally looks like a cartoon or a damn romance novel with the ease in which he has Xyla on his left and Serena on his right. Both of them are laughing, kicking their feet, and trying to tickle him.

"Three drinks and I am assuming at least one of them was laced because they are getting crazier by the second." He stalks over to the couch and throws them both down. Their skin is red and their eyes are bloodshot and dilated. They are having some sort of giggling fit and can't catch their breath.

"We're fine!" Xyla slurs in between gasps of breath. She makes eye contact with Serena and they lose it again. I pinch my lips together to keep from smiling and look at Oz. He glares at me and then bends down to scoop up Serena.

"That one is yours." He says pointing at a pouting Xyla.

"Give her *baaaaack*." She whines reaching for Serena. Oz slaps her hand away and points at me.

"Get her some water and into bed. We have a party to attend in a couple hours and I need her sober." He turns around, Serena draped over him like a scarf before yelling. "Stitch! I need IVs!" And then he disappears around the corner.

Xyla surges up and I grab her around her waist.

"No, no. Off to bed." She slaps at my arms, and I flip her around so she's facing me. "Did you take anything?" I ask her. Her head lolls back and I switch my grip so one arm is around her waist and the other is grabbing the back of her head. "What did you take?" I say a little more forcefully.

"I had two frozen drinks and then a mojito." She enunciates *mojito* dramatically and then starts laughing. "That's a funny word." I tap her cheek to get her to focus and the humor that I feel fades into concern.

"Okay, come on." I start to walk her backwards and her legs give out. I bend down and scoop her up into my arms, holding her against my chest. I climb the stairs two at a time, depositing her on her bed. Her eyes are closed and she's snoring softly. "Hey," I shake her. "Wake up for me." Her body jerks and her eyes open.

"I feel funny." She pouts and I brush hair out of her face.

"I think you had something else besides alcohol. Do you know what it was?" I ask her softly. Rustling behind me has me glance over my shoulder. Stitch is walking in with his medical kit, a bag of saline and yellow liquid in his hands.

"Alrighty, beast. Let's get you fixed up." I watch as he sets up her IV and then draws blood out of her other arm. "I'll figure out what they gave her, but this will help keep her hydrated. She needs to sleep whatever it is off." He instructs and I nod.

"Thanks. Serena?" I ask as he rips off his gloves.

"Already taken care of, got some blood from her also." I nod and he departs, leaving us alone.

The banana bag, as he called it, is steadily dripping yellow liquid into her IV. Her eyes are open, half unseeing as she stares at me.

"When did you get here?" She asks, her voice slurring.

"I've been here." I say, dropping into the armchair I slid over to the bed.

"My head hurts." She says with an exhale before yawning. "I think I was drugged."

"Yeah, I think so too." She scrunches her face and then shoots up.

"Serena!" She says in a panic and then tries to rip her IV off. I grab her frantic hands and pull them away from the needle.

"She's fine, she's with Osprey." She relaxes, dropping to the bed like a ragdoll.

"I think it was the shots."

"Shots?" I ask. She never mentioned shots.

"Junior gave us shots at the bar right before we left." I rub the bridge of my nose with my thumb and forefinger.

"Xyla, you know better." I say softly, not wanting to lecture her, but she really should. "You know to watch your surroundings and to not let yourself get hurt like this." Her eyes line with silver as she stares at me.

"I know." She whispers and blinks as a tear escapes.

"What's wrong?"

"I'm so tired. This was the first time in years Serena, and I got to let loose." She says defensively.

"You were on mission, Xyla." I retort.

"I know!" She yells and then slams her mouth shut. "Sorry." We both take a deep breath and then our gazes meet. "We were being careful, playing the part, and then I saw how much fun she was having. I haven't had fun like that in so long. So, I let loose. I knew Oz was watching, so I figured we'd be fine, I mean they wouldn't do anything in broad daylight, or at least I thought." Her voice seems so soft and so young.

She seems like the old Xyla.

"What do you want in life?" I ask her after some silence. Her eyes widen, almost like she never expected anyone to ask her this question.

"Not this." She says, almost instantly. "Not this, Raven." I reach for her hand, and she lets me take it.

"Then why?" Her eyes wander and she yawns again.

"I just wanted the resources to find you. I wanted to build something you'd be happy to see when you got back. I wanted to build this for—for you. I wanted you to have something." The tears fall freely now as she averts my gaze.

"Xyla." I say softly and she shakes her head. "Xyla, look at me." And she does, her bloodshot eyes growing redder by the second. "I never wanted this either. It was something I felt I had to do. I never had any wants or any desires or any dreams." I pause as she listens. "Until you. Then all I wanted was the life with you."

"Scotland." She whispers softly.

"I wanted Scotland." I repeat.

"Do you still?" She seems so small, so fragile. Not the beast everyone fears, just a young girl who wants love. Wants to *be* loved.

"I will want Scotland until my very last breath. I will only every want it with you." Her eyes close and her body shakes as she starts to cry. Actually, cry hardcore tears. I scoop her up into my arms and climb onto the bed, holding her as tight as I can.

"Everything has gotten so fucked up." She says in between her sobs. I palm her cheek and force her to look up at me.

"I know. I know and I am so sorry."

"How do we even move forward?" Her hand comes up to fist my t-shirt.

"One day at a time. Neither of us are the same people we were back then. But one thing that hasn't changed is that I am so in love with you, Xyla." Her eyes flick back and forth between mine.

"I love you, too, Raven." She says, snot running down to her lip. Tears prick in my own eyes and then my mouth is brushing hers. A soft, gentle, promising kiss.

A kiss filled with tears and snot, but a kiss that foretells the future. The future that everything will be okay and that we will get through this.

I'm the first to pull away, curling her into my chest and rubbing her back until she falls asleep.

# CHAPTER SIXTY-NINE

## OSPREY

Serena pokes me in the ribs, jerking me out of a very deep sleep and I glare at her.

"Stop that." I mutter, throwing my arm over my eyes to shield the setting sun blaring through the window.

"We have to go." She says, her lips brushing my ear.

"We have time." I groan, hating that I haven't gotten much sleep in the last few weeks.

"It's almost 5:30." She repeats and then her teeth chomp on my cheek.

"Hey!" I yell, pushing her face away from me before rolling on top of her.

Her banana bag is empty and her IV already out. She looks tired, but definitely not drugged anymore.

"How are you feeling?" I ask her and she stretches her arms up above her head.

"Sleepy, a little headachey. Hungry." She groans as her ribs stretch and I tickle her stomach. She squeals and pushes at me. "Stop!" She yells and I do, pinning her hands above her head.

"Alright my little lightweight, let's get ready for a party." She rolls her eyes as I slide off of her.

"I'm not a lightweight."

"Three drinks and you're gone." I retort as I step into the bathroom.

"I was drugged and you know it." She yells back at me.

And she's right. Stitch ran their blood and it seems they were roofied. No doubt in preparation to add them to Antonio Senior's long list of sex trafficked women. But thankfully, they ended up okay. Not something Arabella or any of the other girls can say.

But that ends tonight. Tonight, father and son get a bullet in their head, and all those girls go free.

As long as it all goes according to plan.

Right at six o'clock, a stretch limo appears outside the estate. Xyla and Serena are dressed in cocktail dresses, their skin on full display despite the chilly night. Raven and I are dressed up in our usual attire, acting as their bodyguards. She's been to the house, so she'll know where to go.

The only issue is making sure Antonio Senior doesn't see her first.

We climb in, despite my earlier protesting about us taking our own SUVs, and I give the girls a hard stare.

"No drinks."

"Alright grandpa." Xyla mutters before throwing her legs across Raven's lap. Raven squeezes her ankle and then freezes as she catches me watching. A small smile plays at her lips and I return it, giving her a nod.

Maybe things will go back to normal, then.

I brush Serena' hair back before gripping the back of her neck reassuringly. She looks at me with a smirk and then leans in and plants a sloppy kiss to my cheek, no doubt leaving behind a smear of red from her lips.

The Becerra mansion is something alright. It looks like it's houses every single mafia movie set to ever exist. It's ostentatious, huge, and honestly a little performative.

We climb the front steps and the guards at the door take Xyla's name before we are allowed to enter. The front door itself is made from a bright golden lacquered wood, spanning almost all the way to the third story. It leads into a grand foyer and upon looking up, you can see all the way to the fourth floor. I whistle under my breath and Raven slides her sunglasses back on.

Her hair is slicked back like usual, and we are hoping she won't be recognized, although that is likely not the case.

The girls start to walk forward and when we follow them, hands plant on both of our chests.

"Weapons." One of the guards says and I glance at him out of the corner of my eye.

"Fuck that." I say and his hand presses harder into me.

"You want to protect your little doll, eh?" He asks, his thick accent making the words seem sarcastic. "No weapons." He repeats. I glance forward at Xyla and Serena disappearing into the crowd. Xy turns slightly, seeing us held up and stops. I shake my head once, letting her know it's alright and she nods before turning the corner with Serena.

She knows her mission. She needs to get to the girls, and to do that, she might need to let herself become one.

I hesitate only for a second before I unholster my gun and hand it to him. Raven does the same and then they pat us down, relieving me of the blade in my boot and the one Raven kept on her thigh. After checking we have nothing else, they push us forward.

We knew they would check us, that was a given.

But what they didn't do, was check the girls.

# CHAPTER SEVENTY

## XYLA

Despite the dress dropping to my navel in shafts of silver silk, and then dipping down my back, all before ending in a very short skirt that sits right below my ass, I am still armed to the teeth.

I have three blades on my ribs, their thin and curved blades fitting the contours of my body perfectly. Serena is a little more covered than I with her knee-high red dress that flows like water, thanks to liquid organza. That allows more movement, and a better chance at hiding weapons. Which she has.

Since her dress flows down loosely, she has two small pistols strapped to her ribs, and one more on her inner right thigh. All they had to do was barely touch us and they would have found we were ridiculously armed, but no one questions the rich party girl.

We walk arm and arm to the back door, where the party is in full swing out in the backyard.

Antonio Junior walks towards us with open arms. He kisses both of my cheeks before reaching for Serena and doing the same.

"Welcome!" He says theatrically. He snaps his fingers, much like I did this morning, and two glasses of champagne appear on a tray carried by a stone-faced waiter. My stomach rolls at the sight, but I plaster a smile to my face and take it anyway, faking a sip.

"This place is beautiful." I say as I look around in awe.

"My father would like to meet you." He says to me, ignoring Serena. I glance at her and she shrugs.

"Lead the way!" I say excitedly and step forward. He places a hand on my lower back, his thumb brushing my bare spine as he guides me to the other side of the pool.

The edge of the backyard borders a cliff, looking out into the ocean and goddamn it's beautiful. I don't have to fake my awe this time as my mouth parts. I take in the view, ignoring Junior to my right.

"Beautiful, huh?" He says with an heir of superiority.

"Incredible." I reply, because it is.

"Ah, senorita." An older male voice says and I spin around. The old gentleman in front of me looks almost identical to Junior, just aged another thirty years. Tan, flawless skin, gelled back black hair, and frat boy chic apparel. "You are even more beautiful than my son described." He reaches for my hands and gives each of them a kiss on the back.

"Mr. Becerra, your home is so lovely." I say and he smiles wider at me.

"You can thank my late wife, she was the mastermind behind the decorations." My face falls.

"I am so sorry for your loss." I say, offering a sad smile. "I also lost my mother, so I understand the feeling." He places his hand on his heart and nods.

"That is very kind of you, Miss Bader." He replies honestly and I hate that this very sweet man is also a psychopath.

"Please, call me Xyla." I smile and tilt my head as I lean into Junior a little bit. "Your son has been a wonderful host." I compliment, trying to help breakdown any walls that may stand. He looks surprised but quickly schools his features. He's an interesting person to read.

"That is not something I hear often! I think he might finally be growing up." Junior mutters under his breath something I can't catch, and his father shoots him a stern gaze. I fake a small chuckle and then Antonio's smile grows skeptical before schooling himself again. What is he trying to hide?

"I would love a tour, if it wouldn't be much of a bother? I own a real estate agency in the States, and I have a love of architecture. Your home is definitely a prize, one I would love to see more of." I smile and make sure my dimples are on full display.

"Of course! We would love to show you around." He offers me his elbow. "Shall we?" I take it enthusiastically before glancing over my shoulder, meeting Raven's gaze from where she lurks. She nods once, an affirmation that she has my back, and then I am being led away.

# CHAPTER SEVENTY-ONE

## RAVEN

Xyla disappears with the two men, their silhouettes slipping into the house. I feel my pulse quicken as I lose sight of her, but I make myself wait. I count in my head, forcing myself to relax, and once I hit one hundred, I move.

I keep my pace slow, leisurely as I approach the door they disappeared in. A hand grabs my arm before I can slip in.

"No entry, miss." A man says and I grab his hand and wrench it backwards. Before he can scream, I slap my other hand over his mouth and then one quick jerk to the right, and his neck is broken.

His limp body falls into my arms, and I glance around to see if anyone noticed. Party goers are a little too far away to really see what we are doing over here in the dark, so I drag his body a little more around the corner, drop it to the ground, and then slip into the house.

The hallway is well lit and is filled with doors on either side. I reach the end and the archway leads to a sitting room with doors leading in both directions. I slip my phone out of my pocket and pull up Xyla's tracker. I zoom in as much as I can and see she's to my right. I race that way, keeping my footsteps light and silent.

I hear laughing and slow my pace until I reach an open door. I quickly glance in and see Xyla being shown a painting of some old lady. Antonio Junior has his hand on her lower back, his fingers playfully brushing the edge of her dress. She is acting unaware, but I can see the tension in her shoulders that she does a pretty good job hiding. I can also see the catch in her dress where the silver silk has caught on a blade.

*Fuck.*

If they look too hard, they might be able to tell she's armed.

"I would love to see what other treasures you have hiding around here." She says playfully, turning to run a finger down Junior's arm. His father looks at them with approval; a dirty smirk plastered to his face. I sit back, not wanting to watch her flirt with him, even if it's fake.

"I will let you two get acquainted, I know when I am not wanted." The old man laughs and then heads towards me. I quickly backtrack, slipping into a room and silently shutting the door.

The room is pitch black and as I turn around, I realize where I am.

If I go further into this room, I'll find another door that leads down to the girls. But if I do that, I leave Xyla.

I leave her alone with that man who probably has some more tricks up his sleeve.

What do I choose?

"Osprey." I whisper, knowing he can hear me through my hidden mic. I hear a beep, as he hits the indistinguishable button on his jacket sleeve that sends a signal to my earpiece. "Beast and target are together, but a path to retrieval is in sight." Another beep. "Oz." I say again, my voice a little more desperate.

*"Stick to the plan, Ray."* He whispers, his voice a little muffled. And I know what he's saying, Xyla can take care of herself. And so, a single deep breath later, I walk further into the room and open the door down.

# CHAPTER SEVENTY-TWO
## XYLA

"I think you'll enjoy some of the art in the third floor sitting room." Junior says, his voice thick with lust. I bite my lip and nod as he takes my hand and pulls me towards an elevator. The doors ding and we step in. I pull my hand out of his and walk to the other side of the elevator, leaning back against the handrail so that my breasts push out a little more.

"I'm having a lovely time." I whisper, keeping my eyes half-lidded. He licks his lips and steps closer to me. His hand slides to my lower back again, before dipping under the fabric and cupping my ass.

"I think I can make it better." He whispers before leaning down and planting a kiss to my neck. I feign a groan as he needs my backside and sucks on my jaw. I let him get comfortable.

Get hard.

Get fucking ready to destroy me, as the elevator doors open.

He pulls back and a guard looks at us with surprise before stepping aside to let us through.

I let him drag me through the hallways, giggling like a drunk schoolgirl, before we reach a door.

I try to avoid his lips, but they slam into mine and then he's pulling me in the room. His mouth tastes like cigarettes and brandy and I pull away. He grips my arm and pulls me back into him, my ass pressed hard against his erection.

"I wanted you the second I saw you." He whispers in my ear, and I gag in my mouth. I moan and lean back. His hand goes around my neck, and I hold onto his wrist, mostly preventing him from sliding down to my rubs.

"Yeah?" I say, breathlessly and then spin out of his arms. I push on his chest, until he walks far enough back to fall into an armchair. I straddle his lap, his hands cupping my ass again as I lean forward. "I also wanted you." I whisper against his lips. "But for a different reason." I slide my hand down his chest until I reach my own thighs. I lean back and grab the hem, acting as if I am going to pull the thin silk off.

He watches intently, hungrily licking his lips. But instead of pulling it off, I just lift it up enough to expose the blades strapped to my ribs. His eyes widen and he stiffens.

He tries to push me off of him, but a quick jerk and I have my hand around his cock, squeezing hard enough to rip it off.

"Move and I'll fucking castrate you." I spit in his face.

"What the fuck do you want?"

"I want your father." He jerks back in disgust and I roll my eyes. "I want to kill him, you idiot." He fights against me and I slip a blade out, pressing it into his throat. "But I have some questions first." He blanches, keeping as still as possible. "If you're a good boy, I'll leave you be." I say softly and when he doesn't move, I release his cock, the thing still fucking hard. What a freak.

"What do you want to know?" He whispers.

"What does Étienne do for your father?" I ask and his eyes flash.

"What?"

"Étienne. What is the connection?" I repeat.

"He—my father. He gets the girls for him." He stutters and I frown. I knew there was the connection, but I didn't know if it was the drugs or the girls, and well, now I have my answer.

"Are they still here?" He nods. "Downstairs?" He nods again and I smile. "What a good boy you are, Junior." I smile.

"Where will your father be tonight?" He shakes his head, panic filling his eyes.

"Ah, ah." I warn as the knife slides down, pressing into his jeans. "Answer the question."

"I can't."

"Oh, but you can. You're choosing not to." I furrow my brows and pout.

"He'll kill me."

"Not if I kill him first." I shrug and she shakes his head, his hands shaking from where they are *still* planted on my ass.

"Not my father, Étienne." He corrects and I lean back, perplexed.

"Where is he?" I ask again, but this time referencing the mafia don.

"He's here. He's here to pick up the girls tonight. He's downstairs with them right now, counting." Bile surges up my throat. Serena and I were supposed to find the girls, but since I am with Junior, that means she went to find them. But she's with Oz. So that's okay. And Raven is watching out for me.

But, if she is, why hasn't she come in yet?

While I'm thinking, Junior moves, knocking me off his lap. I hit the ground with a thud, my back aching and he lands on top me, reaching for the knife.

"That was fucking stupid." I say just as I slash across his neck and slit his throat.

Hot liquid instantly pours across my chest, soaking into my skin and my dress. His eyes widen as he grabs at his neck, but it's too late.

The door bursts open and a guard walks in. He quickly unholsters a gun and aims it at me.

"Fuck." I curse as I ready the blade to throw it at him. Just as I get ready to aim, the guard drops to the ground.

Oz is standing there, a fireplace poker dripping with blood in his hands.

"Jesus, Xyla." He scolds as Junior slumps to the right, rolling off of me. I smile at him, and sit up, kicking off my heels at the same time as I kick off one of Junior's legs. I pad over to a disgusted Oz and pat his chest.

"Just a little blood, cowboy." I joke and his lips curl. I walk past him and then freeze. "Where is Serena?" I snap as I spin and face him.

# CHAPTER SEVENTY-THREE
## SERENA

My footsteps aren't nearly as silent as Raven's as I follow after her. She hides in a room and I quickly hide, too, as Antonio Senior walks by in a rush, his face looking a little angrier than it was when he walked off with Xyla.

Once he's gone, I step back out and creep down the hallway to where Raven disappeared. I open the door and close it just as quickly.

"Raven?" I whisper, but she isn't in here. I see another half-opened door and walk towards it. I hear someone yelling, a man, and I peer through the doorway.

I see a set of wooden stairs that lead down, and I quickly start to back away before I hear her.

"What are you doing?" Raven yells and then the unmistakable accent of Étienne's comes through.

"I work for myself, *perle*. Do not mistake our mutual goals as a partnership." A shot rings out and I stupidly rush down the stairs.

Étienne's gun is raised to the ceiling, Raven's hand pushing his arm up. I stare at the scene with shock as dust rains down and a chorus of screams echoes around me.

Oh. My. God.

Cells upon cells of naked young girls sits before me. Their bodies are dirty and scraped up. They are covered in literal feces and urine. Empty bottles of water fill the cells, and they are all huddled together in fear.

Bile rises in my throat as the smell hits me and I can't fight it. I puke, tears burning my eyes as I double over. I start to hyperventilate, growing dizzy as I feel claustrophobia sit in.

The cells. The smell. The sight.

This isn't Paris.

But this is still *real*.

I swallow the next breath and force myself to stand. Étienne and Raven are yelling at each other but there is a pounding in my ears, a ringing that is preventing me from hearing. I look at the cell closest to me and see a young girl, maybe fifteen, curled in on herself. Her eyes are red, her body coated in filth, and my heart breaks.

The pounding and the ringing start to fade and I turn to look at Étienne. His gun is on the ground, his lip bleeding. Raven is reeling back, readying to punch him again, but fury courses through me.

"Stop!" I yell and she freezes, stunned. Her eyes widen as she sees me standing there.

"Serena, get out of here." She orders and I shake my head. Étienne stares at me before a smile spreads across his face. I walk over, my own pulse pounding. My head clear for the first time in a while.

"These girls have done nothing to deserve this." I say and he snorts.

"They were put on the planet for a men's objectification, child." He spits and Raven kicks at his knee. He falls to the ground with a grunt and I get closer. My foot hits the silver revolver he dropped, and I look down at it.

"Serena." Raven warns because she knows. Once you make that shot, your life is never the same.

But my life hasn't been the same for two years.

So, I bend down and slip the cold metal into my hands.

"You don't have the guts." Étienne's face hardens as he stares at me.

"Xyla had to honors of gutting Bash like a fish for what he did to me. And while you are not Nathan, and the debt I owe her won't fully be repaid, you still played a part in our pain. In her suffering. In my torture." Étienne struggles, but Raven restrains him, his arms wrenched behind his back so that he's facing me.

I look up at Raven, the gun resting in my hands gently. Her eyes are sad but understanding. Because she, too, knows what it means to suffer. She knows what I endured and how this small thing could bring me some sense of peace.

A little bit of healing.

I lift the gun.

I aim.

Raven slides out of the way.

I meet Étienne's gaze.

Footsteps pound down the stairs to my right, but I ignore them.

My finger squeezes the trigger and as the bullet flies through his forehead, the light fades from Étienne's eyes.

# CHAPTER SEVENTY-FOUR

## XYLA

Shock races through every vein and artery as I watch Étienne's head jerk back with the force of the bullet. He stays upright for a full second before he sways backwards and crumples to the floor.

Serena's arm is still outright, her face focusing on the place Étienne was just a moment ago. Her eyes are unseeing, blank. No fear or pain. She's just existing.

I step forward but Oz pushes past me. Before either of us can reach her, Raven is there. She gently pries the gun from her grip, sliding it into the back of her pants, before she takes Serena's hand in her own.

"What you did was not something that will stain your soul, Serena." She starts, her voice crisp in the silent room. All of the young girls are frozen. In shock, or fear, I don't know. "What you did was an act of mercy for all of the women you just saved. You saved them, Serena. Not me. No one, but you." Serena's eyes drip with tears and she slowly looks up at her. "You saved them." She sniffs once, and then nods, holding Raven's gaze.

Oz walks over slowly and pulls Serena into his chest where she shuts her eyes, burrowing her face into his shirt. Raven sighs and the looks over at me, her eyes flashing with panic.

She rushes over, her hands frantically hovering over me.

"Are you hurt?" She asks, her voice breathy.

"No, I'm okay." I say with a smile. "It's not my blood." She meets my gaze and I see her relax slightly. I lift my hand and pull her forehead to mine. "Thank you, for what you said to her." She doesn't respond, but she doesn't need to.

Her hands wrap around my waist and pull me against her, her lips pressing to mine possessively as if she feared she wouldn't see me again.

"We're okay." She says into my mouth, and I nod before pulling away.

"Now let's get these girls out of here."

We disarm Serena and myself, distributing weapons amongst all of us. Serena doesn't get a gun, but she does get a knife, just in case.

She looks to be in shock, and so we gave her the task of taking care of the girls. We unlock their cages and try to keep them huddled together.

"Arabella?" I call out, trying to find the girl we were hired to save. No one answers, and so I say it again. "Arabella?" A couple girls look at me sadly and I feel it in my gut. "Have you seen her?" I ask and they nod.

"She had them take her instead of Tessa." One of the girls gestures towards the child that looks no older than twelve. "We haven't seen her since." I nod and sigh, we still have to get Antonio anyway.

"Shark is en route, he'll be here any second, if he's not here already." And like clockwork, screams and gunshots ring out above us. Sounds like Shark brought some firepower. The girls whimper and hug each other, the youngest of the flocking towards Serena. And after a few moments, the first of our birds make it downstairs.

"Alright, Miss Serena is going to help these really nice guys take you to safety, okay?" No one moves and I chew on my lip. "These are not the same guys, okay?" Still nothing. God, I don't know what to say to kids, much less traumatized kids. Osprey gets down on his knees and looks at the twelve-year-old.

"My name is Josh, and we are going to take you to your mom and dad, alright? We are here to rescue you. I promise, nothing will happen to you." The little girl's amber eyes are lined with silver and she nods slowly, looking directly into Oz's eyes, as if she's searching his soul for the truth. "Miss Serena is going to take care of you until we find them." She nods again and then gently takes his hand. I pat his back and stay behind to watch as the girls are wrapped in blankets and escorted out.

Once every girl is accounted for, I look at Raven.

"Antonio and Arabella are still out there." She looks at me and then at Oz.

"Go. We'll handle the rest." She says to him. His head jerks back.

"I am not leaving you to finish the mission alone." He says, his voice thick with anger.

"I'm not alone, I have a little beast on my side." She intertwines our fingers and then looks back at Oz.

"Xy?" He asks and I smile.

"One last mission?" He stares into my eyes understanding dawning on him.

"The last one?" He asks.

"The last one, Oz. For all of us." He looks between us and then back at the door leading upstairs to Serena. His shoulders drop and when he looks back at him, he has a smile on his lips.

"One last mission. The three of us."

"The three of us." I repeat and look up at Raven.

"All three of us, then." She parrots as Oz reaches forward and chucks her chin.

# CHAPTER SEVENTY-FIVE
## OSPREY

All of the party guests dispersed quickly, and by dispersed, I mean literally ran away when Shark started shooting at all of the guards. We watched as all of the captives were loaded into vans, headed straight to the hospital where they will be reunited with their families. Serena went with them, Shark watching over her with Jet by his side.

Once they drive away and it's just the three of us, we turn to face the estate. There is only one floor that the birds didn't check, and that's the very top where Radar's floorplans say the main suite is.

We slipped on bullet proof vests, Xyla finally got some pants, and Raven was handed her old Staccato. Her eyes stared at it before she took it, as if she was watching to see if it would explode.

Her grip was light as she tested it in her hand and then I saw the flash of the wild mercenary ignite in her eyes.

The wild, emotionless, monster who raised me to be the person I am today. The monster I call my family. My sister.

Her head slowly raises and when she meets my eyes, I see the pain that is about to come. She smiles a wicked sneer and then turns to face the house.

Xyla watches with curiosity before a small, sad smile slides across her lips. She looks at me and I nod at her, the only comfort I can offer as she sees the woman she loves slip into a killer.

All three of us are killers, but with Raven, it's always been different.

And this will be the last time she'll get the opportunity to shed some blood.

"Let's fucking do this." I say as we head straight towards the elevator.

The ride up to the fourth floor is silent, and we know what it is we are going to see when the doors slide open.

Gun fire erupts as soon as they do and we return fire. I hear Xyla yelp as a bullet grazes her arm and then she sends that man to the ground with a bullet between the eyes. Silence spreads and we stare at the mound of bodies holding the doors open.

Xyla's bare feet step directly on top of them as she moves forward. She looks to her left and to her right, like I taught her, and then she moves. I follow, checking our surroundings as well.

The sitting room is soaked in splattered blood and we keep pushing on. We keep Xyla in the middle, Raven and I taking the outer edges as we clear the room.

There is only one set of double doors and I kick the handles, sending it flying open.

Another wave of people and another wave of bullets.

I get hit in the chest, sending me to the ground with a huff. The pain radiates through my ribs, and I know one of them at least, is broken. But the vest took the brunt of it, meaning I'll live.

I pull myself up and I hear Raven grunt as a bullet rips her pants, slicing straight through her thigh. A bull of a man barrels forward and takes Xyla down.

I lunge forward, my rifle swinging to my back as I unsheathe a blade and send it straight through his temple. I push him off of her and see a thin blade sticking out of Xyla's arm. She's pale, focused as she rips it out of her arm.

"Ow." She says coldly, monotone. Blood gushes and Raven quickly rips her shirt, wrapping it tightly around her upper arm.

Another shot rings out, but it lodges in the door. I look up in confusion and see a trembling Antonio pointing a gun at us.

We are twenty fucking feet away and he can't even hit us. I snort and Xyla looks up and chuckles.

Antonio tilts his head in confusion before furrowing his brow.

"What the fuck do you want? Where is my son?" He yells and it's Xyla who pushes forward. She's wearing pants, but her upper half is still her silver silk thing that could barely be called a dress. And honestly, it's not even silver anymore. The rusty brown and splotches of red hide most of the original color.

"He's just taking a nap." She shrugs and Antonio drops his arm, staring at her. "A permanent one." She adds looking down at her blood stained chest.

"I'll kill you!" He screams and I swear Xyla rolls her eyes. "Do you want money? Is that it?" He yells and I step forward.

"No, we want the fucking killing and the kidnapping and the drugs and whatever the fuck it is you do, to stop." I spit, my voice loud.

"Where is Arabella?" Raven asks, stepping up next to Xyla. Antonio looks bewildered.

"Who?" He yells as if we asked him who the boogeyman was.

"A young girl, barely twenty. You took her and the girls downstairs said she hasn't been seen since yesterday."

"The one with red hair?" He asks, and his tone is pissing me off.

"Yes." Xyla clips and Antonio drops to the end of his bed, the gun slipping out of his hands because he knows his time has come to an end.

"She's dead." He says softly, as if he is almost saddened by it.

"Why?" Xyla's voice cracks as she steps forward, walking right up to him. Her hand grips his hair and forces his head up. "Why?" She asks again and I can hear the emotion in her voice.

"She wouldn't stop fighting. She was a liability." He answers coldly.

"She was a child trying to survive!" Xyla screams and then sends her knife straight into his chest. He gasps and falls backward, taking Xyla with him as the land on the bed. "She was a child!" She screams again as she pulls out the blade and then stabs down again.

I count.

Three. Four. Ten.

Fifteen.

And when she's about to reach twenty times she has slammed that blade into his mottled chest, Raven steps forward and halts her arm.

"She was a child." She whispers, her voice broken. Her soul broken.

And I realize how much all of this has taken a toll on her.

She was always a crazy little thing, but this life has destroyed her. She was full of light, a dancer, and artist. And now, she's a killer. This whole plan was to find Raven, to bring her home, and in the process, she's lost who she was.

I think we all have.

And with this being our last mission, our last time doing this, I can't fucking believe we ever spent our lives doing this at all.

We stopped killers. Psychopaths. Drug lords and mafia dons. We stopped traffickers and just all-around disgusting people, but who did we become in the process?

"We became saviors." Xyla whispers and I realize I said the last part out loud. "We have saved so many people, and the only cost was our souls." She drops the knife, the blade thudding as it hits the carpet, and then she slides off the bed.

She turns and looks at us, taking us in. Both of us bleeding in one or two places before she speaks again.

"My life was never going to be easy, and that wasn't because of you two. That was because of my father, and Nathan. They started all of this, they caused me to become this." She takes a deep breath. "This was our last mission, but not our last kill."

She looks us both in the eye, switching back and forth.

"We have two more."

# CHAPTER SEVENTY-SIX
## XYLA

Authorities and press were surrounding the hospital when we stopped by to pick up Serena. Jet and Shark are meeting us at the airfield with the rest of the men and luggage. I wrap the blanket around me as I curl up on the leather couch on the plane.

Two more kills.

Both of which will be back home.

Where it all started.

Where it will all end.

I start to fade, exhaustion pulling at me, and I let myself give in. I fall fast asleep just as the plane takes off.

I dream of a better life. One where there isn't this never-ending list of men who want to control everything. Men who want to be the top of the food chain and hurt anyone in their way. But even after these last two kills, even after this is all over, it's still going to exist. These men won't disappear, not unless someone makes them.

And someone will.

But that someone can't be me anymore.

I wake up two hours out and take full advantage of the onboard bathroom, taking a steaming shower. Five minutes in, the door opens and Raven steps in. Her slick skin is covered in bruises and blood. She's pale, which she always has been compared to me. She shivers as my eyes graze over her naked body. Her pebbled nipples and her chest moving up and down as her breath shudders.

And finally, I meet her eyes. She's staring at me, a question and a command simultaneously in her gaze as she waits. My hands raise slightly, grabbing hers and then I step back under the stream of steaming water, bringing her with me.

I don't get far before her lips slam into mine. She shoves me against the shower wall, her breasts smashing into mine as she bends down to lift my legs. I wrap them around her, tangling my fingers in her hair as her tongue dives into my mouth. I cross my ankles, keeping me in place as she slides one hand between us.

I gasp as she circles my clit, sending shooting pleasure straight to my core.

"*Fuck.*" I moan as she slides along my slit and then slams that finger inside of me. She pulls out, adds a second, and slams back in. Her lips find mine again as she sets a steady rhythm, my hips moving in tune with her fingers. I bounce against her, feeling my clit rubbing against her lower stomach as she fucks me.

As she makes me feel something no one else ever has.

"Don't stop." I cry into her mouth as I feel the orgasm build. The first one caused by another in two years. Because in the last two years there was no one. Just her. And when I didn't have her, I only had my hands and my memories.

So, I fully embrace this. I embrace every feel of her slightly longer than normal nails scraping inside of me. As I feel the stretching and the pain, and the *pleasure*.

As I feel the scream ready to burst out of my throat as I reach the edge.

And when I do, when I crash through the barrier of our questioning and confusion. Of our wondering of what we are now. My body shudders and I cry out into her mouth, her tongue silencing me as she rides through the waves with me.

And after I calm, and the steaming water starts to run cold. We shower together, taking turns scrubbing each other's hair in the icy water, laughing when the water gets too cold and we have to rush.

And then I show her how much I missed her on the bathroom floor, reminiscent of our first time together. And when she starts to cry out, it's my clit that silences her mouth.

And before long, we are pitching down to landing and we are both exhausted, spent, and laying on the tile floor, tangled in towels and each other.

A place I want to be forever.

# CHAPTER SEVENTY-SEVEN
## OSPREY

"Boss." It's Jet that wakes me. We have apparently landed, a passed-out Serena curled into my side. "We have a problem." I stare up at him, and his eyes are wide as he glances at Serena and then back at me.

I kiss the top of her head before sliding out from under her and gently guiding her down onto the couch. I follow Jet into the cockpit and look at what he's pointing at.

Out on the runway stands Lincoln and—*Bog*? Lincoln has a gun pointed to Bog's temple, a position he seems to be in a lot, but he's alive.

Bog is *alive*.

I rush out of the cockpit, nearly colliding with Xyla. I push past her and run straight down the stairs onto the tarmac.

"Bader!" I yell as I run towards the two of them. I hear Xyla and Raven yelling after me, and then the sounds of their boots behind me. "Let him go!" I yell even louder as I reach them. I am readying myself to barrel into him, when he puts his finger on the trigger.

I halt, my body nearly falling over with momentum and I can see Bog clearly. He's pale, gaunt. He has deep blue bags under his eyes and is covered in wounds. His lips are sliced open and a gash in his eyebrow has one of his eyes swollen shuts. He's favoring his left arm, and it looks like it's out of its socket.

"Daddy?" Xyla says reaching me. She steps forward and I grab her, keeping her back. Her eyes shine with tears as she looks at him. She didn't see how he held Serena, so this is the first time she's seeing him like this. "Daddy, this isn't you." She says softly and he looks like his heart is breaking a little bit.

"You can still survive this, baby girl." He says to her, his southern accent thick with emotion. "Come with me. Nathan is at home; he's waiting for you." She shakes her head.

"The White House isn't my home." She spits and his face softens even more.

"Not the White House, the bunker. He's there, waiting for you." He's in the bunker.

He's in our *home*.

"No." She says, shaking her head. "He can't be."

"He can. I let him in." Her body weakens and I hold her up.

"You didn't." She sounds so defeated.

"Bader, you can fix this. You can walk away and we will leave you alone. Walk away from the Presidency, and your life. You can live if you just walk away." His gaze snaps to mine.

"There is no walking away. Do you know what you have cost me?"

"Do you know what you have cost me?!" Xyla screams, fighting against my arms. "You had mama *killed*!"

Lincoln rears back, releasing Bog in the process who surges forward, right into Raven's waiting arms. She holds him up as all four of us stare at the President.

"How—"

"Nathan told me." Xyla rights herself, her shoulders dropping and I slowly slide my arms off of her. "He told me how it was your idea to kill mama. How you and him orchestrated everything. You planned for Kestrel to recommend Raven to you. You hired her. You planned for us to fall in love so she had a weakness. You planned for all of us to be in your control so you can start a fucking world-wide terrorist organization. Russia, Bucharest, Paris, Mexico. You wanted to be King of it all." Lincoln stares at her and I take a step back, letting Xyla run this.

"Yes." He says simply, shrugging.

"But you didn't account for one thing, daddy." He tilts his head, waiting for her answer. "Nathan wanted it too."

His face falls as shock rolls through him. He truly never considered that Nathan wasn't supporting him, he wasn't just a loyal servant. Nathan was using *him*.

Lincoln looks down as if every moment the last few years is passing through his mind, as if he is trying to figure out how he could miss the signs.

"You were so obsessed with power; you underestimated the most dangerous person in your orbit." I say and I watch as Xyla slides the Glock out of her waistband. He underestimated his daughter.

She lifts her arm and aims at her father.

Her last living relative, besides one person.

"Mira will never know you." Xyla says and Lincoln's face pales. Serena must have told her. All of us turn and look at her as she pulls the trigger and kills her father.

# CHAPTER SEVENTY-EIGHT
## XYLA

I watch as his lifeless body drops to the ground. I watch as the light fades from his eyes just as quickly as his blood soaks the pavement.

I just killed the President of the United States.

I just killed my *father*.

And I feel nothing.

I lower my arm and turn around, facing the others. Their eyes aren't wide with horror; their mouths not twisted in disgust. The look understanding.

They look, relieved.

Probably not that I had to do it, but that I got the chance.

The chance to kill one of the people who ruined my life. Ruined all of our lives.

"Let's go home and end this." I say, my voice not my own. My voice more tired than it has ever been.

And in the silence during the walk back, I expect to feel shame. Sorrow. Pain.

But I don't.

And when I see Serena's tear-stained face, I don't accept her hug or her sympathies.

I climb into the SUV waiting for us, and plan for what's ahead.

Because what's ahead is the final performance I'll ever have. My final dance. My final bow.

My final everything.

Not everyone survives in war, and I a fully comfortable if that person is me. But there is one thing I won't let happen.

And that is letting Nathan walk free.

So, when we finally make it home and the real estate building on top of the bunker is fully illuminated and the bodies of the birds who fought are laying out on the grass, I accept my fate.

Cliff and Deck walk forward, two birds who I was never close with, but still earned my respect.

"What happened?" I ask and Cliff answers.

"Nathan arrived with fifty men. Someone opened the elevator for them all. They started shooting immediately. We were dropping quickly, but we managed to push them outside. We got most of them, before they took over the bunker. There aren't many left, but they have all of the guns. They have access to everything. We are locked out." His face looks solemn.

We had over a hundred guys in there. A hundred left to defend their home.

"How many of us are left." Oz answer and I feel my gut twist and a numbness settle over me.

"We have less than ten." Horror punches through me like an arrow and I double over. Less than ten.

We lost ninety people.

"Oh my god." Serena says behind us.

"It was a blood bath. We weren't prepared." He adds.

My father *did* this.

My father did *this*.

And now he's dead.

And there is one person left.

"Shark. Rally up everyone who is left and who we brought with us from Mexico. Have Stitch start treating anyone left. We need a safe place to house everyone until we get our home back." I reach towards Raven and pull her Staccato out of her holster. I slip it into my pants and she stares at me.

"What are you doing?" She asks.

I reach for Oz's weapons, and he just stares at me, because he knows what I'm doing. He lets me take them.

Not because he wants me to go on a suicide mission. Not because he wants this.

But because I won't give him another choice.

I'm done.

"Keep everyone safe and get them out of here. Call the police, the SWAT, anyone who can be here immediately. This is ending. Now."

I look up at Oz and hold his gaze, a wordless conversation passing through us.

A goodbye.

Because I will burn this fucking world to the ground before I let Nathan walk free.

I look at Serena, her hand over her mouth and she understands and I avert my gaze. I can't say goodbye to her.

So, I walk to Raven, gripping her head and pulling her lips to mine, I give her every inch of my love.

"I won't let you do this." She says. Her grip on me is firm, her eyes angry and manic. She tightens her hands around me, and I feel the bruises forming. She would hurt me to keep me here.

And I would hurt her to leave.

So, I do. I scream as my balled fist hits the edge of her kneecap, dislodging it. Her leg snaps and her scream drowns out mine as she collapses to the ground.

"I'm sorry." I whisper to her as I turn towards the building and run.

# CHAPTER SEVENTY-NINE
## OSPREY

"Stitch!" I yell as I bend down to assess Raven. Her kneecap is dislocated and her ACL has torn. Xyla broke her fucking leg.

She broke Raven's leg so she wouldn't prevent her from doing this.

From sacrificing herself.

"She's fucking psycho!" Raven screams as she rolls on her back in pain. A fist collides with my cheek and I fall over. I look up at Serena her eyes wild as she stares at me.

"You are letting her do this alone? Who the fuck are you!?" She screams and wails at me again. I catch her hands and force her to the ground.

"This is *her* mission!" I yell back. "She needs to do this!"

"She *needs* her partner!" She screams in my face, spit flying.

"Osprey." Raven moans in pain and I look over at her. "Please." Her voice is desperate. She wants me to go. I look between the two of them and yell.

"FUCK!" I push off the ground and run after her.

# CHAPTER EIGHTY

## XYLA

Everything is silent as the elevator descends. I don't bother checking all the floors, I go straight to the bottom.

I have my gun loaded and ready, pointed at the doors as they open.

One shot. Two shots. Three shots.

Bodies down. I step out.

One shot. Another body down.

I press on.

My bedroom door is propped open by what looks like a pillow, but as I near, I see it's not a pillow.

A scream of pain erupts from throat as Miss Dolly lays before me. She's gasping in pain, her breath uneven and choppy.

I fall to my knees; my pants immediately soaked in her blood.

"No, no." I cry as I brush her cheek. Her visible eye flashes to mine and panic seizes her. "I'm so sorry." I cry as I bend down and bury my head in her chest. "I'm so sorry." I say again. I feel the soft brush of her fingers on my head as she holds me.

As she holds *me*.

"I love you. I love you so much." I cry into her and she mumbles something. I pull back and see blood dripping out of her mouth as she tries to speak, gargling instead.

"Ru—run." She gets out, coughing at the same time.

"I'm not leaving you." I say through my sobs.

"Go—baby go." Miss Dolly gets out, her accent distorted by the blood filling her lungs.

"You should listen to the old lady." Nathan says as he steps out of my bedroom and walks over the couch, leaning onto the back of it.

"I'll fucking kill you."

"That's what every man wants to hear from his fiancé." The scream that tears out of my throat is carnal, animalistic as I run at him. He catches me just as we both fly over the couch, landing on the glass coffee table.

Glass shatters under him as I get a good punch in. He throws me off of him, and I feel the glass slice through my t-shirt.

He punches me hard and blood wells in my mouth. I reach for a knife, and he slaps it away before I can get it into him. He bends down as if he's going to whisper something and I headbutt him, hard. Hard enough that I am temporarily stunned, and then I feel the warm trickle of blood on my forehead, dripping down to the bridge of my nose.

He falls off of me, groaning, and I pull myself up and crawl on top of him, weakened, but I get another good punch in. He elbows me in the stomach, and I fall back onto the ground, gasping for breath.

I finally wrap my hand around Raven's gun and aim it at him. He kicks out at the same time, sending the gun flying across the room and my wrist at an odd angle.

We both groan and stay on the ground, catching out breath.

"Why won't you die!?" I yell, reaching for another gun. He briefly closes his eyes, and I aim, pulling the trigger, but his fucking food catches my wrist again, and the shot gets directed upwards.

Cement rains down on us and then silence.

All I hear is out coughing and gasping breath and—wait.

Hissing?

I look through the dust and see a metal pipe exposed in the concrete.

Oh god, it's the gas line.

I sit up, looking for Nathan in the wreckage of my living room and see him crawling away like a fucking sewer rat.

I pull myself up and limp over to him. He's reaching for something and I don't have time to duck when I see it's a gun.

The shot goes off, getting me right below my ribs, under my vest. I fall forward, gasping in pain, but I feel around my back anyway.

And exit wound, thank god.

The hissing grows louder and I start to smell gas. He doesn't notice. I crawl forward reaching for him and he kicks me in the face. I fall, landing on the soaked blue rug.

All of my strength goes to rolling over, to stare up at the ceiling. My eyes cloud and I know I'm dying.

Weight lands on my chest and I see Nathan crawling on top of me. His hands go around my neck and he squeezes.

I kick out, trying to get away from him, but he's too strong, and I am too small.

My hand searches for a weapon, but all I feel is the glass of the coffee table.

*The coffee table*. An idea sparks in my mind, and I know that this last move will kill us both, but I'm dead anyway.

So, I fight against the tunnel vision and feel around, knowing that I had it right on top of the glass.

Right next to the candle.

My fingers brush cold metal, a little square, and I know this is it.

"Any last words?" He says, loosening his grip slightly.

"Why—" I start and he loosens some more.

"What?"

"Why are you such a fucking cliché?" I ask. His eyes widen and then I bring my hand and the object in between us. He glances down in confusion as I flick the lighter and everything erupts.

# CHAPTER EIGHTY-ONE

## OSPREY

The elevator opens and bodies are piled in the hallway. I take one step and an explosion shoots out of Xyla's room. I fall to the ground, the walls and floor shaking. Pieces of the ceiling start to fall, and I scramble to my feet, coughing in the dust.

I run to Xyla's room and try to see through the flames.

"Xyla!" I scream. "Xyla!" I say again, coughing.

"Oz—" I hear her voice to my left and I run, tripping over fallen pieces of the ceiling.

Another explosion rocks the underground bunker, and I fall to my knees, crying out in pain.

"Xy!" I yell even louder and then hear her cough. I crawl my way towards her and see the huge chunk of cement and steel on top of her, only her left arm and face visible. "Fuck. I got you." Her face is covered in soot, blood along her hairline. Her nose is bleeding and I see a crushed skull laying next to her, the rest of the body hidden under the same chunk on top of her.

*Nathan.*

"I got you. Don't move." I grab the edge and pull with every inch of my being, but it doesn't budge.

"Oz." She says, coughing again.

I scream as I use every ounce of my strength, and the slab barely lifts.

"Oz, get out." She says, hoarse. I drop to my hands by her face and stare down at her. Her eyes are dimming, the gold gone from her irises.

"I am not leaving you to die, Xyla." She tries to smile, but fails.

"I am not letting you die with me out of stubbornness." She jokes and then coughs again. Blood splatters across my face and I feel tears burn my eyes. "He killed...Miss Dolly." She gets out and my heart breaks.

"Xyla..."

"I'm so tired." Her eyes close and I panic.

"Stay with me, Xyla." I grab the edge of the cement again and pull. I feel my muscles straining and ripping, and it moves an inch. She screams when it does and I stop. "I have to get it off of you." I say and her eyes roll into the back of her head. "Goddamnit!" I scream. I pull myself to my feet, brace my legs and push instead of pull.

The cement slides before getting blocked from the wall. She's uncovered down to her waist and I relax, catching my breath. I look around for anything, because I will not let her fucking die.

I see the metal arm of her dining table and rush over to it, dodging more falling cement. I drag it over and shove it under the cement. Another scream and I am using the steel beam to lift the slab. I rest it onto my shoulder, nearly crying with the pain.

Fuck. Fuck. Fuck. I bend down as best as I can, grabbing her arm and dragging her out. I lurch forward, the cement and beam dropping to the ground, but Xyla is free.

I shake her and her eyes flutter open halfway.

"Stay with me, Xy. I'm going to get you out of here." She smiles weakly, her face pale.

"Thank you, for being my friend." She whispers.

"Xyla, don't fucking do this."

"I'm not in pain anymore." She whispers and then a sharp inhale cuts off her words. A thick gurgle and then an exhale.

Silence.

Silence spreads as I stare at her lifeless body. I scream. A scream so painful and loud that when the next explosion erupts, I almost think I caused it.

I pull her into my arms, my knees pressing into the debris covered rug, the blue rug she was so excited about.

I scream until the fire spreads, and the only exit is no longer visible.

# CHAPTER EIGHTY-TWO

## RAVEN

My broken leg is throbbing, the explosions around us doing nothing to distract me. Serena's tears are silent as she holds onto my arm, her fingers cutting off my circulation.

"They'll come out." She whispers, but I know she knows. The chances that Oz and Xyla get out of the crumbling building are next to none. But still, here we sit. On the rubble. Amongst the flames. Our shoulders smushed together. Watching.

Begging.

Praying, despite our lack of faith.

We watch as another gas line ruptures, and we shield our eyes as the flames grow so big and so bright, they scald our eyelids.

We watch as the remaining Birds around us all drop to a single knee.

We watch as they all pay their respects to their fallen commanders.

And then, only then, do I finally let the tears spill.

It's as if time slows and a melancholy violin plays somewhere. Signaling their death.

Another explosion and then the top floor finally gives, caving in to the floors below.

"She wanted to end it." I whisper, to no one in particular. "She wanted it to finally be over." Because she did. Xyla risked her life, *ended* her life, in order to end Nathan's. In order to finally break the cycle of war and ruin. Of sadness and pain, and of death. The never-ending game of chase, because someone has to win. And someone has to lose.

But never both. Both sides aren't supposed to lose.

There is always supposed to be a victor.

And for some stupid fucking reason, that victor is me.

It was always supposed to be *her*.

But we watch. We watch as the flames continue. We watch as flashing red and blue lights appear. We watch as the real estate agency that was always just a front, disappears before our eyes.

We watch as the steel and concrete crumble, taking everything down with it five stories below. Five stories down into the earth.

"They built this place to be indestructible. But I don't think they ever considered it being destroyed from the inside." Serena says her grip loosening.

"It's always from inside. We have never operated without someone ruining us from the inside." I respond.

"We ruined ourselves." She answers. And she's right.

Streams of water erupt to our left, hitting the flames dead on.

A terrorist took the body of my brother, and the last few years of my life were taken. I was robbed of normalcy. I was robbed of love. And when I found it, it was orchestrated. And now—now that love is gone.

Xyla.

Xyla is *gone*.

"Stop!" I hear someone call and Serena's fingers tighten one more time. "Someone is coming out!" The water stops and everyone freezes. No one moves, aside from Shark, who slowly reaches for his gun.

Just in case.

A shadow. Just one, through the flames and smoke.

Broad chested, limping. Soot covered skin and hair appear and there he is.

Oz.

With Xyla in his arms.

Serena is off, her feet tearing up the distance between her and him. *Them.*

"Shark!" I order, and his arm goes around me, lifting me to my feet. We meet them halfway, and my gaze stays fully on Xyla in his arms.

Her blue eyes, so bright, shining.

Still.

Unseeing.

"Osprey..." My voice is a croak as I see the blood along her hairline. As I see the blood soaking her chest and abdomen. As I see that same chest not move, just stay.

Frozen.

"Xyla?" Serena whispers, her fingers touching her cheek slightly.

Oz drops to his knees and finally do I look at him. Tears pour down his cheeks. Blood soaks into his shirt, blending with the black ash. *Her* blood.

"I tried. I got there too late. She-she got him. She fought and she won, but the floor above. It pinned her down. She was so strong." His voice cracks and my hand flies to my mouth. "She was so strong until the end."

I shake my head, pulling out of Shark's grip and falling to the floor. My broken leg screams in agony, but all I can do is stare.

"Let's get a medic!" I hear someone scream, and then Oz lays her down.

"She was so strong." He reaches forward, closing her eyes.

She's dead.

Xyla is *dead*.

I reach for her, my hand going to her neck, searching for a pulse. My hands slide to her sternum and then I push up on my knees.

"Someone get a crash cart!" I scream as I start to push. One, two, three, breathe. My lips press against hers, the salt of my tears mixing with the metallic tang of blood pooled in her mouth. One, two, three, breathe.

Someone in red appears to my right, tilting her head back. I watch as they intubate and attach a bag to the end of the tube.

One, two, three. I keep up with compressions. I don't stop.

One, two, three.

One, two, three.

One, two, three.

"How long?" Someone else says. I hear the mechanical whirring of the paddles being turned on.

"Raven, move out of the way." Someone's tender voice reaches me, but I don't stop.

One, two, three.

"About ten minutes." Someone responds. ten minutes? It's been ten minutes?

One, two, three.

"Get her out of here!" A medic yells, pushing my arms away.

"No!" I scream, my fist flying right into his face. Arms go around me, ripping me off Xyla's body. Her *still* body. "No!" I scream. Over and over as I'm held back.

Over and over as I watch them shock her. Again. Again. And again.

I watch as they look down in defeat.

I watch as they look at Oz, who is cradled in Serena's lap. Whose face is a mix of horror and pain. I watch as they finally look to me.

"Time of death—"

"NO!" I roar. "Keep going!" They look at me with pity, but I don't care.

So, they continue. The continue until they finally get a stretcher over.

They continue until they get her loaded in the ambulance.

And they continue for hours more at the hospital, the phrase *code blue* being repeated every few seconds.

She would never stop fighting for me, even when I gave her every single reason to stop. To run.

And I will never stop fighting for her.

Even if that heart never beats again.

# EPILOGUE
## NAOMI
## SIX MONTHS LATER

My eyes stay fixed on the small box in front of me. The box that was my whole world, for years. The box that will always be my soul.

"You ready to go?" Oz says from behind. I grip the white oak to my chest and take a deep breath.

"Yeah, let's get out of here." I turn and follow him out of the hotel room, the place we've called home while we figured out our next steps. Liquidated everything. Cleaned house.

And so, I walk out of the suite and leave everything behind.

I carry nothing with me. Just the box.

I follow Oz into the awaiting SUV, Serena already inside. Shark, and Radar, too. Another SUV sits behind, filled to the brim with suitcases and gear.

Everything we need to start a new life.

To just start over with the people who choose to join us.

The SUV takes us to the private airstrip, where Jet is waiting along with Xyla's favorite plane: number thirteen. I stare up at it, my heart clenching ever so slightly, as I grip the box tighter.

Serena is laughing, walking up ahead hand and hand with Oz. Her giant emerald engagement ring she got a few weeks ago, glinting in the sun. And I smile for them. For their love. For everything they have fought for.

I have only ever cared for a few people in my life. And almost all of them have betrayed me.

My parents, who turned me away when Nathan was declared dead. Who blamed me for his death.

Nathan, who protected me when we were children, and always told me I could be anything and anyone in the world—until he used me as a pawn.

Goose, who was the father I needed, until he, too, betrayed me for a lost cause.

Kestrel, who I loved wholeheartedly, but only saw me as an object to use.

Osprey, who is my best friend, my partner. And the most stable person in my life.

And then Xyla. My soul. My everything. She was the reason I woke up every single day during our time a part. The only reason I kept fighting. The only reason I didn't kill myself long before.

She is my life.

But along the way, every single person I have ever loved has left me. Has chosen to leave when they no longer had a use for me.

Except two.

Oz and Serena disappear inside the plane, and I hesitantly begin to climb the stairs.

"So where are we even going?" Serena says, popping her head back out to look at me. "You never said." I reach the top of the stairs and push her inside, laughing.

"Scotland, obviously." Her crystal-clear voice, like a siren made just for me cuts through the laughter and the chatter. Xyla rolls her eyes at Oz who kicks her feet off his chair before he plops down.

"How did you not guess that?" I say to Serena as I sit down next to my wife on the leather sofa. Her lips are soft as they press against my cheek, the cold metal of her ring chilling the nape of my neck as she holds me close.

"Oh, my bad I wasn't privy to one of your inside jokes." Serena declares dramatically, throwing herself onto Oz.

"We don't joke about Scotland." Xyla deadpans, before laughter erupts and a calm peace spreads. Serena and Oz become entranced with one another, Shark climbs into the cockpit with Jet and Radar makes himself comfortable at one of the tables where Bog is already relaxing with a bottle of beer and his phone. Xyla taps the box on my lap and averts my gaze.

"I think it's time." I say to her as she looks up at me, her brown eyes nearly golden, only a small scar above her brow to remind us of that night.

"We'll throw it off a cliff." She jokes before taking it out of my hands. Her fingers grip the lid and open it, revealing my Staccato.

The raven engraved on the side still perfect. The soot from the night Xyla almost died staining the metal black. The one thing that solely represented my time as Raven.

But that time has ended.

"Well, bosses. You ready to get this bird in the sky?" Jet says from the front, raising an eyebrow.

"Naomi?" Oz says, deferring to me.

"I'm just along for the ride, Joshie. You and Xy are in charge." He scrunches his nose at his government name and Xy pokes my ribs.

"I'm ready." He says and so I turn to Xyla.

"What about you, little beast?" I say, tucking her hair behind her ear and pressing a kiss to the tip of her nose.

"To Scotland?" She asks, her eyes bright for the first time since we met three years ago.

"To Scotland."

# A NOTE TO MY READERS

I have no words for what a whirlwind this duet has been. From being born of intrusive thoughts and an obsession with Killing Eve, I created a world that I fell in love with. Xyla and Raven, Osprey and Serena, they became a family in my mind that is so hard to say goodbye to.

They wouldn't exist without you all. You gave me the time to take a break from fantasy and create a world so different; I had to temporarily jump genres.

So, *for now*, this is goodbye to our psycho little beast and the cunning raven.

# A NOTE FROM THE AUTHOR

This duet wouldn't exist without a select few people.

To Ris and Shay, who gave me the idea to begin with, your support, suggestions, excitement, and love are the reason this world was born. I am forever grateful for the two of you for giving me a safe space to create!

To my best friend, Annie, who is my rock in all things, thank you for constantly being my biggest supporter and the third to my throuple. Without you, I think my love of books may have faded. You constantly excite me, boost my creativity, and keep me grounded in all ways. I love you forever.

To my babies Vee, Heather, Erin, and Jac, you guys are my people. My group, my sounding boards and the people who keep me sane. Not only are you my editor, personal assistants, handlers, and closest friends, you are people that are all behind Celaena. She wouldn't exist without you.

To my friends Sara, Haydn, Dawn, Thea, and to my new agent, Angie, I am so grateful to have you all in my corner. I wouldn't keep going without you!

And lastly, to my soon-to-be wife. The Xyla to my Raven and the Raven to my Xyla, because let's face it, we are both. You are my everything. My family. My home. And the space you create so I can create is something I can never repay. I just hope to be rich and famous one day so I can give you the life you deserve. The life we deserve.

I'll see you all in Scotland, because all good things come to an end, and when they do, I'll be in the highlands.


XO Cel